I0533533

**The NEBADOR series:**

**Book One: The Test**
Spring 2010

**Book Two: Journey**
Summer 2010

**Book Three: Selection**
Fall 2010

**Book Four: Flight Training**
Spring 2011

**Book Five: Back to the Stars**
Fall 2011

**Book Six: Star Station**
2012

# NEBADOR

## Book Three

## SELECTION

an epic young-adult science fiction adventure

by

J. Z. Colby

Nebador Archives

Copyright © 2010 by J. Z. Colby
All rights reserved

Cover art by Rachael Hedges
Illustrations by J. Z. Colby, Mireille Xioulan Powers, and Rachael Hedges

For other print editions, ebooks, dramatic audiobooks, previews, samples, biographies, comments, questions, artwork, writing contests, Ask Kibi advice, deep learning notes, Nebador citizens, and more, please see:

**www.nebador.com**

**Nebador Archives**
**Kelso, Washington, USA**

Library of Congress Control Number: 2010910975
Manufactured in the USA

ISBN: 978-1-936253-24-1
**NEBADOR3PBG2**: paperback, 6" x 9", 179 pages, global edition
 (10-point Georgia type), revision 2

**Greetings, young people of planet Earth,**

In *NEBADOR Book One: The Test*, Ilika of Satamia in Nebador arrived in a medieval kingdom with the purpose of finding a crew for his ship. He selected ten students, nine spirited young slaves and one innkeeper's daughter. One of the students did not understand that teamwork requires trust, and quickly landed back in slavery. Ilika did not, at first, understand how many of the taboos of that society he was breaking, and he and his remaining students were forced to use dark and dangerous ways to escape the walled city.

In *NEBADOR Book Two: Journey*, their bodies, hearts, and minds were tested by nature, personal demons, and human relationships. They came to the first mountain pass transformed, hardly recognizing the people they once were.

Although the journey is not yet over, the travelers have been sorely tested. Strengths and weakness have emerged, some not even known, before the journey, to those who own them. Ilika is getting a pretty good idea of who will make good crew members — and who will not. The students, also, are seeing who will stand at their sides through thick and thin, and who will run away scared.

By the end of *Book Two*, it is a rare young reader who is not seeing part of themselves in one of the students. They might be relating to the strength growing in Sata as she discovers that the universe can be deadly and friendly at the same time. They might be admiring Boro's down-to-earth wisdom and understanding of all things physical, like chemistry and geology. Or they might be trembling a bit, along with Miko, as he wonders what makes a good leader, and why the skill eludes him. Or they might be walking in Buna's shoes as she struggles to learn math and logic.

Although the journey of life can be challenging, we all get through it, one way or another, whether it is short or long. Other tests and challenges, however, are designed by the mysterious powers of the universe so that we cannot all pass. No matter how much we might want to be on the team, we cannot all make the selection.

J. Z. Colby
2010

## Acknowledgements

Wonderful people throughout the author's life provided unique and irreplaceable lessons and inspirations:

Juniper Russell
Vicky Ball
Linda Dezzutti
Jennifer Carolyn Gates
Rachael Bleich
Paula Wells
Sarah Satterthwaite
Ashley Riddle

Esther Smith
Dottie Frisbie
Martha Higgins
Susanne Koller
Charleen Cox
Meredith Herzog
Patricia Sharp
Antonya Pickard

Valuable readers gave the author feedback after digging through early drafts of the book:

Mitchell Bendis
Beth Littlewolf
Ardith Libby
Cecelia Harper
Holly Chalcraft
Karen Pihlak
Brendan Aragorn

Patrick Murray
Deborah Meier
Dan Clark
Karen Oster
Toni Corkran
Shelley Johnson

Excellent critiquers commented on thousands of passages, then provided reactions during in-depth interviews:

Sidney Oster, 8
Sarah Bray, 10
Jessica Johnson, 10
Aditya Srinivasan, 11
Mariah Bruns, 14
Hannah Li Powers, 15
Kathryn C., 16
Brie Polette, 17
Rachael Hedges

Dylan Oster, 10
Joshua Clark, 10
Catherine "Cat" Harper, 11
Jasper W. Romero, 13
Kristen Voie, 14
Alex Chalcraft, 15
Abby Powers, 17
Elwin Aragorn, 17
Winn Barrientos

Careful publishing assistants, proofreaders, and technical helpers brought the final manuscript as close to perfection as possible:

Sarah Bray, 12
Katelynn Persons, 15
Deborah Meier
Tim Kutscha

Joshua Utter, 15
Amanda Herman, 17
Norma Ashley

## Contents

1 A World Apart ................................................................ 1
2 Mountain Paths ............................................................. 4
3 Blind Faith on an Empty Stomach ............................... 12
4 Logic and Inner Sight .................................................. 16
5 Lights ........................................................................... 23
6 Particle Physics and Existential Rules ......................... 28
7 Hardtack and Hard Choices ........................................ 33
8 The Way Down ............................................................ 39
9 A Final Farewell .......................................................... 44
10 Moving On ................................................................. 48
11 The High Desert ........................................................ 51
12 Cattle Town .............................................................. 56
13 Changing the World ................................................... 61
14 Ilika's Big Mistake .................................................... 66
15 A Time of Healing ..................................................... 72
16 The Plan ................................................................... 76

17 The Long Road Home.................................................................81
18 The End of Many Stories ........................................................ 85
19 Choices....................................................................................91
20 Parting Ways ........................................................................ 96
21 The Ship................................................................................102
22 Manessa Kwi.........................................................................105
23 What Would I Do? ................................................................ 114
24 Preparing for Trouble .........................................................120
25 Steward.................................................................................126
26 Engineer ............................................................................... 131
27 Watch....................................................................................136
28 Navigator ..............................................................................142
29 Pilot......................................................................................147
30 Holy Cause............................................................................ 152
31 Flight Preparations .............................................................158
32 First Flight............................................................................163
33 An Old Friend........................................................................170
34 The Last Stop........................................................................174

"I come from a place where everyone has great power, by your standards, and they steadfastly refuse to use it for self-aggrandizement ... anywhere ... ever."

        — Ilika, concerning Buna's plan at Cattle Town

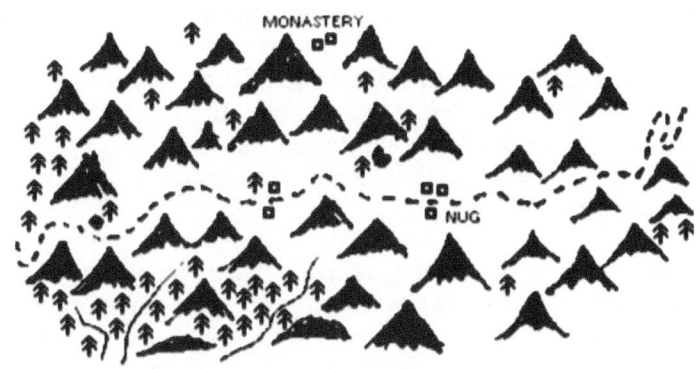

## Chapter 1: A World Apart

After getting out of the bitter wind on the eastern side of the pass, Ilika and his ten companions rubbed their eyes and gazed at the alpine valley ahead. Four mountain peaks soared thousands of feet above, with slopes of bare gray rock and brilliant white snow. About a mile ahead and a thousand feet below nestled a perfect little blue-green lake. Thin, white-barked trees ringed the shore and lined the outlet stream as it wound its way south into a rocky gorge.

From their vantage point near the pass, the students could see a narrow finger of land that jutted into the lake on the far side, and they all pointed to it, anxious to make it their next camping place.

As they descended the trail, the shadow of the mountain to the southwest reached out and covered the lake, turning the water a deep blue. The western slopes of the other three peaks still blazed with golden afternoon sunlight.

※

As soon as the line of eleven walkers arrived at the lake, strange wiry bushes greeted them, offering countless little red berries. After gathering a few, they all cautiously chewed, ready to spit them out. To their delight, the berries were edible, if not as delicious as the large purple ones in the lowlands.

The main trail skirted the southern edge of the lake, and a campsite with fire ring and sitting logs showed long use. Only faint animal tracks weaved through the trees to the far side of the lake.

A thin neck of land, only about a yard wide, guarded their new home. Level places for bedrolls were scarce, but Neti and Miko managed to find a space for two, and Kibi and Ilika had only a small tree between them. Mati placed hers on the edge of a grassy slope that Tera claimed for grazing, Sata was not far away in case her friend needed her, and Boro was among some boulders just uphill. Misa and Buna found places together, and Toli was near, but he and Buna weren't yet ready to resume snuggling. Rini found a niche by himself between some fallen trees where he could look up at the stars.

They saved the open space in the middle of the peninsula for a campfire circle. Boro and Ilika soon brought logs from the forest for sitting, while Miko found rocks for the fire ring and others gathered wood. Mati gave her precious donkey a good brushing as the stillness of a summer evening descended upon the lake.

*

Both the priests' horses sweated and trembled as they staggered down the trail from the pass. The younger priest tried to say comforting things to his mount, but was silenced by the elder.

Not far above the lake, the priest in the lead halted. His horse coughed several times and started shaking, but the man didn't seem to notice as he pulled out a spyglass. He carefully scanned the entire valley, but when his gaze came to the peninsula jutting into the lake, a sudden flash of green light blinded him. He lowered the spyglass and rubbed his eye, then tried again. The same thing happened.

"You see something?" the younger priest asked from behind.

"No, just a reflection from the water. I want to get to that sorry excuse for a town — Nug, I think it's called — by tonight. That's the best place to catch up with the filthy criminals."

"But the horses . . ."

The elder priest turned and glared, and the younger man lowered his eyes and mumbled words of obedience. A moment later, they both set spurs to their horses' flanks.

*

For six days, the lake and its woods were home to Ilika and his companions. Several parties passed by on the trail, but most only stopped briefly to drink at the stream, and never knew anyone else was around.

Those six days were a time of healing for the students who left painful memories behind in the lowlands. Misa helped with chores and even began to pay attention during some lessons. Buna felt she was just about over her math block. Toli believed his fears were a thing of the past, and Miko vowed to never again do anything without careful consideration.

Ilika used those days to review previous lessons and fill in a few missing bits. The students mastered negative numbers, and could quickly spot if they were valid, or if only positive numbers should be used. With Toli and Boro in the lead, they added to their knowledge of chemical compounds and deepened their understanding of ions, always ready to jump into chemical bonds and make new compounds. Neti especially liked ions.

Reading further in *The Adventures of Godi and Tima*, some of the experiences of the young warrior and the elf maiden began to sound familiar. The students wrote compositions about their own recent adventures from both their points of view, and through the eyes of an all-seeing storyteller.

Ilika was rapidly running out of paper.

Also during those days at the lake, each student spent time alone with Ilika, talking about anything they wanted to discuss. Buna had more questions about his bracelet and knowledge processor, to which he said, "I don't know," or "I can't tell you," but always with a smile. Mati was suddenly very confident she would be on his crew, and he could guess why. He had to dance around her questions about how a handicapped girl could work on a ship.

Sata's questions focused on the forces of the universe that could be dangerous if not understood and handled carefully. Ilika had trouble limiting his answers to the dangers present in their kingdom.

As they sat around the campfire during the evenings, people slowly started talking about the fire that had destroyed Lumber Town, and their experiences in the days that followed. *Kibi and the Green Light* was told for the first time, to the amazement of Miko and Neti, who knew nothing of the glowing guide.

Misa just listened for several evenings, but was eventually able to haltingly tell *Misa and the Big Fire*, from smelling the first whiff of smoke, to being found by Ilika in shock and grief.

While Sata grinned, Boro told the story of *Boro and Josa* with great embarrassment. Mati was still silent about events that had recently troubled her heart.

On the group's fifth day at the lake, a family stopped for the night at the campsite on the main trail. After they settled in, Kibi approached, made friends, and brought her companions over to share a meal and stories. The family had lost their home and work in the fire at Lumber Town, and had relatives at one of the few settlements in the mountains. Misa's eyes glistened and her lips pouted as she listened to their story.

*

On their last full day at the lake, the group walked up to one of the snowfields several hundred feet above the lake. Ilika and Toli helped Mati, and Boro carried Misa.

On a patch of gravel beside a snowfield, made warm by the still air and bright sun, Ilika talked about the chemistry of living things.

"Water is the universal solvent in biology, just as it is in most inorganic chemistry. We have now experienced all three states of water . . ."

"Ice is solid!" Buna declared, reaching back and pounding on the hard crust of the snowfield behind her.

Sata's hand shot up. "The oceans, lakes, and rivers are liquid!"

"Steam is gaseous!" Miko announced.

"How do you know, Miko?" Toli asked with a huge smirk on his face as everyone else started laughing.

Miko grinned and held up the hand he had burned, pointing to it with his other hand. "This is how!"

* * *

## Chapter 2: Mountain Paths

Another clear summer day dawned early, but they knew the sun wouldn't get to the lake until mid-morning. Neti used the last of Farmer Koto's oats to make a thin porridge. Comments around the breakfast fire told Ilika they were ready to tear themselves away from the beautiful lake and head for the nearest settlement for supplies.

Tera pretended not to hear until Mati used the do-or-die tone of voice that was occasionally necessary with her donkey. She pulled one more mouthful of tender grass and walked over to be saddled.

✳

By the time the sunshine found the lake, the students and their teacher were half-way up the slope to the next pass. At the top, just a gentle ridge between two peaks with a cool breeze blowing, Ilika announced they were seven thousand three hundred feet above sea level.

"Did you figure that out with trigonometry?" Sata asked.

"No. My bracelet has an altimeter function."

Buna came and stood by Ilika. "What's an al . . . timeter?"

"Altitude meter. It can tell about how high we are above the ocean. I'll do a lesson on it this evening."

"Okay, thanks!" Buna said, grinning with delight at discovering yet another of the bracelet's magical powers.

While Ilika was answering Buna's question, he was also contemplating the scene before them. They could see into two small mountain valleys, to the northeast and the southeast. Both contained small lakes, but neither hosted any kind of settlement.

Ilika's brow furrowed. The trail forked, just a few yards in front of them, with one branch going into each valley. He sat down on the rocky trail and pulled out their map. Everyone gathered around to help him consider the situation.

"The trail on the map looks like it goes sort of northeast about here," Neti observed.

"Yes. That gives weight to the left branch. But sometimes mapmakers aren't careful, and just draw a wiggly line when they know the way is wiggly, without being careful to match the wiggles they draw with the real wiggles."

"That sucks," Boro said with a frown.

"Yes. I'd like some scouts to go down both trails a little way to see if one or the other is more heavily used."

"Me!"

"Me!"

"Me!"

"Me too!"

"All of you, go ahead — the more opinions the better. You too, please, Rini."

Sata, Miko, Neti, and Buna headed down to the right. Rini stood thinking for a moment, then set his feet on the trail to the left.

Kibi sat down close beside Ilika.

"Any idea which way we should go?" he asked her.

Kibi was silent for a long moment. "Which way the settlement is, or which way we should go?"

He flashed her a grin. "There's a reason we're in these mountains. I just can't see it yet."

The group of scouts returned and headed down the left trail.

"What if we get lost?" Toli suddenly asked in a loud voice.

Ilika looked at Kibi. His glance pleaded with her to deal with Toli on this occasion.

"Then we'll just have to find ourselves," she said over her shoulder.

"Thanks," Ilika whispered.

All of the scouts returned, and Rini quietly slipped away down the right-hand trail.

"They look the same to me!" Miko announced proudly.

"Me too," Neti agreed.

Sata and Buna nodded.

"That's what I was afraid of," Ilika said with a slight frown, then went back to staring at the map.

Eventually Rini returned and sat down with Ilika and Kibi. "Not much difference. More moccasin prints, even some bare feet, to the left."

Ilika stood up. "Okay, unless anyone has other opinions, I'm going with Neti's observation that the trail on the map goes northeast here."

Everyone was silent.

"Sata, I'd like you to lead a project."

She came and stood before her teacher, then took a deep breath of the cool mountain air to fill herself with courage.

Ilika handed her one of their last blank sheets, a thick piece of drawing paper. "I'd like you to make a map of all the trails, lakes, mountain peaks, and other interesting things we find, starting back at the first pass. You do the mapping, but let others get compass bearings and distance estimates. I'll give you the elevations."

"This sounds like fun!"

Ilika got out his knowledge processor and selected the magnetic compass.

Sata started drawing. "Um . . . Mati, would you get a compass bearing on our lake? How high was that, Ilika?"

"Six thousand one hundred."

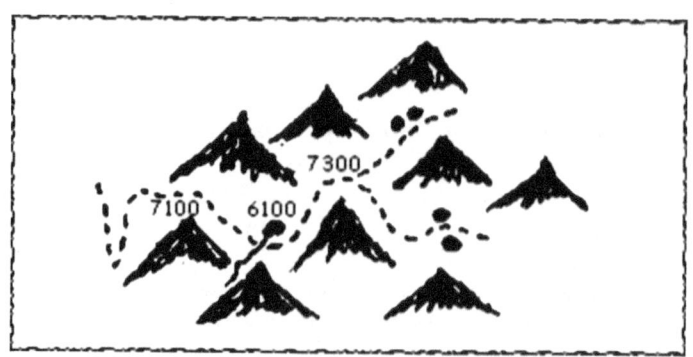

With the help of others, Sata soon had all the information they could remember, or discover from their current location. Having already chosen their path, they shouldered their rucksacks, only to discover that Misa had just taken off her moccasins.

When she noticed everyone looking at her, she pouted for a moment and said, "I heard Rini say he saw bare footprints. I wanted to try it."

Rini smiled.

The rest shrugged and headed down the left-hand trail.

⁕

The little alpine valley they entered was even more beautiful than the first, containing two crystal-clear lakes and a little waterfall in between. When they stopped for drinks, Misa plunged her sore feet into the icy water and dug out her moccasins.

When they came to the far side of the valley, three paths continued onward. One followed the stream southeast, another went over a low pass eastward, and the third climbed a higher pass almost due north. Sata got busy with her map.

"Ilika, what happened to the ONE trail through the mountains on the map?" Neti asked pointedly.

"I guess it's ONE of these," he replied, just as pointedly.

"But which one!"

"The trail down the stream probably just joins the other trail we decided not to take," Toli speculated.

Several people nodded.

"The north way looks . . . hard for a donkey," Mati said, shading her eyes.

"It looks hard for anything!" Boro added.

"Do we have an agreement to take the trail to the east?" Ilika asked.

Everyone nodded and shouldered their rucksacks.

✳

The trail forked twice more before they stopped for lunch at a little meadow where Tera could graze. Boro passed out scraps of stale bread and small pieces of dried goat cheese. Sata worked on her map, asking for estimates of the distances they had walked.

The afternoon brought more choices of direction, more alpine lakes, and plenty of work for Sata. They tried to pick trails that would take them east, but were often forced to go toward the north.

Ilika could see Neti getting more and more frustrated, and Toli was clearly on edge. Everyone else seemed fine, and were picking little red berries at every opportunity.

✳

A group of slender trees beside a tiny lake became their final stopping place of the day. Rini and Buna, both as happy as little children at play, ran off to pick berries, while Boro asked Toli to help him with firewood. Kibi started a soup with whatever she could find in their bags. After updating the map, Sata helped with spices.

"Okay, I promised you a lesson about altimeters," Ilika began as everyone sat around warming their hands at the fire. "Under the influence of gravity, the atmosphere tends to pile up and be denser at the planet's surface. It gets thinner and thinner as you go up. It does so in a very predictable way, so we can make an instrument that tells us how high above sea level we are."

"How can we do lessons when we don't know where we are?" Neti moaned.

Ilika looked at her for a moment before answering. "Because it doesn't matter where we are. We have everything we need, we are safe, and the lesson is just as important here as anywhere else."

Neti rolled her eyes but said no more. Miko put his arm around her.

"The problem with a simple altimeter is that several factors can change the air pressure at a given location from one hour to the next. Wind can cause the pressure to go up or down. Temperature changes cause pressure changes, since a gas is heavier when it's colder. Moisture in the air also changes the pressure."

"So how can your bracelet figure all that out?" Buna asked.

"It can take into account the temperature and the humidity, because it can sense both of those directly, but it has no way of knowing the current sea-level pressure. I can tell it, if I know. If not, it assumes the usual, which is the pressure that will push mercury up about thirty inches."

"Element eighty, liquid at normal temperatures, and there's only four of them," Boro said from memory.

"Right. Very useful, but also very poisonous."

"We're lost, aren't we?" Neti burst out in a voice close to tears.

"Anyone who doesn't like our situation is free to leave," a voice said.

There was a moment of astonished silence. Neti would have expected that from Ilika, maybe even from Kibi, but to hear it coming from Buna was almost shocking.

"I agree, Buna," Ilika said calmly. "But let's give some attention to Neti's concern. Please share with us what you're worried about, Neti."

"It just bothers me . . . that we don't know where we are or . . . where we're going or . . . when we're gonna . . . find food . . ." Her voice broke into sobs.

Ilika let some time pass as Miko held her tightly.

"We've got food for about a day," Boro explained, "two if we cut back and eat like slaves."

Sata shriveled her face slightly, then took a deep breath.

Rini spread his arms wide. "There are berries all over the place!"

"We're going to be okay," Miko said tenderly. Neti buried her face in his cloak and let herself cry for several minutes.

Ilika whispered to the others that he would continue the lesson another time.

When Neti collected herself and wiped her eyes, Ilika was sitting beside her, and to her amazement, put his bracelet on her arm and snapped it closed. Then he peered at his knowledge processor, sometimes touching it with a finger in different places.

Toli and Buna watched carefully but didn't ask any questions.

Ilika frowned. "Neti, I'm not surprised you feel terrible."

"What?"

"You're dehydrated, anemic, and hypoxic. Remember what those mean?"

"Um . . . all dried up . . . and . . . I don't know."

Ilika smiled. "Our bodies don't work well when we're dehydrated. Also you're very low on iron. That and the high altitude are making it hard for your body to get enough oxygen. I bet you've been headachy."

"Yeah . . ."

"You're usually so self-controlled, I knew something was wrong when you became grumpy."

"It's the first time I've ever seen her like this!" Miko said with concern.

"You get *three* bowls of soup for dinner, Neti. Make more if you have to, Kibi. Have you been eating the red berries?"

"No. They're not very tasty."

"Well," Ilika continued, "they may be just what you need, and we can't afford to pass up any source of nutrition right now."

Rini handed her a bowl half-full of berries.

"Remember when I had to eat all those *sour* berries?" Miko reminded her. "These are lots better!"

"Okay . . ."

✳

Miko made sure Neti got plenty of liquids at breakfast the following morning, and lots of berries. She seemed to feel better, but was still weak.

"On a Transport Service ship," Ilika began as they huddled around the morning fire, "every member of the crew reports *any* health problems to the commander. I don't blame Neti, since she wasn't familiar with altitude sickness, and she didn't have a bracelet."

"You mean, even the crew gets bracelets?" Buna asked excitedly with wide eyes.

"Of course. A captain can't expect his crew members to do their jobs unless they have the proper tools. On a ship, we run into so many strange situations, the whole crew has to be constantly watching for anything unusual. A headache could be a clue to something dangerous, like radiation. Men have more trouble than women admitting something hurts or feels funny."

"Does that mean if someone got sick, they could rest?" Toli asked with a hopeful voice. "When we were slaves, we had to work even if we were sick."

Ilika had to think about the question for a minute. "Very different situations. As slaves, you couldn't rest because your masters wanted as much work done as possible. But your work was never critical. No one's lives were depending on you.

"In the Transport Service, your commander will let you go off duty if possible, but there are times you'll have to stay on duty until some dangerous maneuver is completed. The safety of the ship comes first. Without the ship, the crew and passengers are dead. See the difference?"

Toli scrunched his face in thought. "I think so."

"Makes sense," Boro said, nodding. "On the ship, we would depend on each other."

"But even if you couldn't go off duty immediately," Ilika continued, "the commander needs to know about any weakness in the crew or the ship. That way, you'll get what you need just as soon as you can be spared."

✳

For Neti's sake, they took their journey more slowly that day, stopping for drinks and wild berries often, and having snacks between meals, to the extent they could find anything to eat in their rucksacks.

The trails continued to branch every mile or two, and Sata faithfully recorded the details. As often as not, they were forced to go farther to the north than they wanted.

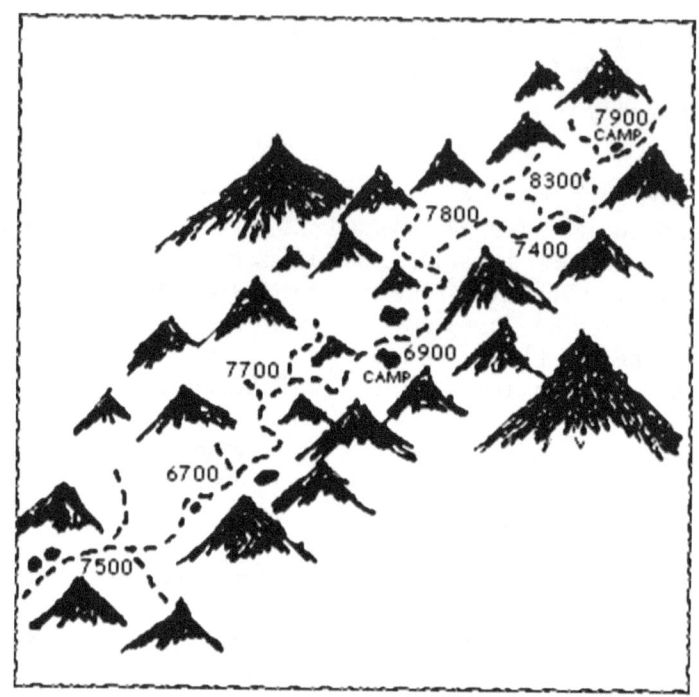

The soup was very thin that evening. Everyone searched their bags. A few nuts and a bit more cheese came to light.

After a bowl of hot soup, most of the group spent time hunting for wild foods, looking in the water for frogs or turtles, or pulling up plants to see if the roots were edible. Kibi brought back a few tender greens, but everyone else shook their heads.

Tera looked up from her plentiful supply of fresh grass and wondered what the fuss was all about.

The teacher and students turned their attention to what was available. Mati stayed to tend the fire as everyone else fanned out with bowls and cups to gather all the berries they could find before dark.

Ilika wore a frown as he picked. Several times Kibi noticed him fingering his bracelet thoughtfully, but each time he would stop himself before doing anything and go back to picking more berries.

As the evening deepened into night, the somber group sat around the fire. Only occasionally would someone share a story.

Kibi exchanged glances with Ilika, then looked around at the others. Rini was, as always, unaffected by their situation. Boro and Sata seemed fine. Other than a little soreness in her good knee, Mati looked okay. But worry lines crossed Kibi's face when she glanced at the other four students and listened to her heart.

As Ilika sat warming his hands and quietly observing his students, he became aware of a change in the weather and consulted his bracelet to verify what he was sensing. "The air pressure is falling."

"Isn't it a little late for lessons?" Toli asked in a testy voice.

Ilika looked up as the first flakes drifted down from the sky and gleamed in the firelight. "Yes, too late for lessons. But a very good time to get ready for snow."

✳  ✳  ✳

## Chapter 3: Blind Faith on an Empty Stomach

Several inches of white snowflakes piled up on their bedroll covers before stopping in the middle of the night. Misa had joined Buna in her bedroll, and everyone stayed warm. Toli had to get up several times during the night, and everyone knew, by the grumbling, that he was unhappy.

During the early dawn hours, Kibi caught little bits of conversation between Miko and Neti. She was feeling better, but their situation still worried her. Miko tried to comfort her, but was powerless to remove her concerns.

The morning dawned gray, with a cloud ceiling so close they could almost reach up and touch it. No one hopped out of bed to build a fire, even though they had piled their rucksacks on top of the firewood to keep it dry.

Suddenly those who were awake heard the sound of footsteps crunching through the snow.

Before Ilika could respond to the sound, the flap of his bedroll was pulled back, and the weathered face of a middle-aged woman looked down at him from deep inside the hood of her cloak. She smiled slightly, and gestured for him to follow.

Rini found himself looking into the eyes of a girl no more than eight years old.

The same happened to all the others, and everyone was soon sitting up, looking at the ten or eleven hooded figures who had returned to the nearby trail. Some wore moccasins, and others were standing barefoot in the snow.

"Who are you?" Miko challenged assertively.

"Where are we?" Neti asked with a shaking voice.

"Where are you taking us?" Toli whined.

None of the figures spoke. When all the questions had faded away, one of the women repeated her hand signal to follow.

"I think we found the monastery," Rini declared.

Kibi smiled. "I think it found us!"

"It must be an order with vows of silence," Ilika said. "My country has those also."

Several of the hooded figures nodded.

Ilika stretched his arms. "We're being offered guidance. Let's get ready and go!"

No one complained. Within five minutes, boots were laced, beds rolled up and strapped to packs, and the donkey saddled.

They kept out their bowls and cups of wild berries, all they had for breakfast and possibly beyond. Toli clutched one of the cups protectively.

Rini picked up the biggest bowl, with about half their supply, and looked at Ilika.

He nodded.

Rini presented the bowl to the girls and women waiting on the trail.

After looking at each other with surprise for a moment, they accepted it with a slight bow. Each of them took a handful of the precious food, then returned the bowl and began to lead the way up the trail.

*

The group walked under gray skies, following their silent hosts ever upward and ever northward into the fog while chewing the remaining berries. At their first rest stop, they all got drinks of icy cold water and put away the bowls and cups.

As they continued, Ilika dropped back to the end of the line. Looking around at the silent and still landscape, he noticed they had climbed above the elevation where the berries grew. He caught occasional glimpses of mosses, lichens, and hearty grasses, but absolutely nothing they could eat. Then he took a good look at Neti, not far ahead. Somehow she was finding the energy to keep going, and was not stumbling too often. He touched the surface of his bracelet with a worried frown, then plunged his hands back into his pockets and focused on the task at hand — getting to wherever they were being silently guided.

*

"I think it's our mountain!" Boro yelled as they rounded a rock outcropping, came out of the fog, and suddenly beheld a snowy peak towering above them in the sunlight. "The thirteen thousand foot one we did the trigonometry with!"

Ilika checked his bracelet. "We're at eight thousand five hundred. You could be right, Boro."

"Look!" Toli squealed. "There's some kind of house over there!"

Everyone looked in the direction he was pointing. Another quarter mile along the trail and just slightly lower, in a sheltered nook on the side of the mountain, a cluster of pine trees ringed a small meadow, currently covered with snow. A simple building perched between the trail and the meadow.

Without word or gesture, their hosts led them in that direction.

*

The monastery's guest house was a one-room rock shelter with a steep roof of slender logs, and slabs of bark for shingles. The door, just a simple opening in one wall, faced east and overlooked the alpine meadow. A small fire pit took up the middle of the room, and the dirt floor gave enough space for all their bedrolls, as well as Tera if the weather turned foul.

Miko spotted the dry firewood and chopping block, and set to work with flint and knife, while Boro quickly organized a team to collect more wood.

While the travelers were getting settled, one of the priestesses sat down out of the way and closed her eyes. The rest of the women and girls of the monastery silently departed.

"Do you think they know we need food?" Toli asked in a desperate voice.

Kibi nodded. "Yes, I think so, Toli."

Overhearing Kibi's firm but comforting tone, Ilika smiled to himself.

Buna came in with the bronze pot full of clean, cold water, and Ilika poured a cup for Neti, warming herself by the fire. Neti accepted the cup and looked into the gentle eyes of her teacher. "You knew we were going to find something, didn't you?"

"I knew we were going to be okay," he assured her, "but I didn't know we would find the monastery."

Rini came in from the meadow with numb hands from helping Tera scrape snow off the grass. The fire was soon built up and they all gathered around. Cups of water were passed, and sparkling eyes met, sharing a moment of happiness even as hunger gnawed at their bellies.

At that moment a large wooden tray appeared, carried by one of the sisters of the monastery — bread, butter, cheese, plums, crab apples, and sprigs of fresh greens. She set the tray on the chopping block by the wood pile, sat down out of the way, and the sister who was already there rose and silently departed.

"Eat slow, everyone," Boro asserted. "You remember what can happen when you haven't had food for a while and suddenly you get some."

"We remember," Buna assured. "You can't be a slave very long and not know that!"

During their meal, more guests arrived. A bushy-tailed gray squirrel begged for a piece of Ilika's apple, then ran and sat on the meditating sister's lap to eat its meal. A sparrow flew in the window, landed on Neti's shoulder, and received a bit of bread. Rini soon discovered his bony knees were preferred by two chipmunks, both of whom received handouts.

Neti smiled for the first time in two days.

*

The teacher, nine students, and one fellow traveler spent the remainder of the afternoon getting everything dry, building up a large pile of firewood, and just resting and talking. Toli paid close attention as Ilika placed his bracelet on each person's arm.

Neti was no longer dehydrated, and her iron had improved a little. Toli's blood pressure was high. Everyone was slightly hypoxic due to the altitude, but otherwise in good health.

Another tray arrived in the evening, brought by a different sister, who stayed and sat with eyes closed. Two squirrels and three chipmunks also showed up. After giving away a small part of his dinner, Boro asked Ilika to continue the lesson on air pressure and altimeters.

Somewhat to Ilika's surprise, all of his students were wide awake. Misa and the five little meadow creatures seemed just as interested. He talked about the weather patterns typically created by different pressure, temperature, and humidity conditions. The chipmunks, however, soon got bored and left.

As they prepared their beds that evening, the last tray was silently carried away, including the two silver pieces Ilika had placed upon it. The squirrels followed the sister out the door, and the travelers were left alone for the night.

\*  \*  \*

## Chapter 4: Logic and Inner Sight

Early the following morning, before the frost had melted from shingled roofs and canvas tents, a woman with hauntingly green eyes appeared in the little mountain town of Nug. No one saw her walk into town from either the west or the east, and the frosty trails revealed no footprints, but they assumed she was from the strange monastery deep in the mountains. Indeed, she told a tale of a group of travelers, with a donkey, who had arrived at the monastery in a snowstorm the day before. They had been given bread and sent on their way, and had returned the way they came, to the west, where the weather was mild and snow did not fall in mid-summer.

As soon as he heard this news, the elder priest yelled at the innkeeper until he hurried to make the morning mush. Then he screamed at the stable boy to saddle the one horse that had survived their first crossing of the mountains, and spurred it back into the west.

The younger priest took to the trail on foot. With a sad face, he watched his poor horse disappear into the distance.

*

The rising summer sun came streaming into the monastery guest house. Rini stretched his slender arms toward the sky and hopped up to see if Tera needed anything. Both his shoulders and Tera's back soon hosted little peeping birds. He lifted his arms so more could perch. Tera, however, twitched so they would take flight. All around them, the snow rapidly melted from tree branches and meadow grass.

Miko was able to kindle the fire from coals, and just as he got it going, a young sister arrived with a tray, her hood back and a small bird on her shoulder. Although she smiled at her guests, she remained silent, and soon sat down and closed her eyes.

"Ilika," Rini asked as he slowly ate his porridge, "do you know what they're doing when they sit like that?"

"I believe they're meditating."

"I don't know what that is."

"Meditation is a way of controlling the state of your mind to avoid unhealthy thoughts, feelings, and attitudes. It's a very common practice in religious orders."

"Is it like being asleep?" Mati asked while spooning a bit of porridge to a chipmunk.

"No, just the opposite. They are more aware than we are right now, because all distractions are ignored. The hardest one to ignore is the chatter of our own minds. It can take years to learn to quiet the mind."

Ilika noticed a variety of reactions to his explanation. Several students seemed interested, but somewhat unnerved by the idea. Toli and Neti both squirmed as if they would rather wash dishes.

✳

"I have taught you all the math that's useful at this point," Ilika began as they sat in the sunshine just outside the guest house. "We'll keep reviewing and practicing, but I need to deepen your understanding of logic.

"You've already noticed many things deductive logic can't handle because it's based on statements that are true or false, all or nothing. So now we have to learn set theory, and its cousin, quantification theory."

Several students tried to get their mouths around the big word.

"Many, many things in life can be dealt with in sets, or groups. Any time we put things in a group, it's because they have something in common. Noni has a set of creatures she calls her flock. The important quality all the members of her flock share is that they're sheep. She doesn't want the sheep shearer to accidentally shear her dog, or her donkey, or herself."

Buna burst out laughing, rolled backwards, and couldn't stop for several minutes. Everyone else laughed or smiled. The meditating priestess tried to suppress her own laughter, without complete success.

Ilika grinned until they regained their composure. "We can also have sets that share something more subtle. Let's say we have a group called 'red.' We could include a red apple, those mushrooms Kibi told me not to eat, a glowing hot coal . . ."

"One of Pica's paints," Mati jumped in.

"Miko's hand after the steam vent," Neti said with a smirk.

Miko looked at her with a loving snarl.

"The sunset with clouds in the west," Boro proposed while smiling at Neti and Miko.

"You get the idea," Ilika said, pulling out a piece of half-used paper. "Now let's see how sets relate to each other. This rectangle is the whole universe, everything everywhere. Circle R is red things, circle E is things we can eat."

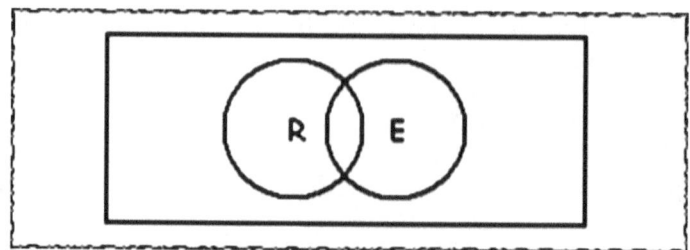

With something to look at, everyone moved in close.

"Two groups creates four regions — things that are red but not edible, things that are edible but not red, things that are both, and things that are neither. Buna, where would a sheep go in this diagram?"

"Um . . . in the E."

"Right. Neti, a red apple?"

"Between R and E, where they overlap."

"Good. Sata, your boots?"

"Well . . . if you were *really* hungry . . . but no, outside the circles."

"Right . . . assuming you aren't *that* hungry. Kibi, Miko's burned hand?"

"If he had cooked it just a little bit more, it would go in the middle with the apple and we could have had it for lunch!"

Miko pouted as everyone else howled.

"But since he didn't cook it enough," Kibi continued with a grin, "it would go in the large part of the R."

Ilika smiled at her. "Let's try three groups."

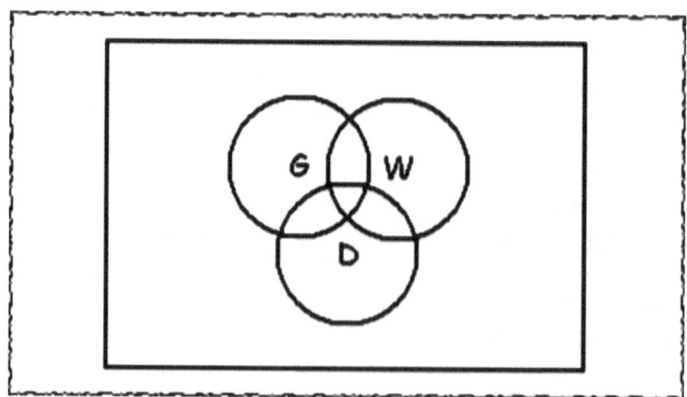

"The groups are green, wet, and dangerous. Algae, Boro?"

"Um . . . it's a water plant . . . um . . . between the G and the W."

"Yes. Fire, Misa?"

She almost jumped out of her skin. It was the first time he had called on her in a lesson, but she quickly recovered and looked at the diagram, determination written on her face.

"Green, wet, or dangerous," Ilika reminded her. "Which of those qualities does fire have?"

"Dangerous!"

Everyone clapped.

"Good. The ocean, Sata?"

"Between wet and dangerous."

Ilika gave them each several examples until he was sure they had the idea.

"We never put anything in the middle!" Buna protested.

"Hmm . . . green, wet, and dangerous . . . can anyone think of anything?"

Everyone searched their minds during a long silence.

"A big, hungry turtle!" Mati said with a huge smile.

*

As mid-day approached, Rini helped Mati brush the donkey, then sat down near the priestess, in the same posture, and closed his eyes. A squirrel climbed onto his leg, making him giggle for a moment, but he soon managed to relax.

Ilika noticed, but continued combing Kibi's hair silently.

The lunch tray arrived, and the sister who had been sitting took the breakfast tray and the silver piece back to the monastery. Rini opened his eyes and rejoined the group.

After more logic practice and an hour reading dramatic scenes in *The Adventures of Godi and Tima*, Ilika left plenty of free time before dinner. Miko and Toli grabbed their sun hats and dashed off to explore the rocks and snowfields on the mountain above.

Rini and Kibi sat down with the priestess and closed their eyes.

The rest wandered about the meadow, drinking icy-cold water, or talking to Tera and the little native creatures. When Sata and Mati started practicing the deep voice of the Mountain King from the story book, their audience of small creatures quickly vanished. Tera just looked at her people and shook her head.

About an hour later, Boro and Mati quietly settled in with the meditators, and Neti and Buna went off to explore.

Sata sat down on a boulder with Ilika and they talked about the solar wind and other topics of mutual interest. After a while, Sata fell silent and scrunched her face. "I don't understand how a ship's captain could have learned all this stuff. We've had captains and officers from ships at our inn, and they're hardly more educated then their crews. The only difference was, they had more money and better clothes."

Ilika smiled at the eleven-year-old beside him, rapidly learning, growing, and experiencing life beyond her years. "You'll find out soon. The stuff I've learned — and am teaching you — is a lot more important where I come from. But if you'd prefer, we could just talk about things that other ship captains talk about . . ."

"You mean ale and wenches? No thank you! That would be as boring as washing tables!"

Ilika chuckled.

✳

At dinner, some students wanted to share their geological discoveries of little caves and gleaming crystals on the mountainside.  Others wanted to share their psychological discoveries of old memories and hidden fears from meditating.  Ilika, who had not taken part in either activity, made sure everyone got a chance to speak.  Toli had trouble paying attention when the meditators were talking, but an elbow from Buna corrected his attitude quickly.  A pair of rabbits showed up, along with the usual squirrels and chipmunks, and they didn't care who talked about what, as long as they got a handout.

"Thank you all for sharing what you discovered," Ilika said as the meal was ending.  "There are many levels to reality, and the physical and mental realms are very different, but we have to know about both of them.  We live in a physical world, but we can only know and understand it through our minds.  If we ignore either one, we can be easily fooled."

After reviewing a number of topics, from latitude and longitude, to the causes of hypoxia, they all settled into evening free time.  Finding no more food, the rabbits departed as the sky began to turn pink.

Ilika noticed Miko, Sata, Buna, and Misa with the meditators.  Only Toli and Neti seemed determined to avoid it.

✳

The temperature plunged well below freezing that night, a dry and windless cold that was easy to bear.  Their stockpile of wood made for a quick morning fire, and little creatures gathered even before the tray arrived.  Hot tea, fresh biscuits, butter, and stewed fruit soon warmed them on the inside.

"Two of the rules of quantification theory are simple and easy to use," Ilika began, "but the other two are tricky and can fool you.  We'll start with a simple one."

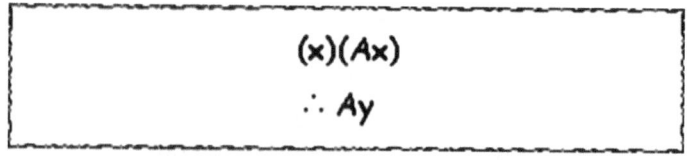

"The universal instantiation," he continued.  "Everything, x, has quality A. Therefore, any one thing, y, also has quality A."

"Everything is cold," Mati said with a shiver, "therefore Mati is cold!"

Boro chuckled.  "That fire sure looks hot to me!"

She gave him a friendly punch in the shoulder.

"Isn't it true that there are always exceptions to everything?" Rini asked.

"Yes," Ilika said.  "Mati's logic was valid, but in the real world we live in, it's hard to find absolutes like 'everything' or 'nothing.'  Most things are relative."

"Everything in the real world is relative. Therefore, cold in the real world is relative."

All those in the circle looked at Sata, the youngest student of all, with amazement. Ilika even noticed the meditating sister open her eyes for a moment, as if curious to see who had spoken.

✳

"It feels funny to be up here when Toli is down there meditating," Rini said as he stood on a rock outcropping on the southeastern face of the mountain a good five hundred feet above the guest house.

"I think Toli would have done anything," Ilika said, "when the sister about his age took him by the hand — wash dishes, stand on his head, anything."

Rini chuckled. "Did you see Buna's face?"

"She was very quick to take his other hand, wasn't she?"

"Yeah. Then Neti couldn't stand being the only one not doing it." Rini was silent for a minute. "This is so beautiful. Thanks for making me come up here."

"That's what teachers are for. Meditation is obviously easy for you."

They were both silent awhile, gazing out over mountain peaks and valleys.

Rini suddenly smiled. "Something wonderful is about to happen, isn't it?"

"You feel it?"

Rini nodded. "But I don't know what it is."

"Kibi senses it too," Ilika said with sparkling eyes. "I think we'll find out soon."

✳

"The universal generalization is very, very tricky. Some things have quality A, therefore all things do."

$$Ay$$
$$\therefore (x)(Ax)$$

Most of the students frowned with suspicion.

Seeing this, Ilika smiled. "Let's say every donkey we've ever seen is blue. We might be tempted to say all donkeys are blue."

"How could you be *sure*?" Boro questioned.

"That's the problem. Sometimes the very definition of the thing makes it a reasonably small number, and you can check them all."

"Like all the magic bracelets in the kingdom," Buna proposed, "can tell the altitude, the temperature, and the humidity."

"How do you know?" Miko challenged. "Have you searched the whole kingdom for magic bracelets? Maybe the healer at Port Town has one in a box somewhere."

Buna became red-faced for a moment. "Okay! All the magic bracelets on

Ilika's *arms!*"

Several looked at Ilika to be sure.

He pulled up his tunic sleeves so they could see he had only one. "Buna just discovered how difficult it is to be sure we've checked them all. What if, like with most things, we can't?"

"If we find one that's different," Mati said, "like Tera, who isn't blue, then we can't do it, we can't generalize."

"Right, Mati. If we find even one counter-example, we cannot make a universal generalization."

"I get it!" Neti suddenly jumped in excitedly. "If we say 'all' or 'none,' that's hard to prove because they're absolutes!"

Ilika nodded vigorously.

"But what if we're really, really, really sure," Rini asked, "but can't check them all?"

"Here's the rule," Ilika answered. "If we have very strong reason to believe that any randomly-selected item has the quality, AND no reason to believe otherwise, AND no counter-example, then we can make a *tentative* universal generalization."

Boro nodded with a look of satisfaction.

*

That afternoon, the priestess sitting silently against the wall of the guest house could sense that all eleven guests had joined her in meditation. The young sister who had reached out to Toli was gone, but Buna was right there to take her place, hand in hand with Toli, eyes closed.

Neti squirmed until Miko took her hand. Just as she relaxed, something small and furry curled up in her lap and fell asleep.

*  *  *

## Chapter 5: Lights

The evening temperature was dropping rapidly as an elder priestess brought their dinner tray. By her dress and jewelry, she appeared to be of higher status than any of the younger sisters. As she entered the guest house, her bright eyes took in everything and looked deeply into each person's soul.

The group could also tell that something unusual was afoot by the quality of the food. Their tray was laden with meat and pot herbs, buttered bread, cheeses, and a small jug of wine.

To their surprise, the high priestess did not sit and begin meditating, but instead took a seat at the fire circle and warmed her hands. She quickly had several little creatures around her, more even than Rini tended to attract.

With a new person at their fire, some of the students fidgeted with discomfort. After gently moving a chipmunk, Kibi sat down beside the woman. Rini did the same on the other side.

Ilika began cutting the meat into twelve pieces. "This is a special meal. I'm sorry we are ignorant of the holy days of the order, and wish there was some way we could learn the meaning of this day."

The elder priestess nodded slowly, but offered no explanation. Ilika held the tray for her, and Neti handed her a bowl.

A slight smile touched the woman's face, and she accepted the first portions of meat, vegetables, and bread.

The meal was eaten mostly in silence, although many glances were exchanged, and the high priestess confidently made eye contact with all her guests. Bowls and cups were wiped clean with bread, and wine was poured.

A shaking voice suddenly spoke from an unexpected source. "I . . . at first I . . . thought that if I closed my eyes . . . I might . . . I don't know . . . I might die or something," Toli struggled to say. "I know it sounds . . . silly . . . but I've never . . . closed my eyes before . . . except when sleep made me do it."

"I can relate to that," Boro jumped in. "Most of us were slaves once," he said in explanation to the high priestess.

She nodded.

"The only way ... I could do it today was because ... someone was holding my hand," Toli admitted. "That hand was like ... the only thing keeping me from ... feeling like I would die."

Buna smiled from beside him on the log.

One by one, the others began to share things they had recently learned or discovered. Rini and Buna spoke of their meditations. Sata explained universal instantiation, and Boro continued with the universal generalization, including how tricky it could be. Miko and Kibi talked about their experiences in the mountains before coming to the guest house, and Mati shared how two sets of things created four different logical possibilities. Neti shared her brush with dehydration and hypoxia, and Misa spoke of the fire that had destroyed her home and probably killed her parents.

The woman listened with sparkling eyes to each person. As stories were told, the sun set somewhere behind the mountain and the twilight faded from the sky.

When the full dark of night was nearly at hand and everyone had fallen silent in their telling, the high priestess rose and motioned for them to come with her. She gestured again, clearly wanting them to bring all their belongings.

They looked at Ilika.

"I think we're being invited to the monastery."

The woman nodded.

"I'm going," Ilika announced. "Anyone who does not wish to go, may stay here. While at the monastery, we must be silent."

She nodded again.

Although some faces showed a little fear, no one expressed a desire to stay. Within ten minutes, everything was packed and Tera was saddled.

They approached the top of the next rise on the trail, beyond which none of them had ever gone. The slight glow of unseen firelight flickered on the rocks above the trail, and a faint throbbing echoed off the mountainside. They could see their breath in the air, and the falling temperature promised a clear, cold night.

As they crested the top of the rise, torches came into view. Not far ahead, the trail passed under a large wooden portal with mysterious carved faces and painted symbols.

Mati could feel Tera's fear, and kept the reins tight. Concentrating on controlling the donkey helped her to ignore the knot in her own stomach.

Ilika seemed perfectly comfortable, and Kibi and Rini hesitated only a little. Boro and Sata stood for a moment before continuing down the trail toward the portal. The rest took a few steps back toward the guest house before mastering themselves and following their companions.

One by one, they all passed under the wooden portal, gazing up at the eerie faces and symbols dancing in the torch light.

The trail, lined with more torches, wound down the rocky slope into a sheltered valley. A large wooden building of three or four floors sat beside a level clearing. As Boro descended the steep path toward the main building, torches sprang to life in the clearing beyond. His mouth opened in wonder as priestesses moved to and fro like ghosts, never speaking a word.

The group of travelers approached the main hall of the monastery, its upper floors towering over them and every window glowing with lamplight from within.

A sister stepped out of a shed, and with gestures she offered to take Tera. Mati thought for a moment, then dismounted, whispered comforting words to her faithful donkey, and received her crutch from Miko.

The high priestess led them into the building. Simple tables and stools filled part of the main floor, while crude rugs and pillows surrounded stone fireplaces. The smell of baking bread came from unseen ovens. The high priestess gestured for them to set down their rucksacks, and then led them on through the building and out the door on the far side.

The clearing just below the main hall, perhaps a hundred feet across, was ablaze with a complete circle of torches. A large iron fire-bowl, still unlit, waited in the exact center. The high priestess led them into the circle, then motioned for them to follow a younger priestess along one side.

For the next few minutes, many more women and girls took up their places around the circle. Finally, with everything ready, the clearing became filled with complete silence and stillness, save for the soft shuffling of nervous feet coming from the monastery's guests.

✳

The high priestess walked with measured steps to the center of the circle, stood for a moment in contemplation, then suddenly raised her arms. The drumming resumed as she began to walk around the inside of the circle, chanting words in another tongue that meant nothing to Ilika or the students. While she walked, all the torches along the trail and all the lamps in the great hall were extinguished by unseen hands.

The chant was taken up by women who came dancing into the circle from several directions. As the chanting continued, seven different priestesses, at seven points around the circle, began dramatic rituals.

To the left of the students and their teacher, a white-haired crone waved a sword, her ritual clearly about conflict and death. To their right, a golden-haired maiden tossed leaves and flowers into the air, and her ceremony spoke of birth and life and abundance. As they peered around with wide eyes, most of the students felt the rituals speaking directly to their hearts, and the meanings were clear.

The chanting gradually became louder and faster, and the words changed as time passed, but always in a strange language. When all seven of the rituals around the circle were complete, another began in the center. Five women and one girl wore simple white robes and no jewelry. Part of the time they lay face-down on the hard ground, later still they kneeled before the high priestess, and finally they walked around the unlit iron bowl with arms outstretched.

Eventually, with the chanting at a fever-pitch, the seven youngest girls of the order, all less than ten years of age, lit hand-torches at the outside of the circle and slowly walked toward the center. All at the same moment, the seven girls thrust their torches into the iron brazier, and purple flames leapt high into the air as all the chanters held the last word of their song in loud, clear voices.

✳

All the sights and sounds of the ritual until now had stirred the emotions of the students more than any public performance they had ever seen or imagined. But what happened next was almost shocking by contrast.

The leaping purple flames quickly died out. At the same moment, the last chanted word faded away and every one of the torches was snuffed. No man-made light remained anywhere on the mountain.

Everyone's eyes were immediately drawn to the sky, but not by the moon or stars. Ghostly green curtains of light slowly danced far in the north, and sounds of amazement escaped many of the students. A few of the young girls, and one of the older novices, also slipped.

The students stood captivated. All of the sisters of the monastery gazed upward, some from their knees, some standing with arms raised. The green curtains faded and a streaky red glow appeared on the northern horizon.

For the next hour, the mind-boggling show continued, sometimes joined by rapidly-moving blue curtains, occasionally punctuated by flashes of purple. At other times the slow green lights returned, or the nearly-stationary red glow.

✳

For Sata, this was the ultimate challenge. She somehow knew that if she was up there, in the dancing lights, she would not survive. She wasn't sure if she would be burnt to a crisp or frozen solid, but it didn't matter. She had learned from her teacher that many things in the world were far greater than her, and yet they were her friends, in a sense, if she was respectful and careful. They could give her beauty and wonder and understanding, none of which she could get if she trembled in fear and buried her head in the sand.

Rini was almost moved to tears. If he had had wings to fly, he would have left the world behind to soar among the dancing lights. But at the same time, he had a deep curiosity about the forces that could cause such a grand display. He knew an artist, like Pica, created a beautiful picture because she wanted to. His mind opened up to the spectacle before him and craved to know what mysterious will could lead to such beauty and grandeur.

Boro was deeply impressed, and at the same time he wanted to know the details so he could help keep everyone safe. He wondered if there was some radiation danger even here, so far from the glowing, shifting curtains and dancing sprites in the sky. From recent lessons he knew it was all in the planet's magnetic field, forty-five thousand miles away. He was tempted to break the silence and ask Ilika about it, but decided that his teacher would say something if there was any danger.

Mati thought of Tera. She was now very glad the sister had taken the donkey into a shed where Tera could not see what they were seeing. Mati knew that ions and free electrons interacting with the magnetosphere were nothing to be concerned about down here. She was pretty sure Tera would not have taken it so lightly.

Eventually the spectacle faded and was gone, leaving about two hundred sisters, and eleven visitors, feeling very small in the midst of the awesome power and beauty of the universe.

✴ ✴ ✴

## Chapter 6: Particle Physics and Existential Rules

After a minute of silence, all the sisters and their guests streamed into the main hall of the monastery, shivering from the cold but elated by the experience. Fires were built up in the fireplaces, mugs of hot tea poured, and soon everyone found warmth and good company. A few small creatures appeared, and bread scraps allowed them to share in the celebration.

Both Miko and Toli had trouble remaining silent, but never got out more than a syllable before feeling a jab from one of their friends. They noticed that some giggling was tolerated in the youngest sisters, but no speech.

Mati felt the need to check on Tera. She glanced at Rini with a worried look. He nodded, gently extracted a squirrel from his lap, and walked out to the shed.

After about an hour, the crowded hall began to thin out as the sisters went upstairs or out to other buildings. One of them showed the group an open floor area covered with thick rugs near one of the fireplaces where they could sleep.

It was not long before the eleven guests, quite exhausted from their long day of studies and the intense evening of unexpected wonders, were fast asleep, dreaming of logic rules and dancing lights in the sky.

✳

The students were again amazed at the level of cooperation possible without speech as they joined the two hundred sisters for a simple breakfast of biscuits and goat cheese, tea and crab apples.

After breakfast, one of the priestesses tapped Kibi on the shoulder, and led her to a corner of the building where a map on the wall depicted all the mountain paths. Kibi got Sata, and together they silently worked to transfer the information to Sata's map. Judging by distances they had already walked, the town of Nug appeared to be a day's walk, perhaps a day and a half, assuming no unexpected snow storms.

Another sister brought them a tray stacked with hard crackers, fully-cured cheese, dried fruit, and other travel foods, enough for about two days. Boro silently coordinated the distribution and packing after handing the woman a great silver piece.

✳

As the group was making preparations to depart, the high priestess appeared. She spent a minute looking into the eyes of each of the travelers.

In most she saw the insecurities of youth but great strength and determination. In a few she saw deep fears that might need more than a lifetime to heal. In all the ex-slaves, she saw the hurt and shame they had suffered, and it almost made her cry.  In Ilika she saw something completely foreign to her, and knew he was from a very different place, one she couldn't even imagine.

To each she gave a silent blessing, tracing a sacred symbol on their foreheads with her finger, before bowing and leaving them with a young sister of eight or nine years.

A clear and bright morning was quickly driving away the night chill, promising a day without cloaks for anyone walking or working.  The young sister accompanied them through the carved wooden portal and up to the top of the ridge.  There she remained, birds on her shoulders, waving silently as the eleven visitors began their journey past the little meadow with its guest house, and around the next bend in the trail.

The questions about the aurora started coming at Ilika as soon as the students were out of sight of the young sister.  He waited until they made brief stops for a drink, a light snack, or just to admire the view.  At each stop, he took the time to tackle at least one question.

Previous lessons about the atmosphere, magnetosphere, and solar wind had been far removed from their everyday lives.  Suddenly, it was knowledge they craved.  They needed to know all about the behavior of free electrons in a magnetic field.  They demanded a drawing, to scale, of the strangely-shaped magnetosphere.  They begged for an explanation of both the incandescent and florescent processes that created the lights.

By mid-day they were in red-berry territory again, and that gave Ilika more opportunities to answer their questions as everyone picked and ate.

"It seems like," Mati began as she sat on a boulder slicing cheese for everyone, "finding the monastery, the meditating, the ritual, and seeing the aurora . . . it seems like it all fit into your lessons perfectly, like you planned it.  But I don't see how you could have."

"I could not have planned it," Ilika admitted.  "None of those events were known to me in advance.  But I do have help, you know.  I hope you don't think I'm all alone in figuring out what to teach you, when, and how."

None of them made any response, but his words echoed in their minds with more power than anything he might say about charged particles or magnetic fields.

Kibi remembered the green lights and the voice that had led her out of the smoke and fire.

*

By mid-afternoon, the questions were beginning to taper off. They took a break at a little stream to drink the icy cold water and eat mouthfuls of berries.

Sata looked at the map, filled in some elevation readings Ilika made, and asked Buna to take a compass bearing. Buna was always happy for a reason to use Ilika's knowledge processor.

That evening, by a small lake at seven thousand two hundred feet, the students finally felt satisfied in their desire to understand the aurora. Rini admitted that even if he had wings, the mysterious lights were so high up that there was not enough air for wings to work, nor enough to breathe. Sata joined Rini in remembering the color shifts and strange shapes, appreciating the beauty of it all with no thoughts of labeling it evil.

When they saw Ilika getting out a piece of paper, one of the last few with unused space on either side, they quickly put extra wood on the fire and gathered to listen.

"The existential generalization is the other rule that's pretty simple."

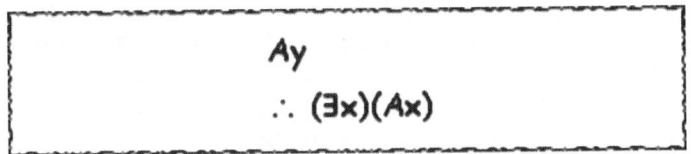

"We know of an individual thing, y, that has quality A. Therefore, some things, x, have quality A. The word 'some' in logic means one or more. But where there's one, there are usually many others."

"So if I could find a purple donkey," Buna began, "then I could say some donkeys are purple."

"Right."

Boro thought for a moment. "That's about as simple as it comes."

*

The night was cold, but not as bitter as it had been at the monastery. In the morning, Miko and Toli worked together to rekindle the fire for hot tea to go with crackers, cheese, and dried plums.

They were all rolling up bedrolls and closing rucksacks when Sata stood up and faced Ilika with a smile of pride on her face. "I figured out the last quantification rule!"

Ilika quickly got out paper and pencil for her.

$$(\exists x)(Ax)$$
$$\therefore Ay$$

"Um . . . it's the . . . existential . . . instantiation," Sata explained, saying the words slowly and carefully. "Some x have . . . um . . . quality A. Therefore . . . a thing y does too!"

"Okay," Ilika began as everyone gathered around to see if Sata had really gotten it right or not. "Good so far. But this is one of the tricky ones. The critical step is how y is selected. How do we know a *certain* y has quality A?"

"Oh . . . crap . . ." Sata began, frowning, ". . . um . . . we look at it?"

Toli snickered.

"Actually, she's right. When we say that some x have quality A, we might be saying that as little as *one* of them, out of all the millions there might be, has that quality. The individual item y must be a specific, *tested* individual item. In other words, like Sata said, we have to look at it."

"Sorry," Toli said in a tiny voice, looking at the ground.

"So if Sata is making a stew," Kibi began, ignoring Toli, "and I show up with a basket of mushrooms and say that *some* of them are edible . . ."

Sata grinned. "I'm not putting *any* of them in my stew until you tell me which ones!"

Ilika smiled. "Excellent example. This is the only one of the four rules that requires an examination of the individual item. And Kibi's example shows how logic is just good thinking habits."

"The price of *not* thinking, when putting mushrooms in a stew," Mati said with big, round eyes, "is a very high price to pay."

Everyone nodded, most of them from personal experience, or the experience of a former friend.

✳  ✳  ✳

## Chapter 7: Hardtack and Hard Choices

By mid-morning they were on the trail again, following the lines on Sata's map toward the little town of Nug on the main path through the mountains. Though they sometimes had to gain a little elevation to go from one mountain valley to the next, they knew they were generally traveling downhill. The trees, few and stunted near the monastery, were getting larger, and tasty berries more plentiful.

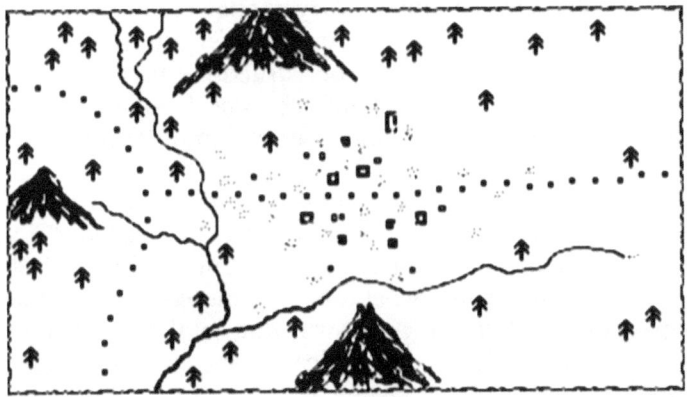

Sprawled in a bleak, nearly-treeless valley at six thousand eight hundred feet, the town of Nug was a shocking disappointment. It had not experienced any natural disaster, but somehow Lumber Town had seemed more inviting, even after the fire.

Rini squinted at the broken boxes and barrels piled everywhere, sometimes mixed with the bones of horses or donkeys.

Mati frowned when she saw entire families living in ragged tents, flies buzzing everywhere, and no stream nearby.

Ilika set his jaw. "Small groups, eyes open, stay close. Boro, quick scout through the town."

Boro tapped Toli on the shoulder. They slipped out of their rucksacks and walked through the entire settlement, finding a few flimsy wooden buildings at its center, but no sturdy stone or timber structures anywhere.

The rest of the travelers waited among some boulders just outside the town. Mati stayed mounted, and had no intention of letting Tera out of her sight.

Suddenly someone came running out of a tent behind one of the wooden buildings carrying a chunk of bread. An unseen voice yelled, "Thief!" From out of another tent someone else ran after the thief and brought him down, and a scrappy fist-fight began. Several boys gathered to watch the fight, but no one else paid much attention. A scrawny dog got the bread and ran off.

Ilika saw that his scouts were well clear of the commotion, so he stayed where he was.

"Lots of poor people here," Sata mumbled.

"No soldiers," Kibi observed.

A few minutes later, Boro and Toli returned to the group. "This place is sad," Boro said with a sigh.

"There's food for sale, just the basics," Toli reported. "Two shops and an outdoor stand."

"One inn, but it's just a few bunks," Boro added.

Suddenly the group realized they were not alone. A skinny girl of about twelve years, wearing little more than rags, had crept close among the rocks. As soon as they looked at her, she bravely stood up and faced them.

"Got'ny food?" she asked with mixed embarrassment and desperation.

Kibi opened her rucksack and looked inside. "Um . . . yeah, a little . . . if you'll tell us about this town of yours."

The cracker that Kibi held out was snatched and consumed in seconds. "Not my town. Hate it here. Someone said they found a little gold in a stream, so my stupid dad just had to drag us up here." She accepted a crab apple from Sata and took a moment to devour it, seeds and all.

"Then he got killed in a fight. He wasn't thieving. It was over who gets to work the streams."

Kibi handed her more crackers. "Why don't you leave?"

The girl cringed for a moment. "Mom's got a business going. You know . . . selling herself . . . wenching. We get about a meal a day." As she spoke, her eyes remained glued to the cheese Buna was slicing.

"Will we run into any trouble if we just buy supplies and then head out of town?" Buna asked, passing the cheese to the hungry girl.

"You got lots of money? Copper don't do no good here. I remember getting a loaf for a copper or two where we used to live, good tasty bread. Here it's hardtack, and it's usually stale, and it's a silver piece. But if you got plenty of money, you'll be okay . . . just watch your back."

The edge gone from her hunger, she began to chew more slowly. Not knowing what else to say, she gazed off across the valley with a hopeless expression.

"You need to get out of here," Mati said from atop Tera, "or this place is gonna eat you up."

The girl looked up at Mati. She almost smiled for a moment, but then her face fell. "No place to go."

&ast;

Mati dismounted and the group got comfortable. They shared the last of their food from the monastery with the girl, whose name was Kali, and told her about some of their adventures.

Kibi asked Ilika to take a short walk with her. She had already realized it would do no good to invite Kali to come with them, as the girl would just be in the same situation in another place in a few weeks, and without the support of her mother. But Kibi had something else in mind. Ilika listened, and felt her plan had a reasonable chance of success, so he agreed.

They returned to the group in time to get the last two pieces of cheese.

"Kibi has asked me for a few hours here so we can give our friend Kali some ideas for her future. During that time, I will get supplies, with the help of . . . Toli and Miko. You'll need an empty rucksack."

Miko emptied his pack, and soon the three were heading toward one of the shops. As they approached the town, Ilika explained that they would rotate buying, carrying, and watching for trouble. Knowing their assigned tasks, they stepped into the first shop.

&ast;

The wooden structure looked like it had seen too many winters and was in danger of collapsing on their heads. The smoke told them it was as close to a bakery as they were going to find.

"Keep the sack on your back until we settle up," the clerk said in a stern voice.

"Okay," Toli squeaked.

Another man, large and muscular, sat on a barrel while sharpening his knife and observing the travelers.

Miko stood back, hands in his pockets.

"How's the bread supply?" Ilika asked.

"Two from yesterday. Eight more out of the oven soon, but I don't put them out 'til the old stuff's gone."

"We'll take all ten."

"You got a great silver?"

"I do. And I want about five pounds of those porridge grains . . ."

✳

After waiting for the fresh hardtack, and adding some dried apples and small beans to the order, they paid and packed without trouble.

"Why is everything so expensive?" Miko asked on the way back to the group.

"It has to be carried up here on someone's back," Ilika explained. "Also, there isn't much competition. And with gold in the streams, at least a few people have lots of money. All of those conditions push prices up. Imagine the most extreme case — you are hungry, you have a wheel barrow full of gold, and someone else has the only loaf of bread."

Toli's eyes opened wide. "All of a sudden the price of bread would be *very* high!"

Ilika nodded as they came to the group, now sitting down among the rocks and almost completely hidden from view. Even Tera was hard to see when she had her head down, looking for something to eat on the stony ground.

As Miko unloaded the rucksack, they listened as the others told Kali about the monastery, its main hall, guest house, ritual field, and everything else they had seen.

Ilika handed his coin pouch to Toli, Miko took up the empty bag, and they headed for the second shop.

✳

Toli successfully purchased several hard cheeses, dried plums, and small pots of honey and molasses. The matron wanted to see silver before she would even take an item down from its shelf. Two of her grown sons stood guard.

"These ceramic pots are heavy!" Toli complained on the way back to the meeting place.

"But just think how good that honey will taste in porridge!" Miko pointed out. "I'll carry one if you'll carry the other . . ."

Toli grinned. "Okay!"

Ilika smiled.

As soon as they arrived at the boulders, Ilika put his finger to his lips. The rest, including Kali, were sitting in meditation. They unloaded quickly and quietly, then headed back toward the center of town.

✳

The remaining shop was just an outdoor stand in what remained of a collapsed building. Miko found several herbs and spices he knew the girls would want, a mixture of dried vegetables, and some small dried peas. He was just about to pay when he spotted something else.

"Is that what I think it is? Candy?"

"It sure is!" the man said as he opened the little wooden box so his customer could see the assortment. "Three silvers."

Miko looked at Ilika.

"Sorry, Miko. I'm just the beast of burden right now. You have to make the decisions."

After a moment of thought, Miko nodded, and the clerk added the box of candy to the pile. Miko brought out the two great silver pieces needed to settle their bill.

"I'm glad I didn't have a wheel barrow full of gold — I might have spent it all!" Miko admitted as they returned to the group.

Ilika and Toli laughed.

✳

As the shoppers unpacked for the last time, Kali was studying the map with Sata.

"Ilika, we don't need this map anymore, do we?" Sata asked. "If I could just give it to her, it would help her find the trail."

Ilika sat down on the ground with the others and nodded.

Kali lovingly received the map. "They've told me how I'm going to wind up a wench or a slave if I don't find my courage and get out of here."

"I think they're right," Ilika agreed. "Your mom is choosing her path. She probably won't last much longer. You need to choose yours, or you'll get stuck. I could see you were strong when you faced us and asked for food."

"I am strong. And Rini told me how meditating will make me even stronger."

"He's right. And the monastery will teach you many things, and it will keep you free. You don't have to stay in the order your whole life. Someday, you may discover that a different path calls to you."

"I wanna stay free."

"The hardest step will be the first step, saying good-bye to your mom and getting out of this valley. Maybe you can't even say good-bye, and you'll just have to go. You must make that decision."

"When she gets back from wenching, she's usually had wine. I'll tell her then, and she won't care. By the time she wakes up the next day, I'll be gone."

"You know it's a silent order?"

"Yep. They told me I should be quiet when I get there and just speak with my eyes, my smile, and my heart. I can do that. And they said I'd learn to work with others without using words."

Ilika looked at his students. "I need three great silver pieces."

They looked in their pouches until the coins were located.

"One is to leave as a gift for your mother," he said, handing Kali the coin.

The girl swallowed and nodded.

"One is for you to get supplies for your journey to the monastery. It took us two days."

"Thank you," she whispered.

"The third is to give to the high priestess of the order, along with a letter I will write. It will help them to know that you are serious about learning and becoming one of them. A weak person would spend the money before arriving."

Kali smiled and clutched the three coins tightly.

The group of travelers spent as much time with Kali as they could, but Ilika wanted to get some distance down the trail by dark. Kibi was tempted to propose they stay for a day or two and see their new friend off. Then she noticed several local people snooping close to the boulders with squinting eyes, so she held her tongue.

As they headed east and passed over a rise, they all shared their concerns that Kali would not find the courage to leave, or she would lose the three coins, or they would be stolen.

Ilika remained silent. Others pointed out that they could only do so much, and that Kali had to take responsibility for herself, or live with the consequences. As they walked along, Kodi's name came up several times, and they remembered a certain gold piece that had not been enough to keep him out of slavery.

Kibi took advantage of the wide main trail to walk beside Ilika at the back of the group. "That's a pretty serious test you set up. I wonder if she'll guess the letter tells them about the great silver piece."

"She'll probably guess, but at least it will test her self-control. I've become rather good at arranging tests during the last few months, haven't I?"

Kibi grinned. "That's for sure! I wonder how many of them I can pass ..."

"Hah! You proved yourself to me the first week we were together."

Kibi's hand found his. "I wish we could visit the monastery again someday, meditate with them, maybe see the aurora, see if Kali made it."

"I think we might be able to do that," Ilika said with a slight smile.

Kibi looked at him with a puzzled expression, but he said no more.

## Chapter 8: The Way Down

For the next two days, the group journeyed east and slightly south. The trail took them from one rocky alpine valley to another, with no sign that the mountains would ever end. When they met other travelers, they were told they would be going down soon enough — the trail didn't follow any of the valleys southward because of impassable gorges.

The group was in good spirits, and Ilika used rest stops and evenings around the campfire to challenge them with complex logic problems. Some required the rules of inference they had learned earlier, and others needed the new quantification rules. When they could think about such things no longer, they got out *The Adventures of Godi and Tima* and took turns reading whole chapters with good story-telling voices and dramatic flair.

They wondered about Kali and her new path, but knew it was no longer in their hands.

※

Finally, on the third day out from Nug, they came to a pass at six thousand eight hundred feet that took their breath away. The mountains abruptly ended, and a dry canyon of twisted and tortured rock outcroppings, through which the trail wound, quickly dropped several thousand feet, leveling out in a prairie far below.

"Wow," Boro breathed. "Now I know what people were talking about."

"Do we still have that rope?" Miko asked with round eyes. "We might need it!"

Rini chuckled. "It's in the bottom of my bag, but I don't think it's long enough."

"Mati . . ." Ilika began.

"I know. If she started running, I'd never be able to stop her."

Buna raised her eyebrows. "She'll do better than Noni's wagon would!"

"This is why no one brings a cart up here," Boro said calmly, gazing at the steep trail below. "Anything that got rolling would soon be splinters."

From the shade of a pine tree, the eleven travelers chewed on stale hardtack and discussed the path before them.  At several points in the canyon, they could see sections of the trail, usually switching back and forth across a steep and dangerous slope.  At many places it was completely hidden, winding through the rocks or disappearing for a time into a side canyon.

Sata received a piece of dry cheese. "This is natural, right Ilika?"

"Very natural.  It's probably the edge of a tectonic plate, an ocean plate colliding with a continental plate, I would guess."

"A *what*?" Buna asked with her squirrelly expression.

"Okay, geology lesson tonight."

After everyone had eaten and rested, Ilika looked at the steep trail again while rubbing the knot in his stomach. "Tight reins, Mati.  Dead slow, and two people walking by Tera's head on all the steep parts."

"That's every inch," Sata observed with a wrinkled brow.

Boro grinned at her, and he and Toli silently volunteered for duty, stepping beside Tera.

After taking some deep breaths and remembering the circle of thieves, the high tide, and the wolf, Mati nodded that she was ready.

Kibi led the way.  Ilika walked just in front of the donkey and her helpers.  Neti and Miko brought up the rear.

Unlike most of the rocky paths in the mountains, this trail soon turned to crumbly yellow dirt, and every few yards little gullies forced the travelers to step over.  Boro and Toli quickly gave up walking beside Tera, and joined Ilika on the trail in single file.

To Mati's delight, Tera seemed perfectly comfortable with the steep path and made no attempt to break into a run, so she relaxed the reins a little.  Tera was not at all bothered by the little gullies, and could easily step over.

When they paused at the first level place, Ilika looked at the donkey with greater respect. "There are many things I don't know about donkeys."

"She's a good donkey, but I still want someone walking in front of her," Mati said.

"You've got it!" Rini said.

Boro smiled at the slender lad, but made sure someone else was in front of the donkey also.

They continued downward in a lighter mood, and soon entered the first of the jumbles of huge boulders, many towering ten or fifteen feet over the trail.

Miko easily climbed one of the jumbles, then found he could leap from one boulder to another high above the other walkers.

"Are you having fun, Miko?" Neti asked with a grin, shielding her eyes and looking up to see the love of her life standing tall on a boulder, scanning the trail ahead.

"I'm king of the world!" he called down. "There's a short level stretch ahead, then a steep switchback."

Miko saw several boulders laid out before him like stepping stones. Some of the gaps required a big leap, so he got a running start.

Moments later, Neti heard his yell for help, then a cry of pain, and finally the thud of something heavy smashing onto the rocks far below. Her blood froze in her veins as she screamed her defiance to the universe.

"MIKO, NO!"

Her scream pierced the silence and echoed through the ravines and gullies of the tumbled land. She bolted forward, almost knocking Tera and Mati off the trail, tears filling her eyes and panic filling her mind. Boro caught her, but was barely able to hold her.

With a sinking feeling of despair, Ilika worked his way through the rocks with Kibi close behind. They soon discovered the place, and it was immediately clear what had happened. The last boulder of the outcrop was just a finger of rock, too far from the others to easily jump to, and too small to land upon. The ground was a good twenty feet down, covered with sharp, broken boulders.

As Neti screamed and fought against Boro, Ilika and Kibi picked their way down to Miko's resting place. Blood poured from gashes on his head and arms, and his breath came in gasps with a gurgling sound.

"Help Neti get down here!" Ilika yelled as he quickly removed his bracelet and placed it on Miko's arm. It emitted several complex tones, causing Ilika to cringe.

All Boro's strength barely kept Neti from flinging herself down to Miko's side. "MIKO!" she screamed as she landed in the rocks beside him, scraping and bruising herself but not feeling it.

"Take his hand and talk to him, Neti," Ilika said, his voice shaking. "You don't have long."

Trembling, Neti took his limp hand in hers. "Miko! Please be okay, Miko. Please . . ." Her words quickly became deep sobs.

Kibi looked at Ilika questioningly. He shook his head slowly in response.

Miko's eyelids fluttered as he gasped for a breath, struggled to say his beloved's name one last time, then lay still.

"He's asleep," Neti said through her sobs. "He'll be okay when he wakes up."

✳

For the next hour or more, Neti stayed with Miko, believing him asleep. She spoke to him, promising him that sleep would heal him, that he would be leaping from boulder to boulder again soon.

Buna, Sata, and Misa climbed down to be with their friend. Taking their cue from Ilika, they let Neti continue to believe that Miko was merely asleep.

Mati and Rini found a place where Tera could get some grass, then found a way down to the scene of the accident that Mati, with help, could navigate.

Toli couldn't find the courage to join them. Miko had been his friend, even when no one else wanted anything to do with him. Now, with Miko gone, he suddenly felt very alone, so he sat on a rock near Tera and silently cried.

✳

Ilika made himself walk around the area to see where they could camp. He found a level place close to the outer edge of the hillside where dirt had piled up against a small rock outcropping, hidden from the trail by the huge boulders.

The place was also, for the moment, hidden from his students.

Ilika fell to his knees and couldn't stop tears from running down his face. With clenched fists he looked up at the sky and let all his guilt and frustration show for whomever might be watching.

About a quarter hour later, after wiping his face on his sleeve, he returned to the site of the tragedy and sat down by Kibi, who took his hand.

"I think she's starting to see," Kibi whispered.

"Miko, please wake up . . ." Neti said in a pleading but helpless tone.

Ilika squeezed Kibi's hand, and then went and sat near Neti. Buna and Sata were still flanking their stricken friend, touching her constantly to remind her she was not alone.

"He's not gonna wake up, is he?" she asked no one in particular in a helpless voice.

"Not in this world, Neti," Ilika whispered softly. "He's going to wake up in another world, and he will never forget you, his beloved from his mortal life. And someday you will join him there, and you can both remember all the sweet times you shared."

Neti was starting to see all the blood and bruises. Miko's skin was slowly turning gray, cold, and stiff. She had held his hand many times when he was asleep, but it didn't feel the same. Suddenly she dropped his lifeless hand and started crying deeply, clutching onto Buna and Sata fiercely.

✳

As evening crept over the land, Neti stayed beside Miko's lifeless body and took tiny steps toward accepting what had happened. Kibi replaced Buna, and a bit later Misa replaced Sata. Mati sat on a rock nearby, but because of her knee, was unable to comfort her friend while Neti was on the ground at

Miko's side.

Most of those not comforting Neti started to move rucksacks to the campsite. Boro took the bronze pot and shuffled down the trail, returning about half an hour later with water. Toli silently gathered some sticks for a fire. After getting directions from Boro, Rini guided Tera down to the spring for a drink, then back up to the camp. No one felt like cooking. A few chewed on hardtack or dried apples.

As darkness approached, Ilika and Boro lifted their fallen friend and carried him to the campsite. Neti walked along behind.

"We're going to need a fire all night to keep animals away," Ilika said softly to Boro as they placed Miko's broken body where a boulder would protect it on one side.

Boro nodded, picked helpers, and looked around for the best source of firewood.

Neti knelt down on the ground beside Miko's body and once again poured out her grief to anyone in the world who cared to listen.

✳  ✳  ✳

## Chapter 9: A Final Farewell

The entire day following Miko's death was spent in nearly complete silence. They had recently visited a monastery where all the sisters took vows of silence, but until this day, none of the students could imagine doing that out of choice. Now, for at least one day, it seemed right.

A dozen or more groups of travelers passed by on the trail that day, some going up carrying heavy loads, others coming down with little, except perhaps a few gold nuggets hidden away. Those going down included two priests on foot, the elder wearing a scowl, the younger a sad look of resignation. None of the travelers on the trail knew what was happening at the hidden camp on the other side of the boulders.

After a sleepless night, Neti sat by Miko's still form all day long, usually in silence, sometimes in tears. At least one of the girls was always with her, and often one of the boys. They all had fond memories of Miko, and needed to deal with their own grief, as well as comfort Neti.

Everyone else took turns getting water, or taking Tera to find more grass, or just poking around half-heartedly collecting a few sticks. At one point in the afternoon, Sata noticed that Ilika was taking the pot to get water, so she tagged along.

"I'm trying really hard to understand what happened, and I want to believe you when you say this place is natural, but a little voice in my head keeps telling me there's a connection between the weird rocks and Miko dying."

"There certainly is a connection. He fell from one of them."

Sata couldn't help but smile. "Okay . . . but isn't it something about the weird shapes?"

"I know what you're trying to do, Sata, but saying the rocks are evil is just pushing a human weakness away from us so we don't have to deal with it."

Ilika let some time pass in silence while he filled the pot at the trickling spring beside the trail.

"Rini finds the rocks very beautiful," Ilika continued. "You, and most of the others, are very careful when climbing on rocks. So you have two choices. You can brush off responsibility by saying the rocks are evil and somehow caused Miko's death. Or you can figure out what happened up there on the boulders, what Miko's weakness was, learn from his mistake, and become stronger in the process. I've already been up on the boulders. It's not hard, and it's not even very dangerous . . . except for the last one that he missed."

Sata was very thoughtful as they slowly trudged back uphill toward the camp.

"One thing I can guarantee," Ilika added, "is that the world will never change itself because of our weaknesses. In fact, it has ways of actually becoming *more* dangerous when we approach it with a bad attitude."

He fell silent as they approached the camp.

On the second day, Neti started asking questions.

Unfortunately, no one had answers to most of her questions. She didn't expect answers — she was talking to herself, to Miko, to all the unknown forces in the world she did not understand.

She was shocked when, a little after a lunch she hardly touched, someone said they had an answer to one of her questions.

"I know why Miko died," Sata announced. "Do you want me to tell you?"

Neti pondered this for a moment, then whispered, "Yes . . ."

Sata took a deep breath. "Ilika challenged me to understand and learn from Miko's death. So I decided to do that. I don't know anything about spirit worlds. Ilika knows about that stuff. I'm just a girl trying to learn where to put my feet . . . and where not to."

Everyone was spread out around the campsite and the nearby rocks. Now they gathered close to hear what Sata had to say.

"Boro, would you help me show what happened?"

"Sure."

Sata looked around. "See that rock that has a sloping top?"

"Yeah."

"Can you stand on it?"

"No problem," Boro declared, and stepped onto the small boulder without slipping.

"Okay, jump down," Sata requested, then got a handful of sandy dirt and sprinkled it on the rock. "Can you stand on it now?"

Boro tried to step onto the rock again, but his boot immediately slid out from under him and he landed on his rump on the ground.

Most everyone chuckled, as Boro was unhurt and smiling. A slight smile even appeared on Neti's face.

"That's why Miko died. I've been up there. The last boulder he jumped from is covered with sand. You can't see it until you're on top of it. He might have made it to the pointy rock if he had a good place to leap from. He might have seen the sand, but was going too fast to stop."

Hearing it described, Neti found herself reliving the moments of Miko's fall. She burst into tears, and Kibi and Rini wrapped their arms around her.

Sata remained silent, not knowing if she should say anything else.

"So . . ." Neti began as she wiped her face and tried to collect herself. "So he wasn't completely stupid?"

"I don't think he was stupid at all!" Sata replied. "He was brave . . . maybe a little too brave for these rocks. I'd really like to blame it on the rocks, or on the sand. But I can't. I know that now. They're just there, doing what rocks and sand do."

*

Neti was thoughtful after Sata's demonstration and didn't ask any more questions for the entire afternoon. She finally ate some soup at dinner.

As the sun set on that warm summer day, everyone started to notice the odor. After dishes were done, Neti finally asked the question she dreaded asking. "What do I do now, Ilika?"

"We need to bury Miko soon. It's your choice where we do that, but it has to be close. And we'll have whatever ceremony you want. I've never done this, so I hope you'll all help me figure it out."

Neti was silent awhile. "I don't know. Is here okay? Or would people be camping here?"

"There was no sign of anybody ever using it when we got here," Boro explained. "Too near the pass."

Rini opened his arms wide. "This is a beautiful place. It's hidden from the trail, but you can see forever!"

"We could bring rocks from where he died," Kibi suggested.

Neti sighed. "I don't know anything about ceremonies. I'll probably just cry. You know about spirits and things, right Ilika?"

"A little. Miko's spirit isn't here anymore. It left as soon as he died, and is resting . . . in a special place. The ceremony and burial are for us, to help us say good-bye."

"I've heard priests talk about funerals," Kibi said with a frown, "and it always comes down to giving them money. What you're saying, Ilika, makes a lot more sense to me. How do you know this stuff?"

"Where I come from, everyone knows."

*

After breakfast on the third day, Boro asked for Toli's help moving rocks. Rini and Buna joined the effort without being asked. They brought all the rocks they could move from where Miko had landed, and then collected more from other areas. Boro could carry many the others could not.

With Neti's blessing, Kibi and Sata started preparing the burial site in the center of their camping area. Ilika found some stout sticks, sharpened them with the knife, and they dug into the dirt as far as they could.

When Sata stopped to wipe the sweat from her face, she found Neti handing her a cup of water and offering to take the stick from her. Sata hesitated, then smiled and released the stick. There were plenty of rocks still to carry.

By the time the diggers started to hit bedrock, they had a hole big enough for Miko about a foot deep, two if they counted the mound of loose dirt.

As the day warmed, they were all motivated by the odor to hurry. Soon they felt satisfied with the pile of rocks they had moved, and gathered around the unlit fire.

"I think we should have an hour of silence," Rini suggested.

Sata wiped her forehead. "I want to wash before the ceremony."

"Me too," Boro agreed, "but after we move Miko."

Others shared their wishes for the ceremony, and Ilika wove it all into a plan. He and Boro wrapped Miko in his blankets, then carried him to his last resting place. They held their breath as much as possible, and when the task was completed, hurried down to the spring.

In silence, most of them washed, some sat in meditation, and a few collected wild flowers. Even Tera was very quiet. About an hour later they gathered around the open grave. The coolness of the earth made the stench bearable.

Ilika tried to swallow the lump in his throat. "Death is a mystery until we experience it. This is a time for sharing any thoughts or feelings about Miko, his death, or death itself. Neti decides when you may speak. When she hands you a pebble, it is your turn."

Kibi set a pile of pebbles in front of Neti.

Neti hadn't expected this, but it felt good. She just wished she could hand Miko a pebble.

Everyone spoke of Miko as a friend, and recounted the many times he had been helpful to them in some way. They all sensed it was a time to forgive and forget little slights, and indeed, no one could think of anything important to complain about. When Miko's weaknesses had gotten the best of him, it had always been to his own harm, and no one else had ever been seriously hurt.

Mati, Misa, and Rini had flowers to place in the grave. Kibi and Toli both had tears to shed as they spoke. Sata had written a few words of farewell on paper, which she placed on Miko's chest along with the flowers.

"I guess I'm the only one left," Neti began with a shaking voice, fingering the remaining pebbles. Tears rolled down her cheeks, but she didn't seem to notice. "I loved you, Miko. I would have been yours forever. Now I can't be. You were a pain in the butt sometimes, but I loved you anyway." She picked up the pebbles and tossed them into the grave.

Everyone took turns putting a rock or a handful of dirt gently onto Miko's body. Ilika and Boro set to work doing the rest, with others handing them rocks. About the time they finished, the sun slipped away over the mountains and left them in shadow.

\* \* \*

## Chapter 10: Moving On

Everyone agreed they should stay one more night and say good-bye to the place the following morning.  Since they had skipped lunch, Buna organized the biggest, richest stew they could make, and others cut bread and cheese, or went hunting for berries.

As soon as Kibi had eaten some stew to take the edge off her hunger, she posed the first question.  "So, Ilika . . . you know for sure there's life beyond the grave?"

He took a deep breath.  "I know that for sure.  But I have obviously not experienced it, so I don't know the details.  I know it's a different experience for different creatures, and even for the same creatures who have developed their souls to different degrees during life."

A long silence followed as they considered his words.

"Does . . . Tera . . . have a soul?" Mati asked timidly while contemplating the piece of cheese in her hand.

"Don't tell the high priest . . ."

Moans and snickers told Ilika there was no danger of that happening.

"Yes, Tera has a soul.  Any creature complex enough to make decisions about right and wrong can develop a soul.  That day she faced the wolf with you, instead of running away scared — that's the kind of day that makes a soul grow by leaps and bounds."

After a long silence, Neti found her voice.  "I hope Miko is somewhere nice, somewhere he can run free and jump from rock to rock."

"Maybe he can fly now," Buna suggested with a gleam in her eyes.  "He'd like that."

"What's a soul?" Rini asked, scraping his bowl with hardtack.

"The part of you — your memories, your decisions, your experiences, your wisdom — that you can take with you when you die.  As you know, you cannot take your body, your things, or other people.  Some people have very small, weak souls when they die, because they've chosen to live empty or fearful lives. All of you, and Miko, have very strong souls because you've had hard lives and are still smiling."

"You mean like when you stand on your own two feet with a smile on your face in the middle of a universe that contains a million ways to crush you?" Sata asked with a smirk.

Ilika grinned, hearing his own words quoted back to him. "Yeah, like that."

Another long silence followed.

"Do slaves often talk about death, and what lies beyond?" Ilika asked.

Kibi laughed. "All the time! It's always right around the corner, waiting for you at the next work site, or coming to take the person sleeping near you."

"But we don't really know anything," Boro admitted, gazing into his bowl. "We just talk bullshit."

"Will . . . Miko . . . haunt people?" Sata asked in a shaking voice.

"Miko liked everyone!" Buna asserted. "Except . . . you know . . . slave traders and masters."

Everyone looked at Ilika for more information.

"Miko will wake on another world, in a new form, and will be able to continue learning. The whole universe is like a huge college, and everyone is always learning new things. Haunting is just not part of the process."

＊

They had more questions about death. Sometimes Ilika had something to say, but more often than not, he admitted he didn't know. Slowly, as they talked and nibbled berries, evening deepened into night.

When the current topic had run its course, more wood was put on the fire and new stories began to emerge that had never before been put into words.

*Mati and the Goatherd* was the touching account of a girl who was beginning to glimpse life beyond the duties of hearth and home. She thanked Kibi for having the courage to help her see what was really happening.

*Neti in the Mountains* recounted her brush with dehydration and hypoxia. She admitted she sometimes forgot to take care of herself, and ended by thanking all her friends for making her eat and drink during the last three days.

Rini told the story of *The Dancing Lights*, and smiles appeared as everyone remembered the beautiful aurora at the monastery high in the mountains. As he was describing the dancing curtains and mysterious colors, he became aware that everyone was looking up at the sky.

He looked up, and saw what had attracted their attention. The aurora was back, shimmering colors dancing and frolicking in the sky above them. "But . . . why is it right over us?" he wondered aloud.

"It's not over us," Mati said without taking her eyes from the sky. "It's over Miko."

They could all now see that it was indeed small and near, unlike the aurora that was huge and far away.

"Ilika . . . why is there a little aurora right over Miko's grave?" Buna asked. "I thought you said his spirit left when he died."

"It did. This is something else. This is a little gift from those who watch over us. They are very happy we have learned from Miko's mistakes and honored his memory, and also very happy we are now ready to move on."

"But . . . *who* is watching over us?" Sata asked with a worried look and round eyes.

Ilika thought about how to answer. "I can't name names, Sata, but I can tell you that you're all very important. It is not often that a group of slaves, and an innkeeper's daughter, aspire to learn the things I am teaching you, make a journey like we are making, and form bonds of trust like we are forming. It is very rare, and very important."

Neti said nothing, but wore a huge smile as she gazed up at the colorful dancing lights over Miko's last resting place.

✳ ✳ ✳

## Chapter 11: The High Desert

Neti was up early, climbing onto the big boulders, leaping from one to the next after carefully judging the distance and looking for sandy places. On the last accessible boulder, which did indeed have a coating of crumbly gravel, she sat and thought about the event that had just changed the course of her life.

After a while she heard others getting up, saw them going down the trail for water, and decided she had spent enough time on the boulders.

Next she visited the place where Miko had landed and died. Most of the smaller rocks had been moved for the burial, but a few large ones still showed dried blood. Tears were close.

From there she went to Miko's grave, and the tears came, but soon the aroma of simmering porridge brought her back to the present. After one more shaking breath, she blinked to clear her eyes and joined her friends picking berries.

＊

As they prepared to depart, Neti had to swallow hard before nodding her approval for Misa to inherit Miko's bedroll cover and rucksack. Most of the weight he had been carrying was moved to other packs. Even when they were ready to depart, with packs on their backs or reins in hand, none of the ten travelers had an easy time leaving the place where one of their friends remained. Most of them spoke farewell wishes one last time, and several couldn't hold back tears even as they turned and set boots to the trail.

The downhill journey was again taken slowly and carefully because of Tera. The donkey was the only member of the group who didn't feel the need to look back while the boulders were still in sight.

＊

The sun glowed brightly in a clear sky, little breeze stirred the air, and the temperature climbed rapidly as the travelers descended toward the hills and prairies below. No one felt the slightest temptation to leap from boulder to boulder when the opportunity presented itself.

About a third of the way down the twisting, rocky canyon, Ilika's bracelet chimed the warning sound they had not heard in weeks. Donkey and rider got behind some prickly bushes in a ravine uphill from the trail, and the rest found little hiding places where they could. As the horses walked slowly uphill, the hot and tired soldiers paid little attention to anything around them.

Farther down the trail, the group paused for berries. A trio of porters, burdened with heavy packs, came trudging up the hill. Quick greetings were exchanged, but the men did not stop, intent on getting to the first mountain pass before the full heat of afternoon.

As the trail descended below four thousand feet, long-needled pines and broad-leafed oaks gave welcome shade. Dry twigs snapped underfoot and unseen insects made constant clicking sounds. Soon a stream came leaping down from the mountains. Following it around a bend for privacy, the group quickly had their boots off, and all their clothes and hair sopping wet. Mati had never seen Tera drink so much water.

As the long, hot afternoon reluctantly gave way to evening, the steep mountain trail finally came to an end. Before them lay barren hills where trees and green grass only grew in low, protected places. Elsewhere, sagebrush ruled. The trail wound through the hills, usually following the cooler gullies, but sometimes cresting a hilltop out of necessity.

A clump of bushes well off the trail hosted the nine walkers and one rider that night. Around a small fire, the promised geology lesson was finally given. As they learned about huge chunks of land that slowly moved and smashed into each other, they began to understand why these hills and mountains seemed so twisted and strange. Most of the students found it hard to believe that the twisting and smashing was going on right now, even as they watched.

Neti just laid her head on Kibi's lap during the lesson, and closed her eyes.

*

The travelers spent most of a day putting one foot in front of the other, going up and down the dry hills as the hot sun burned in a clear sky.

An old shepherd with a small flock of scrawny sheep waved them over to share lunch. His aging dog could still bark a little, but only chased strays in his dreams. The man had no horse or donkey, just a small handcart. He shared what he had in his bag of grits, but the students provided most of the food, and Neti gave him a great silver piece when they parted. The smile on his nearly-toothless face brought a little warmth to her heart.

*

As the sun dipped below the mountains in the late afternoon, they came out of the dry hills and onto the flat prairie where the trail joined the north-south road. A family with a girl and a boy, both not much younger than Sata, came trudging in the opposite direction. At first they seemed afraid of the large group, but Ilika and the others unshouldered their packs at the crossroads and sat down to rest. Seeing no weapons, the man put away his knife and approached to share news. Half an hour later, after hearing of the fighting over mining rights and the cost of food in the mountains, they went off to make camp and reconsider their options.

*

Feeling renewed energy from the evening shade and rapidly cooling air, the group pressed on southward, and Ilika was soon discussing the purchase of dinner and supplies with the matron of a ranch house. Cattle bellowed in the background, neck bells clanging as they grazed.

After a filling meal of stewed beef, potatoes, and new dark ale, the group unrolled their bedrolls in the yard. It was time to consider their own options.

Ilika unfolded the map for the first time since discovering it was useless for navigating the mountain paths. Everyone gathered around to ponder their location and their destination.

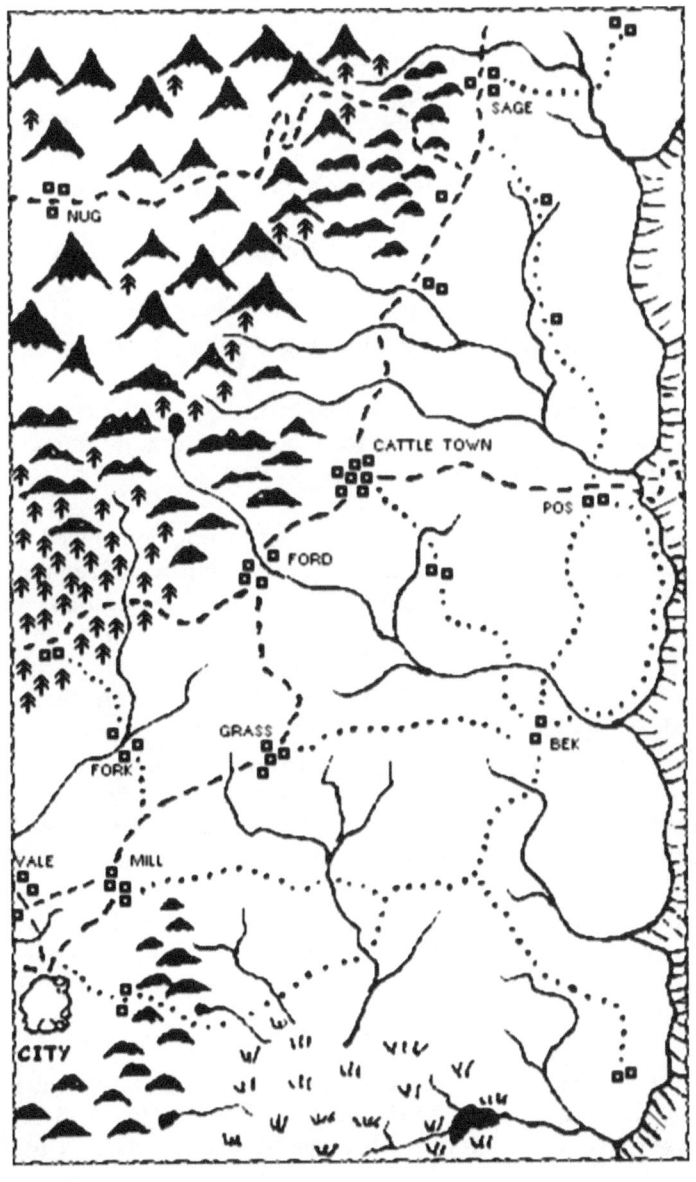

"The matron thinks we could get to Cattle Town in one day," Boro commented. "That means we'll probably take two, with lessons and stuff."

Mati pointed to some rivers on the map. "Looks like water will be a little easier to find as we go south."

"Has anyone been to this town?" Ilika asked.

All the students shook their heads, except Neti who was snuggled close beside Buna with her eyes closed.

Misa timidly raised her hand. "I have. It's dusty, with cows and flies everywhere. It was years ago. I don't remember much."

"Did you stay at an inn?" Sata asked.

"Um . . . I think so."

"How does it compare to Lumber Town?" Rini asked. "Before the fire, I mean."

A moment of sadness crossed Misa's face. "Bigger. More shops and stuff."

Ilika suddenly turned and grinned at Kibi. "Maybe it's a good place for a birthday party!"

Everyone clapped and cheered.

"And for Toli, too!" Kibi asserted, looking at Ilika.

Toli blushed as the clapping continued.

Ilika glanced at Mati and Boro, whose birthdays could also be celebrated because they had no idea when they were born. After a moment of thought, he nodded his approval of Kibi's decision.

Two long, hot days passed slowly as the group journeyed southward. Storm clouds visited the mountains to the west, but whatever moisture and shade they held was completely spent in the higher elevations. Only a few little wisps of cloud escaped to journey over the high desert.

The rivers on the map might have been refreshing in the springtime. Now nearly dry, the remaining water was greenish-brown with algae and mud. Cattle and sheep jostled for a drink, sometimes kicking or butting each other. With Cattle Town nowhere in sight, the travelers went upstream and made camp behind some thorny bushes. Boro dug a shallow well near the muddy stream and dipped out almost-clear water. Ilika reviewed earlier lessons on microbiology, and after boiling the water for several minutes, they made soup.

After dinner, Toli invited Buna to snuggle by the campfire. She accepted, but anyone who looked their way could see she was tense and uncomfortable. It wasn't long before she hopped up to help Misa prepare a place for their bedrolls.

The riverbeds were even drier and more trampled by cattle as they continued south and approached the town. From a high point on the road, they could see rain clouds getting through from the west and watering the grasslands on the southern horizon. Ilika gazed in that direction with a look of longing as he fingered his bracelet.

Twice that day, the bracelet warned them of approaching horsemen. The first was just a team of cow herders, but later a group of soldiers rode hard into the north, and the determined looks on their faces put all the students on edge for the rest of the day.

*

Early afternoon finally brought the weary travelers to the bluff overlooking Cattle Town. Constant sounds of mooing filled the air, even from a distance, and the heavy odor of cattle dung shriveled their noses.

They left the road and found a hidden ravine to survey their destination. The town sprawled below them, stone buildings with thatched roofs spread out on a low plateau. No wall surrounded the town, but many stone fences held cattle. Clouds of dust lingered everywhere, and very few trees blocked the fierce heat of the sun.

Ilika looked over his group. "Let's start with a pair of scouts. I think . . . Toli and Sata. You guys know what we need to know."

Toli was especially touched by the assignment. It was the first time he had been in charge of anything. Every time he was with Ilika or Kibi or Boro, it was clear who would make any hard decisions, and it wasn't him. With Sata younger, he felt like a leader for a change.

Kibi was glad Sata was going along in case any problems arose that required quick thinking. She just hoped Toli would listen.

* * *

## Chapter 12: Cattle Town

"Can you believe it?  There are actually *rewards* out for the capture of the so-called *sorcerers* and *witches* who SET the fire at Lumber Town!" Toli gasped out, red-faced.

Ilika couldn't keep from laughing.

"It gets worse," Sata jumped in.  "You won't be laughing when you hear this."

Ilika tried to compose himself.

"One of the things they're looking for is a young crippled witch who rides a donkey."

Mati frowned deeply, then cracked a little smile.

Ilika grinned at her.  "I'm surprised we got this far without trouble."

"I don't think the witch-on-a-donkey is common knowledge," Toli explained.  "We only know because I read the stuff on the wall at the guard station while Sata was asking about inns."

The pair of scouts continued their report, describing the shops and other businesses, the ever-present smell of cattle, and the dust billowing from countless animal pens.  Then Sata dropped the second bomb shell.  "It's got a slave market."

Dead silence.  None of the ex-slaves had set eyes on one since Ilika led them away toward the bath house.  They had seen slaves at Port Town, and a few at Lumber Town, but had held in their anger and dread.  Now the very worst part, the auction block itself, awaited them in the town that was their destination.  Based on Toli's description of it's location, it would be impossible to avoid.

"And there's another problem," Sata continued.

"Another one?" Boro burst out with wide eyes.  "Did you find the gates of the Underworld itself next to the bakery?"

Sata grinned.  "Almost.  I think there's a . . . what do you call it when lots of people are sick?"

"Epidemic," Ilika answered.  "What do you know about it?"

"I know everything, because I asked questions. It's food poisoning, and it happens every year, late summer and fall, when the weather is hot. We saw children puking right in the streets, and no one cared because most of the adults were doing it too. There's a sour stench all over town."

"I bet it's the meat," Ilika speculated. "Without refrigeration . . ."

"Re . . . what?" Buna asked, squinting.

"You can figure that out!" Toli burst out at her. "Just take apart the word. Re-frig-erat-ion. Place of making cold again."

Ilika nodded, but wore a slight frown.

Buna scowled at Toli.

"Do you have re . . . frigerat . . . ion in your country?" Kibi asked, ignoring Toli and Buna.

"Yes. But there are ways of keeping food good without it . . . and they obviously aren't using them here. Fresh meat is about the hardest thing to handle."

"This town is all about meat," Toli declared. "I think they'd rather die than quit eating meat."

"Sounds like they are. Anything else to consider?"

Sata added some details about the shops, then fell silent.

Ilika took a slow breath. "Good scouting job, you two. We need to do some thinking."

"Yeah!" Kibi blurted out. She already had Ilika's shoulder bag open and the map unfolded in her lap. "I want to have my birthday party . . . right here!" she said, pointing to somewhere on the map.

Everyone gathered around to look. She pointed to a little village several miles to the east on the road to the desert.

"Hmm," Toli considered. "I want to have mine . . . here!" He pointed to another village deep in the grasslands southeast of Cattle Town.

✳

The ten travelers used the rest of the afternoon to work their way eastward. For hours they trudged across sagebrush-covered prairie and scrambled in and out of dry washes. Eventually they found what they were looking for — a well-hidden gully with a spring-fed stream, and no signs of use by people or cattle. A pair of rabbits, nibbling the grass by the stream, bounded away and disappeared into a hole.

Rini scouted southward, and found the road that ran east from Cattle Town only a short walk down the gully. But, he explained with a smile, the stream soaked into the ground before getting that far, so no one would be tempted to explore it.

Once beds were unrolled in the shade of the small, thorny trees, they all quickly agreed on two things — Mati and Tera weren't going anywhere near Cattle Town, and Ilika should stay near Mati at all times, as he was the only one who could fend off soldiers.

Ilika took questions all evening about the ways food could spoil or transmit diseases, and what could be done about it. They had all been sick from bad food many times.  Their masters had usually blamed it on the slaves themselves.  Some of them had heard that evil spirits were involved.

Sata was not exempt from the experience of food poisoning.  She remembered clearly her mother telling her that if food went bad, there was no way to make it good again — it had to go.  She understood why after Ilika taught them about the toxins that remained in spoiled food even after sterilizing it with heat.

Ilika limited his description of food preservation methods to those available in this culture.  He asked them to forget about refrigeration, as it wasn't going to happen here any time soon.  Around the campfire that evening, as the air cooled and the land around them became still and silent, he made a list of things they should not eat or drink in the town, including, to their surprise, water.

✳

Even though Kibi chose not to celebrate her seventeenth birthday party at Cattle Town, she wanted a bath in the cleanest, warmest water available.  As the sun rose in a clear sky, she, Neti, and Boro walked the dusty streets for an hour to learn where everything was.  They often had to make way for groups of cattle driven from place to place.

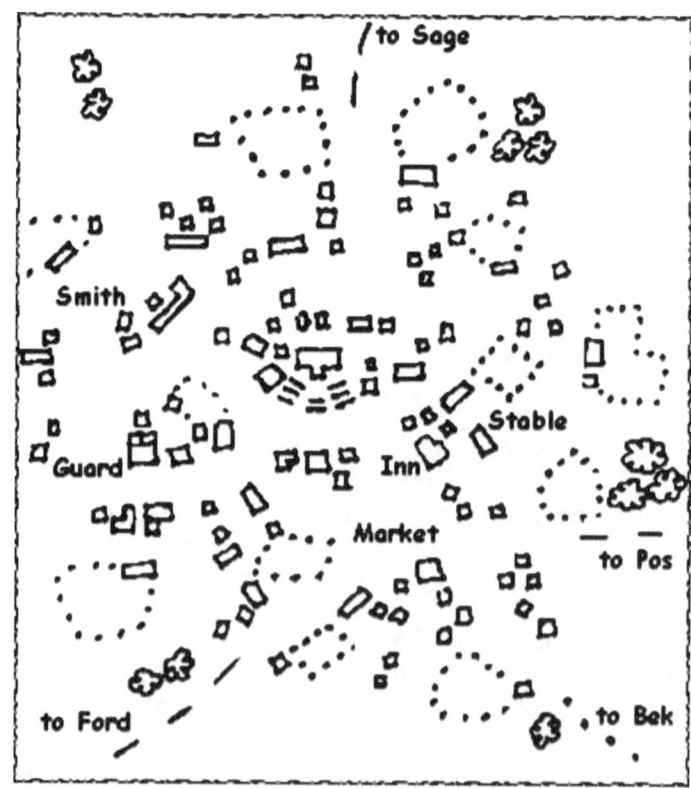

When they walked by the slave market, Neti just stood in the street and cried. The other two led her away, and apple tarts from the bakery brought smiles back to their glum faces.

While waiting for bathing tubs to fill, Kibi bought new wool pants. Neti looked at socks, but had trouble deciding. Boro went off to find a new tunic.

With clean bodies and hair, wearing fresh clothes, the two girls joined Boro at the marketplace, and they soon had a rucksack filled with meatless baked goods, fully-cured cheeses, and sheets of paper for Ilika. As mid-day approached, the three friends headed east along the little-used road toward the desert to share the bounty with their fellow travelers.

※

That afternoon, Toli, Buna, and Misa stood in the street feeling quite sick.

They hadn't been eating meat, soft cheese, or any other dangerous foods. In full sight of everyone on the street, poor women, orphaned children, old men, and the simple-minded of every age were bought and sold, jeered at, and sometimes whipped.

Toli and Buna didn't remember it being so bad when they were the ones on the block. Their survival during those years had required them to numb themselves, not feel, and not think. Now they were free to do both.

The three took baths, replaced worn out items of clothing, sampled the baked goods, and stocked up on dried fruits and vegetables for the group. But in between tasks, and before returning to camp, they kept coming back to the slave market and standing there for as long as they could tolerate, wondering if something could be done.

※

That evening around the fire, Kibi had an idea that was much easier to talk about than the slave market. She suggested they attempt to teach the butchers in the marketplace, and the cooks at the inns, some of the things they knew about keeping food from spoiling.

Most everyone was excited about the idea. They had never before applied what they were learning. This situation, this town, seemed to cry out for the knowledge they possessed.

To their surprise, Ilika didn't share their excitement. "There are many things, besides lack of knowledge, that keep people from living as well as they might. Traditions and customs run deep, and can be very hard to change."

"But don't you think they'd be willing to learn," Toli asked in a defensive tone, "if it would keep their friends and families from being sick all the time?"

"That might motivate some of them. You are welcome to try. I hope you will keep it quiet, one on one, out of sight of the guards. And you can't start until tomorrow afternoon, so Sata and Rini can do some shopping."

The group spent the rest of the evening talking about the methods the people of this cattle-raising area could use to keep their meat and other foods safe. They agreed that if they could teach the people the temperature, moisture, and acidity ranges where bacteria thrived, the preservation methods would be obvious — heating, drying, salting, and pickling.

But as they finally let the fire die down and readied their bedrolls, most of them kept thinking about the slave market.

*

Because of Rini's small size, Boro got an extra trip into town. He didn't mind — he planned a warm bath and some shopping for birthday gifts.

Rini observed the flies crawling on the meat at the butcher stands, and saw gallons of spoiled milk poured into the gutters. He smelled an abandoned bowl of stew, almost as bad as the milk. He saw a little boy lose his breakfast, then run off to look for something else to eat.

All these things made Rini feel deeply, but he remained silent as his friends made plans to teach the people of Cattle Town all the things they knew about food preservation.

* * *

## Chapter 13: Changing the World

Buna nodded when Misa announced that she too wanted to stay in the camp that afternoon. Misa almost always listened to the lessons, and sometimes enjoyed the little games Ilika devised as part of his teaching process. But she found most of the subjects boring, and the microbiology was no exception. To her, it was enough to avoid eating smelly meat.

Kibi and Neti led the way out of camp, followed by Toli and Buna, and finally Boro and Sata.

Mati and Rini, both naturally quiet and a bit shy, enjoyed the reduced population. Misa might have been more outgoing if she had others her age to relate to, but at this point in her life, she did not.

The four who remained at camp lounged on their bedrolls in the shade. Mati re-read a chapter in their book while Misa carved at a stick with the small knife. Ilika was doing something with his knowledge processor.

Rini pulled a small cloth bundle out of his pack and handed it to Mati. "I found the gifts you wanted for Kibi and Toli."

"Thanks. Anyone think the others will have any luck in Cattle Town?"

Misa shook her head.

"No idea," Rini replied. "I didn't go partly because I'm afraid one of them is gonna get in trouble, and Ilika will have to go rescue them with his bracelet."

Ilika chuckled. "You smell that coming too, huh?"

Mati grinned. "My guess is Toli. Neti's been weird, too."

Ilika nodded thoughtfully. "Either way, it'll be good for them, and help me to know what they're made of."

"How close are we to ... you know ... the day you decide about your crew?" Mati asked.

"Two, maybe three weeks. We'll just wander down along the high cliff overlooking the desert, have a couple of birthday parties, and review all our lessons."

Misa held up her carving to examine it. "I'm the only one who's for sure staying here, right?"

"That's right. But you've been a good companion, and I'll give you some money when we part."

The girl grinned. "Thanks!"

Everyone became quiet. Mati finished a chapter and closed the book. As she lay on her bedroll, her face revealed intense thought. Occasionally she whispered one or two names. "Kibi, Boro . . ." Her fingers showed that she was counting something at the same time. One. Two. Then she whispered more names and counted again. Finally, a huge smile flashed onto her face as she took a deep breath of the sagebrush-scented air.

＊

Toli and Buna dragged themselves back to camp in the late afternoon.

Toli wore a long face. "It was useless."

"They kept talking about the way their mothers and their grandmothers did it," Buna related, "and that was good enough for them."

"One cook chased us out of the kitchen with a broom!" Toli added.

Rini smiled at the thought.

Buna jumped in. "One innkeeper said that if he couldn't see it, it didn't exist!"

"I asked him if he could see the air," Toli continued in an exasperated voice. "Then he got very quiet and started fingering his butcher knife."

"We got the message," Buna huffed. "They just don't CARE, Ilika! There's no way to teach people who don't care."

"I agree," Ilika said with a half-smile. "I would *never* want to try to teach someone who didn't care."

Buna began to wind down. "I just wish I knew how to make them care. People are dying. Children and babies are dying."

"I understand," Ilika responded. "But that's the other side of freedom. It includes the option to not care, and the option to die, or watch your children die."

"You mean," Mati said thoughtfully, "that if we forced them to care, that would be sort of like slavery?"

"Yes. I know of countries that have tried that. The government told the people how to eat, how to live, how to raise their children. They passed laws forbidding people to take risks. It doesn't work. People only learn and grow when faced with challenges they *must* solve, or the natural consequences will threaten their lives. If people don't have those challenges, they get lazy."

"But people are dying!" Buna moaned with frustration.

"Everyone dies," Ilika said with a shrug.

Buna started to open her mouth again, but closed it without saying anything, and just sat there, dejected.

Toli put his arm around her. "I feel like a total failure too."

"I think you guys are missing something," Ilika pointed out. "When you were talking to the cooks, was anyone else listening?"

Toli thought back. "Yeah, a son or daughter, or a kitchen slave, or the innkeeper himself once."

"I bet some of *them* will remember your words, and someday make use of them. It's like planting seeds. Sometimes you don't get to see them sprout because you have to move on. But they might sprout just the same."

After he was sure the discussion was over, Rini went for water, and Mati got out ingredients for soup. Judging by Toli's and Buna's experiences, she was sure none of those returning from Cattle Town would be in the mood to cook.

*

Boro and Sata showed up just as the others were sitting down to sliced fruit, bread and butter, and a tasty soup.

"That was so wonderful!" Sata announced to the camp. "I'm *so* glad we went!"

"You mean ... someone actually listened to you?" Buna asked, her eyes wide with surprise.

"Not at first," Boro admitted. "We were wasting our breath with the old butchers themselves."

"But then we left the market," Sata continued, "and were wandering around town thinking about what to do next ..."

"And we started to get the feeling someone was following us," Boro added.

"I was afraid it might be a soldier," Sata went on.

"But it was an apprentice from the market who had heard us talking to one of the butchers."

"And he wanted us to teach him everything we knew about it!"

"So we sat on a wall, ate apples, and talked for hours, and he now knows everything we know about keeping food from spoiling."

"And he asked who our teacher was, and if he could become a student."

"But we told him we were almost done with our lessons and our teacher was going back to his country very soon."

"It was great!" Sata finished. "I'm so glad we did it."

Toli and Buna summarized their less-spectacular results, and everyone turned their minds to eating. No one had any idea how Kibi and Neti were doing, or when they might return.

*

As the sun set and Kibi and Neti still did not appear, Boro took on a thoughtful expression, and soon picked helpers to bring in a good supply of firewood.

As the evening deepened toward night, Ilika made sure he had enough money in his pouch to get his missing students out of trouble, but no more.

His remaining students looked up at him as he put on his cloak, and could see the worry on his face.

Ilika put Boro in charge, then departed.

*

For the next hour, all four who had returned from town shared more details about their efforts. Toli remembered a total of six people who seemed to be listening while the cooks were busy ignoring them. Sata could think of three, in addition to the apprentice, who might have soaked up some of what they were saying.

Suddenly they heard footsteps coming up the ravine, dislodging rocks and snapping branches.

Boro peered into the darkness with big, round eyes. He had a four inch knife to protect Mati and the others. He saw Rini get out the other knife, about three inches long.

"Damn!" Neti's voice could be heard. "When does the moon come up?"

"Not until about midnight," Kibi's voice replied.

Boro, Rini, and the others relaxed.

Soon the two girls could see the fire, and walked into camp.

"Where have *you* guys been?" Toli asked.

"Oh ... in jail," Neti said calmly. "And they *didn't* feed us. What's cooking?"

Mati poured the soup she had saved and Buna tore bread for them. Neti, for the first time since Miko's death, was in a talkative mood, so Kibi let her tell the story.

They had been trying to convince a baker that he shouldn't make meat pies this time of year. They didn't know until it was too late, but his wife had gone for the soldiers.

Once in the jailhouse, they wove a story about living on a ranch far to the north, and their grandmother had taught them how to keep meat and milk from spoiling.

The soldier promised to send a rider to their ranch the following day.

Since Kibi and Neti knew that wasn't going to work for them, they started whining about being needed back at the ranch right away.

The soldier finally got the hint and started talking money. But a silver piece didn't sway him. He was holding out for two or three, and the girls only had one, so they had to use a small gold piece.

Neti ended the story, saying the road wasn't hard to follow in the dark, as they held hands and the stars gave a little light, but the ravine was terrible.

✳

Ilika looked for Kibi and Neti all over the town.

The market was done for the day, and few people were out and about. Most of those were in the process of losing whatever they ate for dinner.

Once Ilika gave up looking for his missing students on the streets, he started asking questions whenever he could. No one claimed to have seen Kibi or Neti, but a baker's wife with squinty eyes said they might know something at the guardhouse.

Ilika glanced into the guardhouse, aglow with oil lamps, where a soldier could be seen playing cards while drinking ale and eating bread and cheese. Ilika didn't want to walk in carrying money, not until a deal had been struck, so he slipped across the street to a dark alley, crouched down to find some loose stones, and hid his pouch underneath.

After stepping into the guardhouse, he noticed the sketch of himself on the wall just a moment before something large and heavy hit the back of his head. Everything went black as he started to fall. He never felt himself land on the stone floor.

\* \* \*

## Chapter 14: Ilika's Big Mistake

Back at the camp, no one could sleep.

They agreed that Ilika must have arrived at the town before Kibi and Neti left, otherwise they would have met him on the road. They tried to guess how long he would search the town. Opinions varied from one hour to three hours. With another half hour for the walk back, they decided he would return by midnight, an hour after at the latest.

But still they could not sleep.

They knew they had, among them if not individually, all the knowledge Ilika had taught them. But that wasn't enough. They wanted their teacher back. They wanted to review all their studies with him, and ask him a thousand more questions. They knew, without a shadow of doubt, they had many more things to learn from him.

Some of them realized they had all his money here at the camp, except for two small gold pieces. But they didn't just want his money. They wanted him to tell them they had completed their educations and *earned* the three great gold pieces.

*

Kibi lay on her bedroll gazing at the fire where Boro, Rini, and Mati still huddled quietly. She was very aware that all her hopes and dreams were tied up with Ilika right now. She could easily let go of the gold, and even the ship. She would not willingly let go of Ilika. If the world took him from her, through death or some other fate she could not overcome, she would deal with it. She would set her feet on the road out of this kingdom.

Suddenly she chuckled out loud, realizing they were camped near that very road. Just a few miles to the east, where the road descended into the desert, the kingdom ended, the kingdom where she had been a slave half her life.

Mati glanced over when Kibi chuckled, but decided it was a private thought that her friend did not wish to share.

But before Kibi admitted defeat, she wanted to see if Boro would have any luck finding their teacher. If he didn't, Kibi would take the tube of great gold pieces she carried, plus the one in her pouch, and go alone to see what she could do. She knew in her heart that she would risk slavery — even her life — before she would give up Ilika without clear evidence that he was beyond her reach forever.

She realized that she loved him.

At about midnight, they could stand it no longer. Everyone was up, ready to take Cattle Town apart, stone by stone if necessary.

But their determination was tempered by the fact that Mati, Kibi, and Neti could not go because of warrants for their arrest, or events earlier that day. Of those who could go, Boro was clearly the leader, and he wanted to go carefully and quietly.

"I want Rini with me. I want Toli near us, watching our backs from where I put him, which will probably be across the street from the guardhouse. I want Sata with him in case we need a runner with a message. And I want Buna in that grove of trees at the edge of town with food and water. Misa too, as another runner. And those of you who have to stay here, be ready to receive us, tired, hungry, and possibly injured. Ilika has always been there for us. Now we're going to be there for him, and we all have parts to play."

Boro took Toli aside, and they agreed on some bird calls that Toli could make.

Buna emptied her rucksack and repacked it with food that could be eaten without cooking. Misa went to the stream for water.

Boots were laced tightly. Except Boro, no one took coin pouches. Cloaks were tied and hoods pulled up. Boro and Rini took the knives, which they knew were useless against soldiers with swords, but they refused to leave any possible asset behind.

"Ilika picked us because we're smart," Boro said when everyone was ready and standing around the fire. "We'll have to be smart to get our teacher back. I can't tell you what to do, because I don't know what we're up against. Each of you may have to make your own decisions, and there may not be time for runners and discussions. Be smart. Let's go!"

The team of rescuers groped their way down to the road, then had an easy walk as the moon rose behind them. They passed along the road silently, as no one could think of any questions for which anyone else might have answers.

When they arrived at the edge of town, Buna and Misa silently slipped into the grove of small trees. They got comfortable in a sandy area where they could look toward the town, now well-lit by the rising moon.

Boro led the rest along a winding route through the town so they approached the guardhouse from a tiny alley across the street. He looked at Toli and Sata, and they understood.

The door to the guardhouse was open and lamps flickered within. Having come this far, Boro couldn't think of anything else to do but go in.

"Hello," he said as he filled the doorway with his muscular body. Rini waited behind.

Only one soldier, of no apparent rank, sat with his feet up on a box. A mug of something sat on the barrel beside him, along with tattered playing cards. Papers, quill pens, and a lamp were neatly arranged on the only sturdy table, currently unattended. A few mismatched swords and one crossbow dangled from pegs on the walls.

Boro's eyes were drawn to the two heavy wooden doors on the back wall of the room. He had the feeling they didn't lead to the outside.

"What do you want?" the soldier asked, bringing his feet down.

"I'm looking for a friend. Taller than me, thinner, light hair, wearing a blue tunic . . ."

"What's he mean to you?"

Boro swallowed. "He owes me money. Heard he was in town, but can't find him."

The soldier seemed to relax a little.

Just then Boro heard Toli's bird call that meant another soldier was coming. Boro stepped in and to the side, and Rini did the same.

The second soldier entered and took in the situation. "What's up?"

"Fellow says our prisoner owes him money."

The second soldier sat down on a crate and started oiling his sword with a rag. "How much?"

Rini's eyes sparkled with an idea. "Three . . . gold . . . pieces," he said slowly in the most serious voice he could muster.

Both soldiers whistled.

"I *saw* one of those today," the second soldier said.

"Where?" the first inquired with interest, forgetting Boro and Rini for the moment.

"Captain got it for letting a couple of rich girls go."

"You guys ever had gold?" Boro asked, stoking the fires of greed that appeared to be their best hope of freeing Ilika.

"Huh! In this puking town? We just *dream* about gold. Captain gets any that fools let fall."

"What's gonna happen to your prisoner, the one who owes us money?" Boro asked.

"Well . . . he's not in very good shape . . ."

Rini could feel Boro tense up.

"He's wanted at the capital, *if* he lives long enough to get there."

"How about if we say he died tonight," Boro suggested, "and you gave his body to a couple of friends to bury."

"But we'd miss out on the reward we'll get tomorrow when the captain gets here!" the second soldier complained.

"How much reward you gonna get?" Rini asked.

"Probably a silver each."

"Wanna change that silver into gold?" Boro prodded.

Suddenly he had their undivided attention.

"That way we can still get what he owes us," Rini explained, "but now he'll owe us five!"

"Are you fellows saying you'd lay down gold pieces — one for each of us — right here and now, if we give him to you?" the first soldier asked with big eyes of amazement.

"IF he's alive," Rini asserted firmly.

"Come see for yourself!" the second soldier said and walked toward one of the doors on the back wall.

Boro tapped Rini on the shoulder, and the small lad followed the soldier.

Rini held his breath when the cell door opened. Ilika lay on the hard dirt floor, not moving, a large swollen bruise on his head, one side of his face covered with blood. The cell reeked of vomit and other odors.

Rini's mind raced. He had to know if Ilika was alive. He remembered lessons from months before, and felt for a pulse under Ilika's jaw.

"He's alive," Rini called out.

Boro turned his head and whistled. A few seconds later Toli filled the doorway, almost scraping his head on the timber above.

Boro opened his pouch, then held up the two yellow coins. "Do we have a deal?"

The soldiers looked at each other. "Sure!" they both said at once.

Boro handed the coins to Toli, then went to collect Ilika.

While Boro gathered Ilika into his arms, Rini watched for any double-cross.

The soldiers, with swords handy, also watched for a double-cross, but relaxed when Boro, half-way to the door, told Toli to set the gold pieces on the table.

Boro stepped through the door sideways with their motionless teacher in his arms. Toli came out next.

As the two soldiers picked up and admired the first gold pieces they had ever owned, Rini bowed slightly, turned, and slipped out the door.

✳

Sata met them in the dark alleyway. "Oh, poor Ilika!"

"I think I can carry him to the trees. I want you three behind me, spread out in the shadows, watching to see if those soldiers change their minds. If they do, or anyone else follows me, I want to know about it fast."

Boro didn't wait around any longer. Just holding their teacher in his arms was taking every bit of his strength, so he headed off down the alley at a brisk but silent pace.

Even though his arms screamed at him, he forced himself to take a round-about path that would make it nearly impossible for anyone to tell which direction he was going.

Boro's arms were burning and shaking by the time he got to the edge of town, but he took one more detour, going north around a cattle pen as if heading for the stable. Then he slipped into the woods from the back side.

Finally he heard Buna's voice. With no strength left, he collapsed, his own body cushioning Ilika's fall.

While Boro lay breathing deeply, Buna did her best to get Ilika into a comfortable position. By the mottled moonlight, she could see the blood and the huge bruise.

"He was . . . alive . . . at the . . . guardhouse," Boro gasped out. "Check his . . . pulse."

"He's still alive," Buna announced with relief.

"Misa . . . go get . . . Mati and Tera . . . and blankets . . . and rope."

The young girl dashed off, hoping she could find the ravine that would lead her to the camp.

✳

Kibi's patience was sorely tested when she discovered she and Neti were the only ones who couldn't do anything to help Ilika. But she knew it wasn't right to leave Neti alone, and if they both went, animals would get their food unless they packed up everything and took it with them, and that would take too long. The others would probably have Ilika back by then.

So she busied herself with the soup Mati had started as she watched donkey, rider, and guide disappear down the ravine. As she stirred the soup, she consoled herself with the knowledge that Ilika was alive, free, and on his way home.

✳

Boro was soon on his feet, but his arms wouldn't quit shaking and burning. He had to ask Buna to pull back his hood.

Sata, Toli, and Rini crept into the grove one at a time, declaring that all was well and the soldiers appeared completely happy with their new-found wealth.

Even though Boro couldn't do anything himself, he began supervising the construction of a stretcher that Tera could drag behind her. Rini and Sata went out, and returned about a quarter hour later with long poles. Rope was harder to find, but a few short pieces were discovered unattended.

Since Toli was good with knots, he volunteered to do the tying. Rini found a fallen branch to use as a cross-bar near the bottom of the stretcher. Sata went out again for more rope, but had little luck.

Finally Mati and Misa arrived, so Toli had plenty of rope to finish the stretcher while Rini tied the upper ends of the poles to Tera's stirrups. Mati stayed mounted to keep Tera right where they needed her.

Buna, with Sata's help, wrapped Ilika in blankets, but reported no improvement in his condition.

As Boro's arms were still useless, getting Ilika into the stretcher took serious thought. Toli and Sata worked together, and Rini and Buna moved his legs. The task required another quarter hour, and they constantly feared they would do him more harm.

When they finally left the trees and took to the road, the night was windless and quiet, and the stretcher made a loud scraping noise on the hard, rocky ground. Toli quickly picked up the bottom ends of the poles, and they proceeded to navigate the first hill east of Cattle Town in silence, save for the faint sound of donkey's hooves.

✳   ✳   ✳

## Chapter 15: A Time of Healing

Kibi lovingly tended Ilika all the next day, even though she had not slept a wink the night before. As the others looked on, helpless to do more than bring her things, she washed him and applied salve to his wound. When she could do no more, she kissed his silent lips and let her tears fall onto his pale skin.

Toward evening she became more assertive, informing him in a stern voice that he must wake up to eat and drink, or he would die.

And still he slept.

As darkness crept over the prairie once more, Kibi could no longer keep her eyes open. She curled up close beside Ilika and cried herself to sleep.

✳

Ilika lay in a pool of blackness for an unknowable length of time. He did not experience pain, but neither did he know joy. He was not, in this place, able to think, or reflect, or remember. He just was.

At some point during the eternity of his existence, he began to hear a familiar voice.

*Ilika, time to wake up! You are not released from your duties yet. There is much to be done, much to teach your charges, and much to learn from them. Wake up, Ilika! Kibi and all the others are waiting for you. Wake up!*

He didn't understand what the voice said, but somehow, listening to the voice, the notion came to him that he could do something. He could move. He could move upward toward . . . he didn't know what, but it just seemed the right way to go.

The darkness all around him was thick and heavy, like black sand, so he dug his way upward. After an eternity it became more like a liquid, so he swam. An eon later the blackness was even thinner, and he felt himself floating or flying, ever upward, not knowing why, but trusting that this was what the voice wanted him to do.

＊

Dawn was already in the sky when Ilika started twitching and thrashing.

Kibi flew out of some dream of despair and was on her knees beside him a moment later.

"Boro! Anybody! Help me! He's moving!"

Sata, on watch, arrived first.

Rini was there a moment later, and seeing Ilika's violent thrashing, cradled his teacher's head in his hands.

"Ilika, I'm right here!" Kibi cried. "Please come back to us! Sata is here, and Rini, and we want you to wake up so you can eat and drink. Then you can sleep again if you need to. Boro is here now, and Neti and Misa. Here comes Buna and Toli, and here's Mati. We love you Ilika, and we need you. Please wake up!"

Suddenly Ilika sucked in a huge breath of air, as if he had just surfaced from deep under water, and his eyes snapped open. He gasped repeatedly, and his unfocused eyes gazed up toward the dawning sky.

He heard Kibi's voice, and after a few minutes started remembering names and faces. Blinking his eyes, they slowly began to focus, but felt scratchy and dry. He tried to move his lips, but found them parched and cracked. Slowly, almost painfully, a concept formed in his mind, something he desperately needed. He opened his mouth to try to speak the word. "Water . . ." he barely whispered.

Within moments Boro and Toli helped Ilika sit up, and Neti reached out with a cup of water.

Ilika tried to take the cup, but spilled it all over himself.

"That's okay," Kibi said through tears of joy. "We'll help you until you're strong again."

Another cup of water was poured, and this time Neti held onto it while Ilika drank.

＊

By sunrise, he was starting to speak a few words and recognize his students, but his speech was slow and labored. They asked what he wanted for breakfast, and after a long moment of thought, he requested soup.

Kibi was at his side constantly, and when he remembered his bracelet, still on his wrist, she handed him the knowledge processor. With shaking fingers that were slow to remember their skill, he selected the medical functions.

"You really need to teach me how to use that thing," Kibi scolded gently.

"Very . . . soon," was all he said as he pondered the symbols on the knowledge processor. "No wonder . . ."

"What?"

"Concussion . . . dehydration . . . low blood sugar . . . blood pressure not much better . . . do we have any honey?"

"No. Just molasses."

"Feed it to me . . . before I black out."

Nobody could remember where it was. Kibi dumped the contents of several rucksacks before she located the prize, and was spooning the dark syrup to Ilika less than a minute later. He took another cup of water, and in a short time was speaking more clearly.

"The soup still sounds good, but I need to eat some fruit first."

Neti and Buna located all their fresh and dried fruit, and Ilika was soon chewing small pieces of apple.

"Tell us everything we can do," Kibi coaxed. "Buna, Sata, and Misa can still go into town without getting into trouble . . . I think."

Ilika let out a slight chuckle. "Fruit, soup, eggs . . . sour berries . . . powdered bones."

Rini got paper and wrote as Ilika spoke.

"How much did I cost?" Ilika asked, lying back down to await the soup.

"Two small gold," Boro said from the fire pit, "plus whatever was in your pouch."

"Pouch is hidden in the alley across from the guard station. Under rocks."

"I'll have Buna and Sata look for it," Kibi promised. "I just want them to eat breakfast before they go."

"Yes. Breakfast is good. Walking into a guard station without someone to watch your back is . . . just plain stupid."

Boro, Rini, and Toli all grinned.

✳

For the entire first day, Ilika was dependent on his students for everything. Kibi tended him, and everyone else did whatever they could to help. Sata created a hearty soup, but cooked it well.

She and Buna headed for town shortly after breakfast, promising to stay out of trouble. They knew the list of students who could safely enter Cattle Town was getting short.

Ilika ate, drank, and slept. At his insistence, Kibi woke him every two hours, and he consulted the knowledge processor. Based on what he saw, he asked for different foods, or more water. They would have loved to ask him questions about the nutrients he was selecting, but he didn't yet have the energy to teach.

Buna and Sata returned with Ilika's coin pouch, powdered cattle bones, and many other foods, but had failed to find sour berries.

Ilika asked for the powder to be added to everything he ate. Then he slept again.

✳

On the second day, Ilika was able to sit up longer and talk with his students more. He explained what happened when he went to look for Kibi and Neti, and they filled him in on events he missed, including his own rescue. He nearly cried when he heard how much effort it took to get him back. His fellow travelers smiled proudly.

Buna and Misa went into town with a new list, including supplies for the next leg of their journey. They returned grinning and dangling a bag of dried sour berries from a woman who was happy to part with them when silver was offered.

Everyone smiled at Ilika's concave cheeks and squinting eyes as he sucked on a mouthful. Neti's eyes became moist as she remembered Miko in the same situation.

Later that day, after a nap, Ilika took their questions about his medical condition, and explained why he was trying to get more calcium and ascorbic acid. Then Kibi had a different kind of question.

"I was wondering . . . the person, or people, who help you plan our lessons . . . and who led us out of the fire . . . and made the aurora over Miko's grave . . . can they help you when you're injured?"

Ilika was silent for a moment as he struggled to remember. "They did. When I was unconscious, they told me when it was time to wake up. But they never help when you can take care of things yourself. They didn't rescue me because you guys were there to do it."

✳

On the third day after waking, Ilika knew, by the foul smell following him around, that it was time to bathe. After sitting by the fire to eat breakfast with his students, he slowly dragged himself to the stream with Kibi at his side.

The coolness of the water nearly took his breath away, and he quickly sat down so he wouldn't fall down. He managed to get himself reasonably clean and refreshed, and Kibi helped him into clean clothes. On the way back to camp, he started shivering and had to bundle himself in blankets again.

Sata and Buna had much less shopping to do that day. After returning from town, Buna looked very thoughtful about something, but was not yet willing to talk about it. Sata and Misa knew, but weren't going to say anything until their friend was ready.

That evening, Ilika predicted that after one more day of rest, he would be able to do some traveling. They discussed their route, and no one could think of any reason to alter their original plans. They all looked forward to seeing the high cliff and the desert below, and having two more birthday parties.

✳ ✳ ✳

## Chapter 16: The Plan

On their last day in the ravine, the stream saw almost constant use. Everyone wanted one more bath before taking the road across the dry prairie toward the desert.

After a stew made from fresh eggs and vegetables, Ilika was savoring a tasty peach when Buna sat down in front of him.

"I have something important to talk to you about."

"Okay. Here, or in private?"

"Here is okay. Some of them already know."

Ilika finished his peach and then gave Buna his complete attention.

"Every time I go into that town — which has been a lot recently — I stop and look at the slave market ... and wonder what I can do about it. I know I'll never have the money to buy them all."

"I went through the same feelings back in the capital city," Ilika admitted.

"So you know what it does to me to see people up there bought and sold ... young people like me, and even children."

"I will never know as well as you, because I have not been a slave. But I can try to imagine how it makes you feel, and I certainly respect your feelings."

Buna blinked several times, then remembered her train of thought. "So ... every time I go into town, I try to think of something I can do. And the only thing I can ever come up with ... requires your help ... or at least ... your bracelet ..." Her face twisted into its unique squirrelly expression as she let her thought dangle in the air.

Ilika remained silent so Buna could fully express her idea.

"Your bracelet is perfect for the job, because it doesn't hurt anyone ... unless they fall off a cliff or something. You ... or whoever you trusted with it ... could just put everyone to sleep, we could carry the young slaves to a safe place, and when the slave traders and people woke up, the slaves would have just vanished into thin air!"

Ilika remained silent and attentive.

"Isn't it perfect?"

By now, everyone else had gathered around to listen. Most of them felt very sympathetic toward Buna's idea, but weren't ready to make bets on Ilika's response.

"It's very tempting," Ilika said in a kindly voice. "But it has some tactical problems, and an ethical problem . . . at least for me." He took a moment to look around at their expectant faces. "The tactical problem is that you might have to put the whole town to sleep. If you just did the people at the slave market, then what happens if someone across the street sees everyone on the ground? If you put him to sleep, what about someone a stone's throw down the street who sees *him*?"

"I see what you mean," Buna said, the excitement draining from her face.

"And of course, if you do the whole town, then you have to watch all the roads and trails."

"I understand," she said, looking at the ground.

"Please tell us about the ethical problem too," Rini begged.

"It's actually much more important. My bracelet represents power, at least here in this kingdom. If I wanted to, I could put all the soldiers and guards to sleep, take their weapons, walk into every money changer and take all the money, steal any art work or sacred relic I wanted, kill the king and his court, take his symbols of power, and soon everyone — of those I let live — would be groveling at my feet, begging to serve me."

The campsite was so quiet, the leaves of the trees could be heard rustling in the breeze.

"But you'd never do that," Rini finally said, breaking the spell.

"That's right. I come from a place where everyone has great power, by your standards, and they steadfastly refuse to use it for self-aggrandizement . . . anywhere . . . ever."

He let his words linger for a few moments.

"So that brings us to the next question. Is Buna's proposal self-aggrandizement? Is it for her own personal gain?"

Buna was on the verge of tears and wished she could run away. But since she was sitting directly in front of Ilika, and several people sat behind her, she didn't move a muscle.

"No, not really," Ilika said with a slight smile. "Buna's heart is pure, and her intentions are good. If this task could be done using tools that were native to your kingdom, I would not be opposed to it.

"But since she is asking to use something of mine, that I brought from my country, I have to apply the ethical standards of the Transport Service. These are the standards you would be subject to if you became members of my crew, so think about this carefully over the next few weeks."

Buna began to recover from her momentary crisis of feelings, and everyone else was paying close attention.

"In the Transport Service, we have to be able to move between many different countries and among many different . . . kinds of people. We have to do this, as much as possible, without interfering with the lives of those people. We can protect ourselves, and anyone under our care, but we must always use the least possible force. That's why my bracelet only puts people to sleep. I'm not trying to hurt or kill anyone. I'm just trying to stay alive and do what I came to do."

He took a deep breath. "It's nothing terrible to help an individual now and then. We've done it many times on our journey. But even that comes close to interfering, and there are times and places it isn't allowed. Luckily, right now, in your kingdom, it's okay.

"But trying to help an entire group of people, in most cases, would be crossing the line. In many countries, people live in terrible conditions for one reason or another. Slavery, famine, economic collapse, military rule, ecological imbalance, natural disaster, resource depletion, and many other things, can befall a land and its people. Your kingdom is pretty lucky. Of all those things I mentioned, you only have one right now — slavery."

After a moment of silence, Ilika took Buna's trembling hand in his. "I want you to know something before I take a nap. Your idea is good. You are a good person. Slavery is rotten. The ethics of my profession don't allow me to help you, but I think highly of you for having the courage to ask. Thank you."

Ilika curled up on his bedroll and Kibi put a blanket over him. Buna headed up the ravine to walk and think, and Misa ran after. Everyone else filtered away to think about what had been said, and to start packing, knowing they were breaking camp the following morning.

✳

Around the evening fire, most everyone had thoughts about the slave market issue.

"There's a part of me that will always hate slave traders," Boro said. "But I want to be able to work around all kinds of people. I remember when Ilika told us he had to have dinner with the slave master to make the deal for us. I bet that was hard."

Ilika nodded. "I got out of there when they started smoking!"

Everyone chuckled. They associated smoking with slave owners who had way too much money in their pouches.

"I'm glad I don't have a bracelet like Ilika's," Neti said. "I'd never hurt anyone, but I couldn't resist freeing slaves, helping mistreated children, and letting caged animals go."

Ilika looked at her. "I understand. There's a part of me that would be right beside you, helping to cut the ropes and open the cages."

"Don't you wish Kibi had never suffered through all her years of slavery?" Buna asked in a touchy voice.

Ilika looked at Buna. Then he looked at Kibi. They exchanged tiny smiles. "No. Kibi would not be the person she is today without those years. She would not have the strength she has. And I would probably never have met her."

Rini and Mati nodded understanding.

"Hardship is a funny thing," Ilika continued. "You can't wish it on someone you care about. You can't plan it. But without it, people are weak. I know of a country where the people were rich enough to let their children grow up without any hardships. In the end, it destroyed them."

"How?" Sata asked.

"A series of natural disasters came along. No one knew how to take care of themselves. They just kept asking their leaders for help, but the government was powerless because the problems were so wide-spread. There was a huge die-off, and the civilization regressed several thousand years, back to little tribes of desperate, hungry people."

A thoughtful silence lingered as the students tried to imagine the situation.

"My parents could have let me play all day," Sata said softly. "But I remember my father telling me that if I didn't learn to work, I'd be nothing."

"I wouldn't have tested you if I hadn't glimpsed your strength and self-discipline," Ilika admitted. "Those years of working at the inn were the price of getting this education and a shot at the Transport Service."

Sata smiled and looked up at her teacher from the other side of the fire. "It's been worth it . . . even if I don't get onto your crew."

Sometime after midnight, but before moonrise, a shadow crept toward Ilika. It was careful to not step on any twigs.

It had watched carefully on several occasions to know how to do what it was about to do. Now Ilika and Kibi were both fast asleep. It could get what it needed and do the job before anyone was awake. Then it would put back what it had borrowed.

The little cover on Ilika's bracelet opened easily. The shadowy figure touched three tiny keys in the right order and the bracelet snapped open.

A moment later, a loud beeping sound began that instantly woke Ilika and everyone else in the camp.

Ilika instinctively grabbed at the shadow and caught a slender arm. A word spoken in his own language caused the bracelet to pour out a bright light that revealed all.

Toli's face twisted with guilt and shame. "I'm sorry!" he burst out as he crumpled to the ground, a crying, shaking little boy, caught in the act. "I shouldn't have done it! I'm sorry!"

Kibi was quickly on her feet, ready to pound anyone to pulp who was trying to hurt Ilika. Boro and Rini, both with knives out, ran over from their bedrolls. Others quickly gathered to see what was happening.

Seeing that Toli wasn't going anywhere, Ilika released him and snapped the bracelet back onto his arm. The beeping ceased.

"I'm so sorry . . ." Toli kept saying through his sobs. "I'm so stupid . . ."

"Yes," Boro spat out, sheathing his knife. "Very stupid. Do you know what you just threw away?"

Mati leaned on her crutch. "I think Toli just threw away *at least* three great gold pieces."

"Toli, how could you?" Sata moaned. "We were becoming such a strong team."

Buna shook her head. Rini wore a frown.

"Creep!" Misa spat.

"I'd like to speak in Toli's defense."

Everyone looked. Kibi was the last person in the world they expected to defend someone who had just violated Ilika's trust.

Ilika, now sitting up, motioned for everyone to relax. They found places to sit around the scene of the crime.

Kibi waited until Toli's sobbing died down. "I agree. Toli probably just lost any chance of being on Ilika's crew. That's up to Ilika. But I know why he did it."

Toli was still shaking and sniffling, but his mouth opened in surprise.

"He did it for love. Toli is a lonely boy with a lot of love in his heart. He did this foolish thing to try to impress Buna by freeing the slaves in Cattle Town. He has a lot to learn, but he's not a bad person."

In the silence that followed, Buna moved over next to Toli and put her arm around him.

"Toli ... you *are* a good person. I've never given my heart to any boy, although I was thinking about it for a while with you. But I've discovered ..." She stopped, and several shades of doubt visited her face. After a deep breath she went on. "I've discovered that boys just aren't right for me. They're okay as friends, but not for ... close personal relationships ... for me."

After a moment, Kibi went on. "I believe Toli is harmless. He knows now that what he was trying to do is impossible. I think he should be allowed to stay with us as a student, and earn his three great gold. He will probably remember more of what Ilika taught us than anyone else."

Several people chuckled.

Kibi fell silent and snuggled against Ilika.

Ilika looked around. "Although I am not ready to make any decisions, I agree that Toli is harmless. Let's all get some sleep. Tomorrow we will walk a little, find somewhere to camp, and I will listen to anyone who has opinions about this. Good night."

Ilika kept the light on for a minute so everyone could find their bedrolls. He shared a kiss with Kibi, curled up under his blankets, and was soon asleep.

✳

Toli lay on his bed, alone, trembling, wondering how he could have been so stupid.

About an hour later he was still awake when a shadow appeared and someone laid their bedroll beside him. A soft hand found his, and a moment later he heard a gentle voice he knew.

"Good night, Toli," Neti said.

✳   ✳   ✳

## Chapter 17: The Long Road Home

Because of the event the previous night, a somber, serious mood filled the camp that morning. The sun had been up for hours when Sata stumbled to the stream to wash her face and fill the pot with water. She returned to find Boro brooding as he kindled a fire, so they worked together silently to make porridge.

When Toli awoke to find Neti still sleeping beside him, he finally accepted that the shadowy visitor from the night before had not been a dream — but he couldn't bring himself to believe that Neti was expressing anything but kindness. She was a pretty girl, the kind that all the boys liked. He had no fantasies that a pretty girl like her would ever have anything more than sympathy for someone like him.

Buna and Misa sat near the fire slicing apples. When they had nine pieces, they stopped and looked at each other, then reluctantly cut one more.

While others shook out blankets and rolled up bedrolls, Ilika stood, stretched his stiff and sore body, and smiled at Rini who was taking Tera down to the stream to drink and graze on the tender grass growing along the banks.

Ilika set the tone at breakfast, and for the remainder of the day, by chatting about the beauty of the early fall morning, and making no mention of Toli and his actions. Even with Kibi helping constantly, Ilika moved slowly and was clearly in no hurry to pack, and once packed, was obviously not aiming to put many miles behind them.

As they meandered along the road eastward, they greeted the occasional travelers they passed, and always warned them about the food poisoning epidemic in Cattle Town.

Five times that day Ilika listened to his students, always out of earshot of Toli, express their willingness to keep him as a student. But they also strongly hinted that if he was still being considered for the ship, they were no longer available.

Ilika discovered that he only had strength and energy for about a mile of walking before he needed water, food, and a nap. They covered about three miles that day before making camp.

On the second day out, Ilika felt better and began to teach short lessons about the geology or the weather as they walked along. The group was moving from a high desert prairie in the rain-shadow of the mountains, into a grassland that received more moisture. Its eastern edge was a geological fault line where the land was rising compared to the low desert far below. The grassland sloped down to the south, and eventually became a swamp near the capital city.

The village of Pos appeared on the side of the road about mid-day, a cluster of little cottages, but no inn or shops. To make extra money, the wives and daughters ran a simple kitchen for travelers, with a single large table under the eaves of one cottage.

With nothing to remind them of tainted meat, soldiers, or slave markets, and with a certain other topic still off-limits, everyone smiled and chatted as they ate lunch. Kibi talked with one of the women, who agreed to make a rich chicken stew that evening. The older girls of the village begged to help, and when Kibi learned they could bake pies, she requested one apple and one berry. Younger girls and boys ran off to gather the fruit.

For the first time in Kibi's life, a celebration would be held in her honor. For the first time in her life, she believed a happy and meaningful future might lie ahead. She smiled and pranced around on light feet as they set up camp among some bushes just outside the village.

As they sat in a circle sharing thoughts and presenting little gifts to Kibi, Boro didn't feel like mincing words. "I know you didn't come to our kingdom for treasure, Ilika, but you found it anyway. Kibi is not the kind of girl who could love just anyone, or be loved by most men."

Kibi turned several shades of red, but was still smiling.

"She's more like a Fairy or Sprite. Anyone who tries to love her had better be strong and true of heart . . . or he'll get burned. I don't know where your country is, Ilika, but I know your trip here, and all the money you spent, and this journey to teach us, will all be worth it even if you just take Kibi."

Ilika couldn't help but grin, and used that pause to present to Kibi a small gold broach in the shape of a dragon in flight.

Kibi clutched it lovingly to her breast and shivered with delight. Then she reached out and gave Boro a sisterly hug, and Ilika a kiss so long and deep he almost forgot others were around, snickering.

Everyone else had words of appreciation and respect for Kibi. They had all been aided in one way or another by her caring attitude and strong leadership skills.

Toli's gift for her, a flower made from ribbons for her hair, was a mere trinket compared to Ilika's expensive gift. He presented it with trembling hands, and could only sputter out a few clumsy words.

To his utter surprise, she thanked him with a warm hug, and he instantly turned red with shame.

A little girl interrupted to announce that dinner was ready, so they hopped up and headed for the village.

The remainder of Kibi's seventeenth birthday party was marked by good food, more kind words, and additional small gifts. Later, around the campfire, many of their favorite stories were retold. Mati attempted the tale of *Kali's Decision* for the first time, and added her wish to see the monastery again someday. Several others nodded.

When everyone had fallen silent and Ilika was beginning to yawn, Buna asked him what he was going to call his own story that took place at Cattle Town.

He thought for a moment. *"Ilika's Big Mistake."*

They all laughed as Boro put more wood on the fire.

Ilika, however, said good-night and headed for his bedroll.

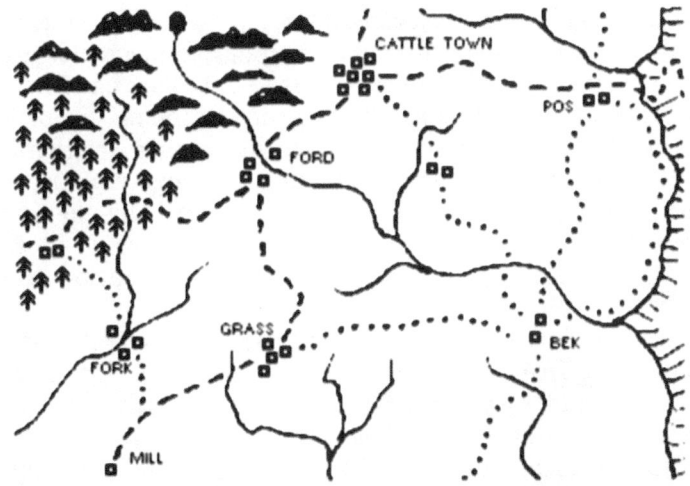

Just beyond the village, the road wound down into a canyon for the long, steep descent to the desert far below. A little-used trail followed the top of the high cliff southward, and a boy was happy to get them started for a copper piece. It was, as they could see on the map, a much longer way than the main path across the grasslands to the next village, but Ilika had many topics to review with his students.

By noon they gathered near the edge of the rocky cliff with the desert spread out three thousand feet below. Several of the students swayed with dizziness for the first few minutes, and had to hold onto bushes or rocks to avoid feeling sick. Tera shook off some flies, found a patch of tasty grass, and began pulling and chewing.

"Wow," Toli breathed. "The gray rocks at the bottom have tiny bushes growing on them."

"Alluvial fans," Ilika explained, "can be hundreds of feet thick, and build up where dirt and rocks wash out of the canyons. Those bushes might be spiny cactus plants taller than people."

"The white stuff in the low places, is that salt?" Mati asked.

"It could be a sodium salt, a magnesium salt, or something else."

"If it's sodium chloride," Rini pondered aloud, "they could use it to salt meat at Cattle Town."

Buna shaded her eyes. "Those piles of sand look like ripples on a beach, but I bet they're a lot bigger."

"I can see places where rivers made deep gullies," Boro said, "but they're all dry now."

"Rivers sometimes flow in the desert during rainstorms," Ilika explained, "but they don't last long or get very far before sinking into the ground."

Kibi sat silently gazing at the mysterious barren landscape below that had somehow fascinated her long before she laid eyes on it.

✳

Ilika's educational review consisted of complex math problems, difficult logic questions, tricky chemical transformations, and challenging written essays. The students had all the basic skills — now they had to apply them. With each problem, after time spent in silence scribbling on paper, smiles would flash and hands shoot into the air, but Ilika always waited for Boro and Buna, and in some subjects Kibi and Mati, to get the answers also.

Neti was happy for her friends, but could not find the energy to do any more lessons, other than the dramatic reading. She would most often sit close beside Toli while he and the others worked on their review problems.

✳

Spending so much time on lessons, the trek along the high cliff took three days. Kibi used her free time to sit and gaze out over the desert. Sometimes Ilika joined her, and they sat with arms around each other as evening shadows crept over the sand dunes below.

"It calls to me, Ilika. It's where I'm gonna to go if . . . anything doesn't work out with your ship."

"If you can wait a couple more weeks, you'll get both. We'll do some of our training down there."

"You mean . . . before we get on the ship?"

"No. We'll take the ship. Everything will be done on the ship after the four extras go their ways."

"Ilika! *How* are you going to get a ship into the desert?"

He grinned. "You'll see."

✳   ✳   ✳

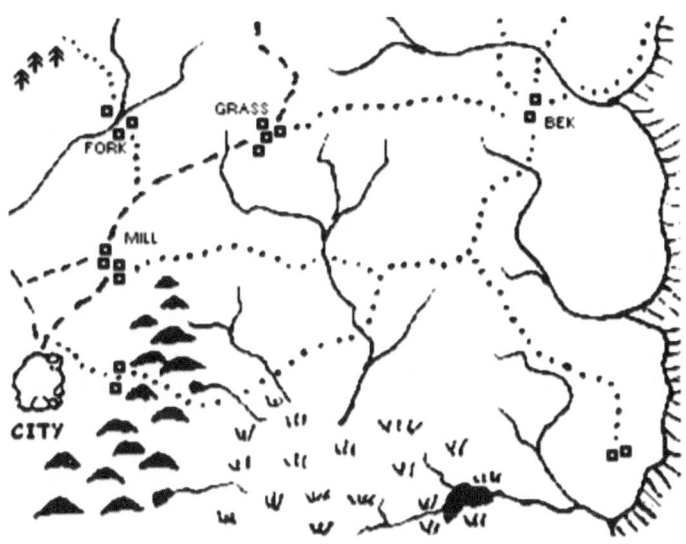

## Chapter 18: The End of Many Stories

Kibi said a silent good-bye to the desert when a canyon forced the trail back to the west. From that point, the group continued westward toward the village of Bek, deep in the grasslands.

Ranches and farms dotted the gentle, green land. Rain refreshed the travelers that night, the first they had felt since leaving the coast weeks before. The muddy river they waded across the next morning crept along slowly, as if reluctant to arrive at its fate in the desert sands below.

When the group walked into Bek, they could feel the fear and suspicion. The people knew their little village was not on the way from anywhere to anywhere. There was simply no good reason for anyone to be on those trails, save the few who had relatives or business in the village.

Since Toli still felt like an outcast, the chilly reception made him wish he could cancel his birthday party.

But to the children of the village, the arrival of ten travelers was too exciting to be ignored. They came pouring out of every cottage and hut, and the teacher and students found themselves pelted with questions about who they were, where they had been, and where they were going.

The travelers set down their rucksacks, Mati dismounted, and soon Toli had two excited children sitting in his lap, and three or four more close at hand, listening to him tell about the ocean, a mysterious place none of them had ever seen.

Surrounded by a similar number, Neti spoke of the beautiful snow-capped mountains, and the children's eyes opened wide with wonder.

It wasn't long before the matrons, old men, and anyone else not at work in the fields, gathered around to glean some news of events in the wide world beyond their grassy home. They only knew of the fire at Lumber Town by the smoke on their western horizon.

Boro talked about the rumor that sorcerers had set the blaze, but swore it was false, as he had seen the mill where the inferno started. Misa, a former resident of the town, added her opinion that no sorcerers were involved. Then she grinned knowingly at Buna.

When the matrons of the village learned the group wanted to celebrate a birthday, and a nice meal for ten with dessert was worth two silver pieces, they immediately went into action. One ingredient was located in one cottage, another somewhere else, a needed spice in yet another hut. One farm wife offered to stoke up her oven, apparently the only one in town. Boys ran to animal pens, and girls spread out in kitchen gardens to find whatever their mothers called for in loud voices.

Toli was embarrassed. A fuss for his sake was the last thing he wanted. But it appeared that Kibi and Ilika were going to keep their promise to celebrate his twentieth birthday in this village. Their kind treatment of him, combined with Neti's affection, made him feel more guilty than ever. He had violated their trust in a stupid attempt to impress Buna, who, he now knew, didn't even like boys. It was hard to imagine a situation that could make him seem sillier or feel smaller.

Kibi conferred with the head matron, who pointed to an area of soft grass where the group could set up camp and pasture their donkey. When men started coming in from the fields, they looked askance at the strangers until scolded by their wives and told about the silver pieces.

As the group settled down to present Toli with little gifts, he was surrounded not only by his teacher and fellow students, but also eight or nine curious children who could all think of an excuse to avoid chores for a while.

Ilika admitted he was unprepared. He assured Toli he was working on a gift, but that his recent injury had put him behind schedule and it was not quite ready.

Toli remembered Ilika lying as if dead, and then sleeping long hours for several days. What amazed him was that his teacher would want to give him anything.

As they started sharing words and stories of appreciation, Ilika said nothing about the bracelet, and Mati didn't mention the wolf. Everyone knew that Toli's mistakes had eliminated him from Ilika's crew, and no further taunting would serve any purpose other than to make him miserable. The one or two people who were tempted to do so, kept their mouths shut.

To Toli's relief, the older girls of the village shooed away the curious children when they began to serve the feast their mothers had prepared. Toli was again embarrassed, but not disappointed, when a big pot was opened to reveal a stewed rabbit surrounded by herbs and dumplings. Freshly baked bread, soft cheese, and a light malty brew completed the feast, followed by tasty custard.

*

Once the men of the hamlet convinced themselves the strangers were harmless, and heard from the children of all the traveling they had done to the far corners of the kingdom, they humbly approached and asked if the travelers could share any more stories and news.

Ilika looked at Toli to know his pleasure for the evening.

He had already received his gifts, heard many kind words he didn't feel he deserved, and feasted. He nodded, knowing it would help remove him from the embarrassing limelight.

So it was that many of their favorite stories were told that evening, excluding those that involved Ilika's bracelet or the fact that they were wanted criminals. Their audience of about twenty-five seemed to be the vast majority of the local population.

To everyone's surprise, Neti told of the death of Miko, including a detailed explanation of what happens when sand covers the top of a boulder. The people of the hamlet paid close attention, just as if they were hearing of the movements of armies or the doings of the royal court.

Toli went to his bed that night very happy with his birthday party. He was even happier when Neti unrolled her bed next to his, snuggled close, and placed a kiss on his cheek before saying good-night.

❋

The people of the village were delighted to earn another silver piece by providing breakfast. They knew it would be a long time before anyone else wandered through their little corner of the world with silver to spend and stories to tell.

With an autumn nip in the air, clouds crept in from the west even as the group saddled their donkey and shouldered their rucksacks.

Ilika had no more lessons. He knew many questions would come up, and he wanted to leave plenty of time for stories. This was the home stretch. They could probably get to the swamp in two days, but he planned to take three or four. They were approaching the end of the process, and they all knew it.

❋

A few miles south of the village of Bek, Rini sat alone in the grass after lunch, chewing a piece of dried fruit and pondering all the things he had seen and done since Ilika's fateful test day. The overcast sky above him looked ominous but had not yet released its burden of rain. He lay back and closed his eyes.

The faces of a laughing bootmaker and a vengeful high priest visited him, along with a beautiful farmer's daughter and a bubbly shepherdess. He could almost smell the stinky hot springs and the salty ocean. A timber wolf's yellow teeth loomed large in his memory, as did the sinking despair of Mati choosing to stay with the goatherd.

A minute later a pair of real voices made Rini open his eyes. The sound of a crutch swishing through the grass made him smile.

"I want to make sure you understand," Ilika's voice was saying, "that for

me to consider you for my crew . . . and I assure you I want to consider you
. . . there is something you must be willing to let go of . . ." After that, Rini
could no longer catch the words.

But a moment later he clearly heard Mati crying her eyes out. Rini smiled,
easily guessing what had been said. He continued to listen, and eventually
the crying changed to sniffling as Ilika spoke again.

Suddenly Mati was cheering and clapping, and her earlier sadness seemed
to be completely forgotten. Rini couldn't guess what would make Mati so
gleefully happy, but he smiled for his dear friend before going back to
pondering his own life.

✳

For the next three days, the group journeyed southward, and the
mountains behind them slowly shrank while the hills near the capital city
grew larger. The rains came, but fell mostly at night, leaving the afternoons
and evenings for the students to ask questions about their favorite subjects as
they walked or sat around the small evening fire.

And there were stories still to be told.

On the first of those three evenings, six students wove a story called *The
Stubborn Cooks of Cattle Town*, a mixture of frustration and humor, deadly
seriousness, and playful mischief.

On the second evening, as the teacher was telling *Ilika's Big Mistake*, he
realized it contained an important lesson, so he cleared his throat.

Neti rolled her eyes, but Ilika didn't notice.

"I messed up and came close to getting myself killed because . . . one of
the people I was trying to find was Kibi. I should have realized I wouldn't be
thinking straight. Leadership is much more difficult when you're emotionally
involved with someone. Those involvements are impossible to avoid on a
ship because we're like a big family, but there are times to let others make
decisions when someone you care about is in danger. I should have taken
Boro to lead and a couple of others to watch, leaving me to use my bracelet if
needed. I caused a lot of trouble for a lot of people by getting hurt and
captured that night. I'm very sorry, and I'm indebted to all of you for pulling
my ass out of that fire."

Grins all around the circle showed that no grudge was held. Neti even
smiled at his choice of words.

Buna snickered. "That's the first time you've used one of our juicy words!"

Ilika laughed. "I'm learning. But you know, the most important part of
that story must be told by others, because I wasn't awake."

Boro called it *The Rescue of Ilika*. He let others jump in any time they
wanted because so many people had been involved. Kibi had the honor of
finishing the story, telling of the joy and relief she felt when Ilika finally
awoke more than a day later.

On the third evening, the mood was light as Kibi and Toli told *Two
Birthdays in the Middle of Nowhere*.

Suddenly a strange feeling filled the camp. Their telling of stories, for the first time, had caught up with their lives. They knew it was necessary, because they would soon be split into two groups — six on a ship, and four . . . elsewhere. They needed to tell all their stories before the separation. After that, it would be too late.

✳

The next day, heavy clouds covered the sky. As autumn approached, darkness came earlier, and little firewood could be found on the open grasslands. Ilika knew they were only a few hours' walk from the end of their journey.

One more story begged to be finished, and they had all grown to care about the people in it almost as much as they cared about their friends. The group of ten travelers made camp early to finish their beloved book before they parted.

Mati was reading.

*"Godi sat on a boulder lost in thought. It tore at him that his people could not accept Tima, even though they owed their very lives to the help and protection they had received from her and the other elves."*

Mati handed the book to Rini.

*"Tima knew in her heart that she loved Godi, and that she would gladly live a simple, mortal life if she could spend it with him. But she knew he had to choose her. He had to let go of those who were too small-minded to accept the love that had grown between a young man and an elf maiden."*

Rini could see Toli squirming, so he handed him the book.

*"Suddenly Godi jumped down from the boulder and began to saddle his horse. 'I am going into the wilderness. I want nothing more to do with people, even if they are my people, my family. I will live with the wolves and the birds, and I will build a house where anyone will be welcome, no matter what color their skin, if they have the courage to journey so far.'"*

Toli passed the book to Sata.

*"Tima asked, 'Are you going alone?'"*

*"Godi replied as he cinched his saddle, 'If I must. But I would like it more if you came with me.'"*

Sata knew Boro would do best with a small paragraph, so she handed him the book at this point.

*"Tima smiled, . . . shouldered her . . . quiver, and grabbed Godi's hand to pull . . . herself onto the horse . . . behind him."*

For Boro, that much had been a serious effort, so he handed the book to Kibi.

*"So it was that a cottage was built deep in the wilderness, about half-way between the human and elvan realms, and that cottage grew into a house, and that house grew into a village. Children were born there who learned to speak the languages of both men and elves, as well as the tongues of the forest animals. Stout people, from both realms, slowly made their way to that special place, and often they stayed."*

Kibi handed the book to Ilika. It seemed only right that he should have the honor of finishing the story.

"*Godi and Tima loved each other for the rest of their mortal days, and were laid to rest together on the hill near their beloved home in the wilderness.  Of course by then it was no longer wilderness, and they were no longer the only ones with strong children born of two different peoples. The End.*"

*

They took a break for dinner, but were all very quiet, pondering the last scenes of the story.  After getting hot soup and bread into their bellies, they read the entire last chapter again.

When the light finally faded and mist began to fall, they reluctantly put the book away, but went on discussing their favorite parts for hours from under their hoods as Boro and Toli tried to keep their little fire going.

*  *  *

## Chapter 19: Choices

After an easy morning walk, the ten travelers made camp in a secluded low spot between grassy mounds not far from the swamp — a perfect place for a group of wanted criminals to divide up their loot and plan their getaway. Ilika laughed at the thought.

Boro saw that firewood was once again plentiful. He, Sata, and Toli brought in a good supply for a long and possibly rainy evening.

When they had done everything they could to prepare their campsite, they gathered quietly around Ilika, looking at him to know his wishes for this tense and important moment in their lives.

"We have become a family, and this is going to be painful," he began. "I want to give all of you a chance to speak your minds on any subject. After dinner I will ask you to give me, in writing, your final intentions. I'll sleep on what you tell me, and announce my decision tomorrow after breakfast."

"Is this where we're splitting up?" Buna asked.

"Yes. The capital city is just over these hills." He pointed to the west.

"Also, that last trail junction we passed goes west and avoids the hills."

"Are you going to give us more tests?" Toli asked.

"No. I think I've tested you guys to death."

They all laughed or smiled nervously.

"Right now I want you to open your pouches and make a pile of coins so I can see how much we have left. The ship will need some supplies, but I'll give as much as I can to those who are staying."

They dumped their coins onto Ilika's bedroll cover, and Kibi added the tube of great gold pieces she had carried so long and faithfully.

The others chatted among themselves as Ilika sorted and counted the coins, but several pairs of eyes remained riveted to the pile of glittering wealth.

"Having us keep a great gold piece all these months, without losing it or spending it . . . that was a test, wasn't it?" Buna asked, eyes still on the yellow coins.

Ilika smiled slightly. "In addition to preparing for emergencies."

One by one the students fell silent as they realized Neti had her hand in the air. "Um . . . I want to say thank you to Ilika for something. This may sound silly . . . but, thank you, Ilika, for making the rule about sex. I'd probably be pregnant from Miko now if you hadn't made that rule. But Miko wasn't the right boy. I know that now. He was determined to get himself killed, if not at the boulders, then somewhere. I want to have babies someday, but with a boy who knows how to stay alive. Thank you for giving me that chance."

"You're welcome, Neti."

*

Ilika finished sorting the coins, then got everyone's attention. "I'd like to share some thoughts about the two paths that lie in front of you."

Everyone gathered close.

"Staying here has the advantage that you know this land, even better than most people after our journey. You know the laws, the customs, and the money. You speak the language, and now you can read and write. You will be the most educated people in the kingdom, except for a few old scholars in their subjects of expertise. You know the wild foods, and you know where *not* to eat meat during the summer."

They all howled with laughter.

"Now the downside of that. As you discovered at Cattle Town, even though your knowledge may bring about changes someday, it's not going to happen exactly when and where you want. If you use your knowledge to stay out of trouble, find places to live and ways to quietly make money or grow food, and teach others when you can, you'll be okay. If you think you can strut around and impress others with your knowledge, this kingdom will slap you down and you'll be *lucky* if you wind up as slaves again."

Toli swallowed.

"Now for the ship. Those who are interested, and whom I select, will have to learn a new language, spoken and written, as well as a new number system and mathematical symbols. There will be completely new laws and customs to get used to. The learning you will do to become my crew will make the last few months look like child's play. And you will be stepping into a civilization in which you will be the *least* educated."

Several of the students smiled sheepishly.

"On the other hand, the language was designed to be easy to learn. The mathematics will seem simple compared to the clumsy system you now use. And you will actually *like* the laws and customs of Satamia in Nebador."

Most of them squirmed with hopeful excitement.

"What if we . . . are selected," Boro began, "but we discover we don't want to work on a ship all our lives?"

Ilika talked about the requirements for citizenship in his country that would allow them to learn other jobs, even other professions.

Neither Boro, nor any of the others who would soon be selected, intended to ever leave Ilika's side. They just needed to hear again that they were not slaves, would not be slaves in Ilika's country, and that whatever they did would be because they chose to do it.

*

When Ilika could think of nothing else to tell his students, and they had no more questions, Kibi, Buna, and Misa pranced away, mischievous smirks on their faces. Rini knelt at the fire circle to build a fire and Boro hovered near in case he needed help. Ilika went off by himself to consult his knowledge processor and make some notes.

It wasn't long before the three girls returned carrying their hats brimming with treasure. Using the broth Sata and Mati had already started, a rich mushroom soup was soon cooking.

As the ten travelers shared their last supper together, they looked into each other's eyes, and saw there the joy of traveling and facing dangers together, and the pain of knowing they would soon be separated into two or more groups.

Nothing remained in their rucksacks to make dessert, but Buna announced she had found mint growing near the swamp, and would brew tea later.

Ilika handed out sheets of paper and pencils, as he had done countless times before, to everyone but Misa. This time, however, it felt very different. "Question one. What is your name?"

Many of them smiled, recalling clearly when they couldn't write their own names, and remembering with fondness the large room at Doko's Inn where their educations began.

"Question two. Do you want me to consider you for the crew of my ship? 'Yes' means I think about it. 'No' means you are staying here by your own choice."

Tension filled the air for the next minute. Rini could almost see the life-paths branching out from this moment into the future.

"If you answered 'no' to question two, you are done, and can give me your papers and relax."

Buna and Neti set their papers in front of Ilika.

"Question three. If there is another person in the group that you absolutely refuse to be separated from, such that you would not want to be selected if they were not, put their name down. If not, leave it blank."

Of the six who still held paper and pencil, most seemed to be writing a name. Buna sat with bright eyes and a mischievous grin, trying to guess them all.

"Question four. List the people you would most like to share a cabin with. Please give me at least three names, first choice at the top."

This required considerable thought and several minutes passed before everyone was finished. Neti had her head on Toli's leg, her eyes closed.

"That's all. Give me your papers, and enjoy the rest of the evening. I must keep to myself while I do what I must do, but I'll join you later for tea."

*

Evening was fading to night and Ilika didn't want to do his work by the fire, so he found a place to sit and set his bracelet for a dim light.

His first glance at the six sheets caused him a double-take. Kibi refused to be separated from Mati, but was not interested in sharing a cabin with the handicapped girl. After a moment of reflection, Ilika remembered a certain private discussion between the two girls behind a goat shed, and smiled with understanding.

He admired Toli for having the courage to try one last time, and set that sheet aside with Buna's and Neti's.

Boro and Sata would not be separated, but Sata most wanted to share a cabin with Mati. Ilika nodded.

Mati would not go without Rini, and Sata was her first choice for a cabin mate. Ilika was not surprised.

Then he looked at Rini's sheet, and frowned. The lad had indicated Neti, Buna, and Mati as possible cabin-mates. Ilika sat in confusion for several minutes as he pondered this. Finally he got up and wandered over to the campfire.

"Rini, would you go on a little walk with me? I need you to help me understand your sheet."

Rini stood and followed his teacher out of earshot of the others.

"I'm confused by your list of possible cabin-mates."

"Me too. I just . . . have feelings for both Neti and Buna . . . even though I know . . . they'd never want to be with me, even if I stayed here."

"I'd like to tell you some things, and see if that helps."

"Okay."

"Neti and Buna, as you know, are not being considered. I want Mati to be on my crew, but she won't go without you. And when we get back to . . . my country . . . the doctors there will be able to fix her knee as good as new. She'll be able to walk, run, dance, everything. Knowing these things, does that help you with your list?"

Rini was trying not to grin, but couldn't help it. "Um, it would make me want to be with Mati!"

"Okay. Thank you. Will you keep these things to yourself until tomorrow morning?"

"Sure."

They returned to the campfire in time for mint tea. Everyone else tried to read the expression on Rini's face, but could not.

✳

Ilika sat beside Kibi and sipped his tea, knowing the decision he had dreaded for so long had finally been made.

Actually, it had been far easier than he expected. Neti and Buna had helped greatly by removing themselves from consideration, even though Ilika would miss them both. Toli . . . had a lot of growing up to do, and Ilika's ship was not the place to do it.

Ilika was now very glad he had gotten to know twice as many candidates as he actually needed, and wondered if there had been unseen forces at work arranging that situation. He would probably never know.

✳

As evening deepened into night, Mati rejected offers from both Rini and Sata to help her brush Tera. Once they had gotten the message and headed for their bedrolls, Mati spent more than an hour caring for her beloved donkey and speaking in soft whispers.

Tera's heart beat a little faster deep in her chest from all the attention and kind words. She sensed that some kind of change was about to happen to her people, but didn't know what or why. However, she clearly felt drops of water fall onto her thin summer coat during that hour, and knew it wasn't raining.

✳   ✳   ✳

## Chapter 20: Parting Ways

Neti lay awake as morning light crept into the clouds.  She knew Toli was not going to be accepted, but didn't blame him for trying one last time.  She did, however, plan to make him feel okay about it.

She had been thinking long and hard about him, and Miko, and other boys she had known.  Toli was a survivor, even if it meant running away from danger.  Neti, in recent weeks, had decided she wanted to spend her life with a survivor.

So she welcomed him into the new day with kisses when she saw others were up and a fire was going.

✳

As they sat around the campfire eating porridge, Buna said what most of them were thinking.  "I have knots in my stomach because I *know* what's going to happen, but it just hasn't quite happened yet."

Boro smiled.  "I like you, Buna.  You always find the courage to say things before anyone else."

"That's me!"

"Isn't this the biggest story of all?" Rini posed.  "Even though we won't get a chance to tell it while we're all together, this is what we've been waiting for . . . the moment we find out what path we walk down."

"But what if you don't get the path you want?" Toli mumbled.

Mati looked at him and blinked.  "Sometimes what you want is not what you need."

"I know what you mean," Kibi jumped in.  "I remember Ilika saying I wouldn't be strong without my years in slavery.  He was right.  I'd be an emotional brat, and I wouldn't have been ready for the test, or this journey."

Ilika, sitting next to her, smiled and put his arm around her waist.

Neti looked far away over the swamp.  "We're never *really* free, free to do anything we want.  I wasn't free to bring Miko back to life.  Now I have to live my life without him, and it's going to be as good, or better, or I'm going to die trying."

Kibi grinned, then spoke softly. "I think you'll succeed. He's just torn between two paths right now. He'll get over it."

Neti gave Kibi a slight nod. Toli was poking a stick into the fire and didn't seem to notice.

Misa took a deep breath. "We're all really lucky. We're alive and we have paths we can walk down. Miko . . . and my parents . . . weren't so lucky."

While they talked, Ilika started collecting empty dishes. Before anyone realized, he had gone down to the stream and returned with everything clean.

Kibi looked guilty. "Ilika! You're so sweet!"

"Remember, where I come from a ship's captain is a servant, not a master. I want you all to go from this place with glad hearts. I want you to remember me fondly, even though I've had to be firm with you. This is a huge day for all of us, one we will remember for the rest of our lives. I'm happy to give you plenty of time to talk."

Suddenly no one could think of anything else to say.

Buna chuckled. "I think we're as ready as we'll ever be."

"Anybody not ready?" Ilika asked, just to be sure.

No one spoke, so he got his rucksack and shoulder bag and seated himself on the ground not far from the fire. "I'd like four very lucky people to come and sit before me. Neti, Toli, Buna, and Misa."

Toli's face fell, but he took a deep breath to prepare himself for what must be. The other three sat before Ilika with happy and expectant faces. Toli's mood improved when he felt Neti take his hand. All the others gathered around to watch and listen.

First Ilika spoke to all four of them. "You are very lucky in many ways. Like I said yesterday, you know this land and its people, and everything I have taught you can be useful here, in your kingdom. I am parting with you because you need this land, and you would not be happy on my ship. Also, I have discovered that we have more money left than I expected, so I'm giving my students five great gold pieces each, except that in some cases I'm lowering that to four."

Buna wiggled with excitement. Neti had a quiet smile on her face, and Toli was starting to look more comfortable.

Ilika turned to Neti. "I am very sorry for your loss, dear girl, but it looks like you're going to take life by the horns and be its master, not its victim." He opened a pouch, removed the coins, and set them in front of Neti, along with the pouch. "You quit doing lessons after Miko died, and that's understandable, but to be fair, I'm only giving you four great gold pieces."

"I understand," Neti said softly. "Thank you."

"You're welcome. I also have a gift for you, as I have a hunch you will be teaching others to read someday soon." He brought *The Adventures of Godi and Tima* out of his shoulder bag and handed it to Neti.

Everyone else clapped. They could not think of a better place for their precious book.

When all was again quiet, Ilika turned to Toli.

"You have a very powerful mind, Toli, and after you get settled into life a bit, which I believe this young lady beside you is going to help with, I'm sure you will take what you've learned and do great things."

Toli squirmed with embarrassment.

"But I am also giving you only four great gold pieces because you violated my trust in a way I can't ignore. I think you'll remember that lesson better if it costs you something."

Toli was looking at the ground and Neti could feel him shaking, but after a few deep breaths, he looked up. "That's . . . one more than I ever thought I'd get."

Neti squeezed his hand.

"And I have a gift for you also." Ilika pulled a small, thick book out of his bag.

Toli brightened noticeably as he read the cover of *Tables and Formulas*.

"I found it at Lumber Town, before the fire, and I've been going through it, making notes in the margins, correcting things that are wrong, and adding a few things I want you to have."

"Thank . . . thank you. Thank you very much!"

"Buna. You are just brimming over with secrets and plans. Can you share any of them?"

"I'm going to be a shepherdess!"

Ilika smiled. "You're going to be the most well-educated shepherdess this kingdom has ever seen."

"And the richest!" Boro added.

Everyone chuckled.

"Even though you have often struggled with your own demons, you have, without any doubt, earned five great gold pieces."

Buna clapped and bounced up and down where she sat.

"And there's a gift for you also."

Mati was ready. She had slipped away a few minutes before, but had heard everything. Now she came hobbling forward, Tera at her side. "Buna, a shepherdess needs a good donkey."

Buna rose to her feet as if in a dream, her mouth open and her eyes wide. "Wow! I ... I promise ... to always take good care of Tera, and never let anyone hurt her."

"I'd trust you with my life, Buna," Mati said with tears in her eyes, "and I couldn't give her to you if I didn't."

Buna grinned from ear to ear as she hugged her new donkey.

Ilika took a moment to give the three departing ex-slaves their bills of freedom, then turned to the youngest of his companions. "Misa, you were not my student, but I'm sure you picked up a few things from our lessons. After you got over pinching people, you were a good traveling companion."

"I learned that when you need people, you'd better be nice to them."

"A very good lesson to learn. I have two great gold pieces left for you."

Misa's eyes almost popped out of her head as Ilika set the coins in front of her.

"But I want to give you some warnings."

The girl got serious and listened carefully.

"I know you and Buna are very close."

"I'm going to be a shepherdess with her, and we're going to try to find Noni!"

"Good. But I want you to remember that these two coins are completely *yours*, and it is *your* decision what to do with them . . . or not do with them . . . not Buna's decision."

Misa nodded thoughtfully.

"Buna, I hope you'll help her with money changing, and understanding the value of the coins, and *always* respect that these are completely hers."

"I will, I promise."

"And I have a small gift for you, Misa. It sounds like you'll be doing some traveling. This will help." Ilika brought out their map of the kingdom and handed it to the girl.

"Thank you!"

"Misa . . ." Neti began with mixed feelings, "you don't have a money pouch. I guess . . . I don't need two. You can have Miko's."

The young girl smiled.

✳

Everyone stayed busy for the next few hours.

Buna and Misa spent much of that time with Mati and Rini. They received the saddle, saddlebags, and other gear. In exchange, Buna presented Mati with her rucksack. Mati and Rini shared everything they knew about Tera, her moods and needs, her strengths and weaknesses. Finally, Mati and Buna shared a long embrace, while Rini gave Misa a kiss on the cheek and whispered something that made her blush.

Ilika asked them to unpack all the food and cooking gear so it could be divided among the four who were staying. After some negotiations, Toli received the large knife, Neti the flint, Buna the cooking pot, and Misa the small knife. Both of the pairs who were sticking together planned to visit the capital city for supplies, and they all agreed to journey together at least that far.

In addition to what they had earned, Ilika gave each a few silver and copper pieces, just so they could get in the city gate before needing a money changer.

Kibi stayed with one of the four almost constantly, helping them pack, sharing hugs, or just talking. She would miss Neti the most, but the other three were special to her also, each in his or her own way.

The good-byes and tender moments lasted until they all knew there was nothing else to do but share a simple meal, and then get on with their lives. A feast would have been nice, but they had only bread, cheese, and a little dried fruit. Somehow it seemed fitting that their time together would end with simple food, just as it began at a slave market.

Everyone was very quiet as they ate. Those friends who were parting took special pains to break bread together one last time in symbolic farewell, sometimes even feeding each other.

Buna and Misa tied their rucksacks to Tera's saddle, but planned to walk. Misa announced with pride that she was getting boots in the capital city, as her moccasins were nearly worn through.

Toli's and Neti's rucksacks were both very light, but even so, with eight great gold pieces between them, they were already talking about horses.

Finally, nothing remained to do but put one foot in front of the other. The four conferred, and decided to take the grassland trails instead of the hills.

All six members of the ship's new crew climbed to the top of a grassy mound and waved until the four were out of sight.

✳  ✳  ✳

## Chapter 21: The Ship

Kibi, standing beside Ilika on the top of the grassy mound, turned and looked at him. He was crying, but trying to wipe away his tears. "That was the hardest thing I've ever done," he whispered.

Kibi wrapped her arms around him and held him tightly. The others slipped back down to the camp to give the pair some privacy and pack what was left of their belongings.

Eventually Ilika dried his tears. Kibi smiled at him with eyes that weren't much drier. Below in the camp he saw Boro, Sata, Mati, and Rini. The four he could not take with him on his ship, and the donkey, were gone. It had not been a dream.

After a few breaths, Ilika walked hand in hand with Kibi down to the camp. He sat on the grass and the others joined him to make a small circle.

"Look around you. This is what I came here for. This is the new crew of a beautiful little ship of the Transport Service. These are the people you can count on to stand at your side, share the work, and watch your back."

They all looked around. The eyes that met theirs had already been tested. The ones they could not count on were gone — Miko, with his craving to lead without the necessary wisdom — Neti, who obviously wanted to settle down and have a family — Toli, who was going to take a long time to grow up — and Misa, who was just too young. They would have liked to keep Buna, but she had her moments of weakness, and had chosen a different path.

"There are many things I can tell you now that I couldn't before, like how a girl who needs a crutch can work on my ship. Mati already knows. The healers in my country will be able to fix her knee, as good as new."

Mati grinned while the rest clapped and cheered. No one doubted that Mati wanted to be a reliable crew member, but some doubted her ability. Now they were satisfied.

"But we have two or three months of training to get through first, and

Mati will have all her basic responsibilities during that time. That's possible because my ship is much easier to operate than any ship you have ever seen . . . or imagined."

Mati pouted slightly. "I just wish I could have kept Tera until we got near the ship."

Ilika smiled tenderly. "We *are* near the ship. It's about a five-minute walk from here."

Kibi squinted and looked at Ilika askance.

"A swamp ship?" Sata suggested with a shrug.

"Our ship can go just about anywhere it needs to go. You have all been picturing a wooden ship, with sails, floating in the ocean. It would have been impossible to tell you the truth without actually showing you . . . and I wasn't allowed to do that unless I planned to take you with me.

"The truth is . . . the next hour is going to be extremely challenging because you will see and learn things completely outside your experience. You will have to trust me. I hope I have earned that trust. If not, you will run away screaming."

Boro frowned. "Us? We'd follow you anywhere, Ilika!"

The rest nodded.

"In return for that trust, I promise to never lead you anywhere without good purpose, and always with as little danger to ship, crew, and passengers as possible. But there will occasionally be dangers, and we will face them as a team."

"*Life* has dangers," Rini said, throwing up his arms. "We could ask for no more than you are giving us."

Ilika nodded.

"Can you show us the ship now?" Mati asked, brimming over with some of Buna's curiosity.

"Yes. Let's get packed and say good-bye to this little place."

*

As soon as Ilika and Kibi got their bedrolls tied to their packs, all was ready. They looked around to see if anything had been forgotten while Boro made sure the fire was out. For the first time, there was no donkey to saddle, no cooking pot or bowls to stow, and no food to pack.

Sata looked around. "I hope the ship really is close, or we're eating raw mushrooms for dinner."

Ilika laughed, then led them slowly toward the swamp. Boro carried Mati's new rucksack over one arm, and Sata walked hand-in-hand with her handicapped friend.

They came to the edge of the swamp and Ilika recognized the very place he had first stepped onto solid ground months before. The fresh spring growth he remembered was gone, and the bushes and vines were past their prime and preparing for winter. Unlike the bright sky of the previous spring, it was now overcast and threatening to rain.

Ilika looked toward the place he had left his ship, and saw a slight mound in the swamp covered with mud and vines.  "My mistake at Cattle Town wasn't my first, you know.  When I arrived in your country, I thought I could just walk across this sticky mud."

The others laughed deeply, releasing some of the tension they felt.  Eventually everyone was quiet again.

Sata looked out over the swamp.  "We don't see any ship, Ilika."

He opened the little cover of his bracelet and began tapping at the tiny keys within.  "I'm waking it up now."

Kibi stood beside him and looked in the direction he was facing.  The swampy mound started rising.  A few moments later the head burst free and rose into the air on a long, shiny neck as globs of mud fell back into the swamp.  Soon the large body of the beast could be seen, still mostly covered with black muck and tangled plants.  Finally, when the body had lifted clear of the surface, the dragon leaped into the air with its stout legs and hovered above the swamp, trying to shake off the rest of the mud.

Kibi swallowed hard and wondered what in the world she had gotten herself into.

※　※　※

## Chapter 22: Manessa Kwi

When the ship judged it had freed itself from the mud and vines enough for normal flight, it slowly changed back to a perfect sphere about eight yards across, golden orange but still smeared with black goo.

Ilika's five students stood frozen between wonder and terror. If they hadn't just promised, minutes before, to trust him completely and follow him anywhere, they might be running away as fast as their legs could carry them.

"Kibi?" Ilika's voice attempted to penetrate her fright. "You okay? Mati?"

"It's ... beautiful!" Rini breathed, pulling himself out of his momentary shock.

Seeing that Rini wasn't afraid, the others struggled to master their fears. Boro blinked his eyes and closed his mouth, but could barely swallow.

"Sata?" Ilika tried again. "It's okay, really. It's just a little deep-space response ship of the Nebador Transport Service."

"Ili ... Ilika?" Kibi managed to stammer. "Y ... you need to tell us a lot more about your ship."

"That's why we're here, dear Kibi. I can tell you everything now. And it's your ship, too."

"It's ... dirty," Mati declared, inspired by Rini to let go of her fear. "We need to ... wash it."

Boro found his voice. "Um ... didn't you say there was a little lake up there in the hills?" He pointed to his right without taking his eyes off the ship.

"Yes ..."

"Can you make it ... go up there?" Sata asked.

Ilika smiled. He could see that his chosen crew was going to recover very soon, and were already showing signs of attachment to the ship — the same ship he hoped they would accept as their home, their workplace, and their pride and joy.

✳

Sata helped Mati up the trail to the lake and Rini brought her pack. The others walked backwards part of the time, watching the mysterious sphere, completely amazed that the ship would just follow them up the trail like a big golden soap bubble floating on the breeze.

Ilika had been to this place and remembered washing his muddy boots before continuing on to the capital city. Now he looked at it with a new purpose in mind. A grassy level place on the far side would do nicely for a landing site, but first he tapped at his bracelet to direct the ship into the water, then selected the flattest possible shape.

Kibi, Rini, and Sata soon had their rucksacks, boots, and outer clothes off, old pieces of clothing out, and were climbing onto the thin circular disc floating on the lake. Ilika and Boro ducked underwater to clean the bottom of the shiny craft as best they could. Mati waded into the water with her crutch and rinsed out cloths that became too muddy to use, then tossed them back to those on the ship.

"Top's clean!" Kibi declared as the three slid off and splashed into the water.

"Can we build a fire?" Sata asked, shivering in her wet underwear. "I'm cold!"

"How about a nice warm ship instead?" Ilika proposed as he worked with his bracelet to maneuver the ship to the grassy area. It changed back to a sphere, sprouted legs, and settled to the ground.

The six of them collected their belongings and circled around the lake. As they approached the clean, shiny ship, Ilika tapped another code into his bracelet, a round hatchway appeared on the side, and a ramp seemed to come out of nowhere. He walked up the ramp, then turned and stood in the opening.

"In the entryway are racks for outdoor shoes," he explained, stowing his boots, "a dirty laundry chute," he pointed out while tossing his clothes in, "and our packs go in this luggage area. On this wall is a shower, you touch these symbols to control the flow and the temperature," he demonstrated. "This blue liquid isn't water, so don't drink it." After quickly rinsing himself off, he opened a cabinet. "Clean robes for everyone. Next person?"

For a moment, no one moved even though three of them were trembling from the cold water of the lake.

Finally Kibi took a deep, slow breath and stepped up the ramp. She then helped Mati, shaking like a leaf, into the shower. Soon Sata found the courage to come up. Boro and Rini passed up the wet clothes and Kibi slipped them into the laundry chute.

Before long, everyone was warm from the shower, wearing a clean robe, and standing on a soft floor just a few steps above the entry hatch, wondering what to do.

Ilika spoke a few words in a strange language and gentle lights came on, allowing the crew to see the interior of the ship.

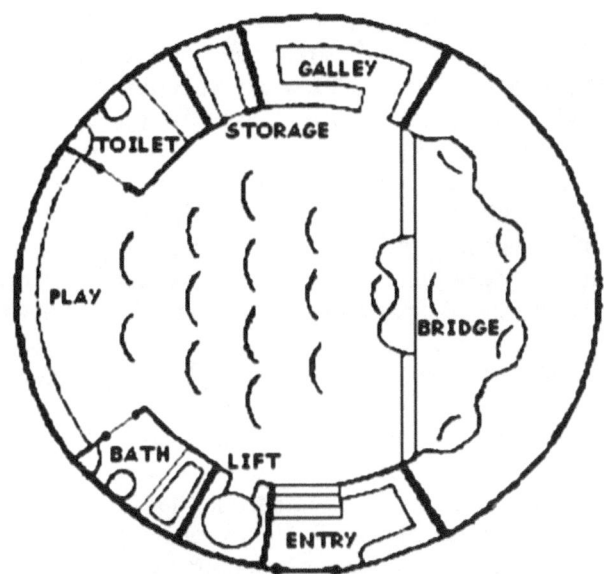

Straight ahead and extending to their left, an open area contained a dozen seats with high backs, almost like royal thrones. Ilika stepped to a mysterious table half-way across the room, touched something, and the seats started moving all by themselves.

Kibi and Sata jumped with fright and collided with Boro and Rini.

Ilika smiled as the seats rearranged themselves so five lined up side by side in the front row. He sat down in the seat at the strange table and swiveled it around to face the others. "Come in and sit. I'm sure you have questions."

With the wide eyes of frightened rabbits, they hesitantly filled the seats. The room remained silent until Kibi found her courage. "It's ... not a dragon?"

Ilika chuckled. "I can see how someone might think so. It's a living creature named Manessa Kwi Habishu Glinta. But it's not a will-creature — it cannot make its own life decisions. Nor can it reproduce, so it's not male or female."

Boro frowned. "It? That's what we say for things that aren't living."

Ilika nodded. "There's no pronoun of respect in your language for something that isn't male or female."

"Ships are always ladies," Rini informed.

The other new crew members nodded.

"So ... can we call her ... Manessa?" Mati asked timidly.

"Yes. I usually do. It's ... she's a deep-space response ship designed to go just about anywhere, and very quickly, although, as you can see, she isn't very big. Twelve passengers comfortably, many more in an emergency, but they'd be sitting on the floor. Over here to my right is the galley, in the back is a little play area and two toilet rooms, one with a bath. Over here beside the entryway is the lift to the lower deck, and I am sitting at the steward's station. Behind me is the bridge, which we'll talk about tomorrow when I introduce your jobs. But today, I'd better show you how to use the toilet rooms."

For the next ten minutes, Ilika explained the technologies of the toilet and bath while they poked their heads through the doorway. The same blue liquid flowed in the sink and the bathtub. The five new crew members took everything on faith, as they could not imagine how any of it worked, but it obviously did, and they would need to use it, or go outside and find a bush.

"You mean . . . we can take a warm bath every day?" Sata asked with a grin.

"You sure can, unless we're too busy running the ship. These toilet rooms are for the passengers, but there's another on the lower deck."

Questions slowly came out as the students relaxed. Ilika promised they would not be crushed when the ship changed shape. When they started asking how everything worked, he pointed out that they could use fire and water long before they knew chemistry. He promised they would slowly learn all the workings of the ship, but even he could not explain them all from memory.

*

As evening approached, a hard rain began to fall, and they looked out through the open hatch to see it pounding the surface of the little lake.

"The ship will protect us from the weather . . . and other things, right Ilika?" Mati asked.

"Yes. This ship is our home, our sanctuary."

"Even from soldiers?" Boro questioned with narrow eyes.

Ilika laughed. "If one was chasing you, you could step inside, touch this symbol . . ."

The hatch didn't close, it vanished. All the students jumped in surprise. Ilika touched another symbol and the opening reappeared.

"I think you've earned a nice meal. Stay in your seats, everyone!" he commanded, turned to the steward's console to touch a control, and the seats started moving again.

Four of the new crew members gripped the sides of their chairs with white knuckles. Mati, very used to a moving vehicle under her, just grinned, but looked up with frightened eyes when the ceiling started coming down.

Soon she relaxed, seeing that only part of the ceiling was descending, a large flat oval. It stopped at table height. By that time, the twelve seats were arranged evenly around it.

"Kibi, would you help me in the galley?" Ilika asked, going that way.

The little kitchen could only hold one person, two at the most. Ilika entered and pulled a stack of trays from a cabinet. Kibi spread them out on the counter.

He handed her six little cartons and showed her how to open one. The other courses came in large packets that became hot, or cold, all by themselves when Ilika pulled a tab. He handed each to Kibi with a serving spoon and she did the rest. Soon they worked together to carry the trays to the table.

"Your beverage is pinkfruit juice from Natavia Two," Ilika explained.

They carefully sipped it, rolled it around in their mouths, and smiled.

"Your main course is a rice and bean dish from Ubalora Three. The vegetables are from Alpha Shumentia Two, and your dessert is duma cakes from Rontilia Four's moon. I picked things that are similar to foods you know. I hope you like them."

Four ex-slaves and one medieval innkeeper's daughter had little chance of being picky eaters, and they trusted Ilika to only feed them good food, just as he had trusted them to select wild edibles on their journey.

"You know, Ilika . . ." Kibi began as she ate, "I don't know all the names of the other lands . . . but did you say something about our dessert coming from the *moon?*"

Ilika smiled around his bite of vegetables. After swallowing, he took a deep breath before answering. "Your duma cakes don't come from *the* moon. They come from the moon of a planet in another solar system. All the other foods you are eating come from other planets too. Nothing on your tray is from this world. And . . . my country is not on this world either."

Not even the sound of chewing penetrated the silence as five pairs of eyes looked at him.

Since they were all still seated and not yet screaming, Ilika gathered his courage and took the thought a step further. "This ship is quite capable of moving on the water, under the water, or in the air. But its main purpose is to journey among the stars. By passing my tests, you have earned the opportunity to jump ahead of the people of your little planet by . . . several thousand years. It will take strong hearts and sharp minds to succeed at this. I think you have the necessary strength and intelligence . . . or I would not have chosen you . . . but only you can decide if you are willing to go where I go, and to work in the Transport Service as I do."

"Count *me* in!" Rini announced instantly, clearly happy with everything he was hearing. "I've been looking up at the stars all my life. To go and see them . . . would be the most wonderful thing that could happen to me!"

Sata grinned from ear to ear. "My parents are going to be so proud of me!"

"Sorry, Sata. Because you have a family, you have a burden the others do not. You cannot tell your parents or your brother, just as I could not tell the other students."

"Oh . . ."

"You can tell them you successfully completed your studies, and were selected for the ship, but you must let them think the Manessa Kwi is a wooden sailing ship, just like they already imagine. They are people of this world. Telling them anything more could be confusing and frightening. Also, it would be showing off, and my crew needs to be grown up enough to resist that temptation."

Sata cringed for a moment, then recovered. "That's okay. It'll probably be a long time before I see them again."

"Actually, you'll probably see them . . . um . . . day after tomorrow."

"Really?"

"I'm sorry to have bad news, but we don't have enough food from other planets for the training period. We'll have to buy food in the marketplace and cook."

"I think we can handle that, Ilika," Kibi said with a smirk.

"I figured you could," he said, smiling back at her. "Tomorrow I'll introduce your jobs, and then I'll spend one day teaching each of you the basics. While I'm doing that, the rest of you, except Mati, will walk into the capital city to buy food, visit Sata's family, Pica, Doti and Tibo . . . anyone else you want."

"And if we run into Toli, Neti, Buna, or Misa?" Boro asked.

"You can't tell them anything they don't already know."

Boro nodded.

*

After Ilika and Kibi cleaned the dinner dishes, again using the blue liquid, he called everyone over to the lift. They stared at the hole in the floor with bleak expressions, the bottom clearly visible about eight feet straight down, and not a ladder or rope in sight.

"I'll go first." Ilika stepped into the hole, then floated slowly downward. "Your cabins are down here!" his voice came up to them.

Kibi took a deep breath and put one foot over the hole. Suddenly she was reminded of stepping barefoot onto a sheepskin rug, long ago in her childhood. She held her breath, stepped out with her other foot, and was just about to scream when she realized she wasn't falling, but only floating downward.

Soon Ilika came into view, smiling at her. "You can breathe now."

Sata arrived next, as if she'd been doing it all her life.

Then came Mati and Rini together, his arms around her, her eyes tightly closed.

"Is there any other way to get down there?" Boro called from above.

"There's an airlock to the outside!" Ilika called up.

"Can I use it?"

"No!"

Sata stepped into the lift and started to rise. "I'll get him."

Ilika chuckled.

Boro arrived a minute later with his hands over his eyes.

"You can come out of the lift now, Boro," Kibi coaxed.

"Are you sure?" he questioned, eyes still covered.

She reached out and touched him, and he peeked out between his fingers. Rini and Mati smiled.

Sata was back down a moment after Boro stepped out of the lift. They all looked around at the pleasant circular room with cabinets on the walls, two tables with short stools, plenty of pillows and cushions, and several doors. The ceiling glowed with a gentle light.

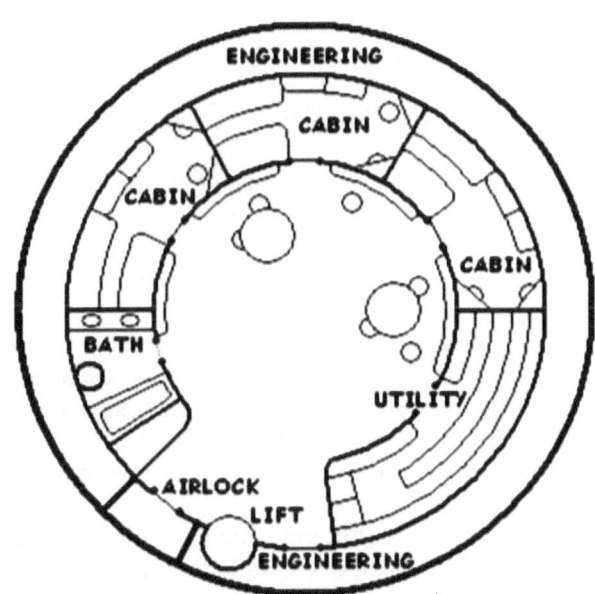

"With rare exceptions, passengers don't come down here. Toilet and bath room over there. This is the utility room with supplies and spare parts, and the laundry machine."

"Did you say laundry *machine*?" Sata asked, a gleam in her eyes. "I had to do all the laundry at the inn because I'm a girl," she explained, rolling her eyes.

Ilika smiled. "It's late, so we'll just get our cabins today."

Mati yawned. "Yeah."

They followed him past the toilet room to the first of three cabin doors. Ilika touched a symbol and the door slid open to reveal a pair of beds, little closets, and two desks. Ilika stepped in and pointed out all the features of the vacant room. "Light above each desk, and a knowledge processor. Reading light over each bed, and storage underneath . . ."

"Ilika," Mati began, "me and Sata want to share a room and just, you know, invite the boys over sometimes. Is that okay?"

"That's what I figured from your sheets yesterday."

Boro nodded. "Me and Rini get along."

"Okay," Ilika continued. "This cabin is for Mati and Sata!"

The boys and Kibi clapped as the two girls entered and sat down on their beds.

"I'll bring our bags down in a minute . . ." Sata said as the rest moved on.

Ilika showed Boro and Rini their cabin, then he and Kibi were left alone in the circular room.

＊

Ilika cleared his throat outside the last cabin door. "This is a very special moment for me. When I left my ship, I didn't know I'd bring back . . . a girl I love."

Kibi smiled shyly. "I never imagined I'd love . . . a boy from another world!"

Ilika bit his lip for a moment, then touched the door control to hide his embarrassment.

Kibi floated in, as if in a dream. To Ilika's surprise, she showed no interest in her bed, closet, or desk, but instead began to touch and smell the clothes in his closet, and look at the objects on his desk. She picked up a shimmering crystal in a little display case.

"A souvenir from my first deep-space mission," he explained.

"Do you have a souvenir from this mission?" she asked with a shy smile.

"Yes," he said, slipping his arms around her.

She giggled, twirled away, and picked up a plush animal doll on his bed, but frowned with confusion.

"Something I kept from my childhood, a moba-temu from Susavita Five."

Kibi smiled and shrugged. "I've never had anything like this."

"When you go into the capital city for supplies, you could look for something special."

She set the plush creature back on Ilika's bed, returned to his arms, and began kissing him deeply. After a time they parted and she looked into his eyes. "That rule you made . . . is over now, right?"

"Yes . . ."

"So . . . if you love me like I love you . . . then I need to go outside and look for a certain herb . . . or we're going to start something tonight that we might not be ready to start . . ."

Ilika smiled as he continued to gaze into her eyes. "I do love you that much. Wait here."

He left the cabin and returned a moment later with a small bottle, sat down on his bed and offered his hand.

She joined him on the bed and snuggled close.

"I'd be very happy and honored to . . . um . . . have a child with you someday . . ." he began in a quiet voice, "but right now, it would make your training difficult."

Kibi nodded and licked his neck.

Ilika shuddered with pleasure. "The only problem with these pills is that . . . if the boy takes one, he has to wait an hour, but if the girl takes one, she's protected right away."

"In that case," Kibi whispered, looking into his eyes again, "*I'll* have to take the pill."

\* \* \*

## Chapter 23: What Would I Do?

Ilika's new crew members slowly crept out of their cabins the following morning, stretched, used toilets and bathtubs, practiced using the lift, and began to peek in all the cabinets they could find. They discovered some things they recognized, like toy balls and bath towels, and many others completely foreign to them.

They thought about building a fire, fetching water from the lake, and rolling up bedrolls, then laughed at themselves.

Last of all, Ilika and Kibi emerged, new-lovers' smiles glued to their faces. They managed to find a free bathtub, and once again shared the space.

Soon, with pinkfruit juice and a hot cereal mix from Katamela Two on their trays, Ilika took up his new role. "During meals, a captain usually deals with problems and briefs the crew about upcoming tasks. So . . . I guess . . . I should do that. Any problems with the cabins?"

"Are you going to show us how to use the . . . knowledge . . . processors?" Sata asked.

"Yes, when you start learning the language."

Rini began chuckling. "I tried to blow out the light last night. Boro remembered how it worked."

Ilika smiled.

"Can we . . . buy things to keep?" Mati asked.

"Yes. Since you can't go into the capital city on these shopping trips, you could ask someone to get you something. Just remember, half a cabin is your entire private living space, and we'll be visiting many places where you can get souvenirs."

Mati looked thoughtful during a moment of silence.

Boro raised his hand. "I'm okay with the lift now."

"Me too," Mati added.

"Good. Any other problems?"

Everyone was silent.

"Okay," Ilika began. "Today I'll introduce your first jobs. You'll eventually learn others, even the captain's position if you want." He looked around. Five faces, nearly bursting with excitement, looked back.

"I've picked the positions that will be easiest, as you'll also be learning many other things at the same time. Every one of your jobs will sometimes be easy, and sometimes hard . . . sometimes exciting, and sometimes boring. You might feel jealous of someone else's position. I expect you to be grown-up about it, and put it on your wish-list for the future. Childish jealousy is one reason Toli is not on this crew."

Everyone nodded as Ilika and Kibi grabbed all the trays and quickly did the breakfast dishes.

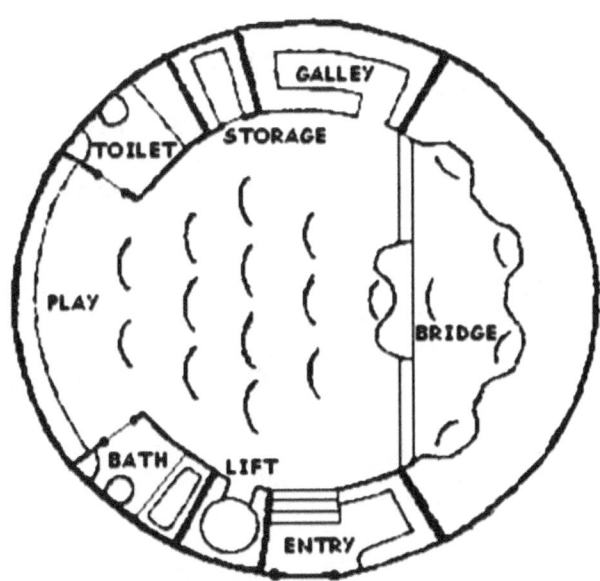

Ilika sat down at the only control console on that part of the upper deck. "The steward has a complex job. He or she is responsible, in many ways, for the *entire* ship, AND the landing site. Safety, air to breathe, water, food, waste, supplies, laundry . . . the list is long.

"None of it is very hard as long as it's just us, but the steward also takes care of any passengers. He or she has to understand people, and have good language skills.

"Most of the steward's duties aren't highly critical in an emergency. Much of it is done before a voyage, and the passengers can take care of themselves if they need to. So the steward is also second-in-command. If anything happens to the commander, from going to the toilet, to dying, and he or she hasn't appointed a new commander, the steward is automatically in command."

Ilika stood up. "I would like Kibi to be the first steward of our little ship!"

Everyone clapped as Kibi, biting her lip and smiling at the same time, rose from her seat. Ilika pointed to the steward's chair, and with some hesitation, she seated herself.

Kibi looked up at Ilika. "You're going to teach me all this stuff, right?"

"Yes. Starting tomorrow."

She smiled back at the young man she loved.

✳

When Ilika spoke a strange word, the bridge lit up from unseen sources of gentle, warm light. He descended two steps to a station not far from the entryway, on the right side of the bridge. Kibi stayed in her seat and the rest moved closer and perched on the steps or sat on the floor.

"This is the engineer's station. This ship has nine different types of engines that use seven kinds of fuel. Some of those engines, the ones you'll learn first, are for travel in air and water. Others are only used in space. One is for jumping between the stars.

"The engineer spends part of his or her time here, but just like the steward, has responsibilities on other parts of the ship. The engineering ring completely surrounds the lower deck, where most of the engines are located, and the engineer keeps them all working perfectly. He or she also stocks all the fuel and spare parts.

"But the engineer never makes use of the engines directly. He or she is providing a service so that others can make the ship go where it needs to go. The engineer must be a person who can handle power without ever being tempted to misuse it. He or she must indeed be a gentle giant, and I can't think of a better person for the job than Boro!"

Everyone clapped as Boro turned red and grinned. Ilika pointed to the chair and the fifteen-year-old came and filled it.

"Um . . . if you think I can do it . . ." Boro said in an unsure voice.

"I do."

Boro took a slow, deep breath. "Then I'll do my best!"

✳

Ilika went to a station on the other side of the bridge. Boro and Kibi stayed in their seats and everyone else gathered around.

"The only term for this person in your language is 'the watch,' but it's very inadequate. This person is responsible for *knowing* everything that's going on outside the ship. He or she uses instruments, knowledge the ship already has, and many different tools to make information available to those who are planning the mission and piloting the ship. This station is the eyes and ears of the ship, and without it, we are completely blind, except for maybe poking a head out the hatch to see what we're about to hit."

His entire crew smiled.

"Important things outside the ship include the land itself, weather, objects in space from grains of sand to stars, and many different forms of energy. This position requires a person with perception, imagination, and clear thinking. I feel confident asking Rini to learn this job!"

Cheering filled the ship as Rini took his seat with a humble smile on his face. He immediately started asking questions, but Ilika just folded his arms.

Rini smiled sheepishly.

✳

Sata and Mati looked at each other. They were the only ones left without jobs. Ilika moved to one of the two stations at the very front of the bridge, the one on the left side.

"This is the navigator's station. He or she is responsible for figuring out how to get from one place to another within the limits of the mission, such as time, fuel supplies that Boro manages, dangers that Rini tells us about, and possibly the needs of Kibi's passengers. To plan routes through space, the navigator has to be very comfortable with mathematics and geometry.

"In addition to navigation, this person also communicates with other ships, star stations, and space ports, so good language skills are necessary. I would like to have Sata learn this job!"

Everyone clapped as Sata proudly took the seat. "There would be no way to tell my parents without sounding like I was making it all up!"

Everyone laughed.

✳

When Ilika moved to the other front bridge station, he noticed silent tears running down Mati's face where she sat on the steps near Rini.

"Mati . . . what's wrong?"

Rini joined his friend on the steps and put his arm around her.

"I . . . just can't think of anything . . . left for me to do . . ." she mumbled in a sad voice.

Ilika knelt down. "Let's think about this together, shall we?"

"Okay . . ."

"Kibi up there is taking care of the ship and the passengers. Boro has the engines purring and ready to go. Rini is telling us what's outside. I have explained the mission and Sata has figured out the best way to get there. And you know what?"

"What?"

"We haven't moved an inch. We still need someone who actually puts her hands on the flight controls and tells Manessa where to go."

Rini grinned.

Sata raised her hand.

"I know!" Boro blurted out.

Ilika put up a hand for silence, then looked at Mati. "I knew, when I saw you riding that donkey, that you were going to be the one who actually touched Manessa, just like you did with Tera. Will you be our pilot, Mati, and guide our little ship among the stars?"

Two different emotions fought on Mati's face. Doubt was soon conquered by joy. Ilika rose and extended his hand to the handicapped ex-slave. She took his hand, and a moment later he lowered her into the pilot's seat.

"How soon 'til we fly?" she asked, turning to Ilika with a bright smile and wet eyes.

He spoke to all of them. "I will do your introductory training in the same order I used today. On the sixth day, we'll fly Manessa away from here and briefly visit a number of places in your country. Then we'll move down to the desert to do more serious training."

All five faces around him, seated at their stations, looked at him with gleaming eyes, ready to learn whatever it would take to become the real working crew of a deep-space response ship.

*

Ilika sat down in the remaining seat on the bridge, the one in the center.

"This is the commander's chair. Notice that it doesn't have any complex control panels or display screens, just this little one on the arm that doesn't do much. The commander is the one person who has to keep a broad perspective on the ship and the mission, and not get lost in the technical details. He or she is the coordinator, the helper, and the servant of any crew member who is having trouble.

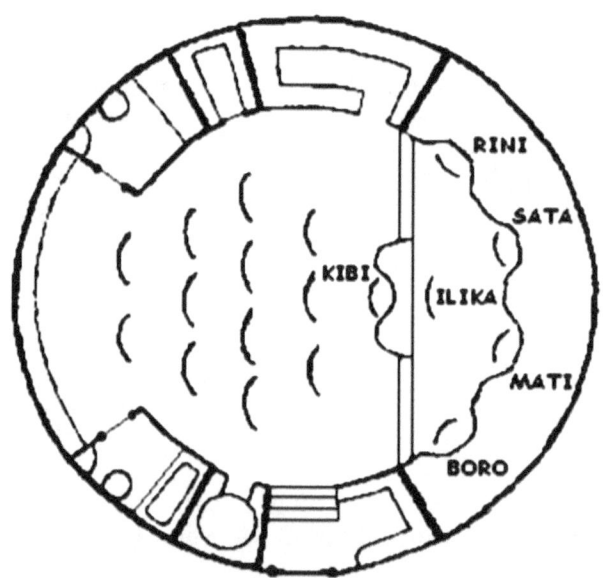

"And I want you to notice some important connections between the work stations. The steward is my second-in-command, and from her station, she can keep an eye on the bridge and be ready to take command in an emergency."

Kibi winked at him.

"There's a natural information flow from the watch, to the navigator, to the pilot, and they're all in a line. The navigator and pilot are at the very front because they deal with the most immediate needs of the ship. The rest of us support *them*."

Sata and Mati smiled at each other.

"Some of the most critical communications happen between the pilot and the engineer, and they're right next to each other."

Mati and Boro looked at each other with deep respect.

"It's also a nice coincidence that Sata and Boro know each other well, because the navigator has to work closely with the engineer during mission planning. It does no good if the navigator plans a route for which we don't have enough fuel."

Boro flashed Sata a cheesy grin.

"Look around you. Get a feel for how the bridge is laid out, where everyone is in relation to everyone else. These are your primary work stations for the next year or more. You know these people. You know they will all do their jobs as well as they can, and if there is any weakness due to inexperience, I'll be there to fill the gap."

He waited a minute while everyone took in the layout of the bridge, physical and personal. "Shall we have some lunch?"

"Yeah!" everyone said at once.

✳  ✳  ✳

## Chapter 24: Preparing for Trouble

Kibi helped Ilika serve a seafood casserole from an ocean world, a vegetable salad from another planet's moon, and nut milk from the fourth planet of yet another solar system.

Suddenly she smiled. "I know why I'm helping you in the galley all the time — it's part of my job!"

"Yes, but after you learn it, you'll only be in charge. You won't have to do all the cooking. We'll take turns."

"So . . . can I start making shopping lists?"

"Please do. You know what's in the marketplace. I'm sure everyone will help."

Suddenly the main hatch vanished and a warning tone sounded.

"Well, well," Ilika began, "let's see what Manessa spotted." He went to the steward's station and touched several symbols. "The hatch is set to repel small creatures with a static electric field, and close when anything large approaches. Hmm . . . something about the size of a man. Let's take a look."

By this time Kibi was at his side and the other four were gathering around. An image of the grassy area outside the hatch appeared on the console's small display screen.

"I started the playback about a minute ago," Ilika explained.

They waited. A moth could be seen flitting about in the grass. Suddenly a robed, hooded figure approached the hatch, then quickly ran away.

"A priest!" Boro gasped with wide eyes.

Ilika nodded. "There's a symbol on his robe I'd like to see. Let's try increasing the contrast."

The scene played again, and this time they could clearly see the symbol, the same as on the high priest's robe the day Ilika was almost arrested in the capital city.

Sata swallowed. "D-does that mean the ship's in danger?"

"No, Sata, we're in no danger, as long as we're careful. We knew we were near a trail. Many kinds of missions require us to land in places where people or animals might threaten us. We must defend ourselves, but harm no one without need."

Ilika and Kibi went back to serving lunch.

"I want everyone to take a pill after lunch," Ilika announced.

"The same kind I took last night?" Kibi asked with a confused expression.

Ilika laughed. "No. These pills will place unique tracer molecules in your bodies that the ship's sensors can locate."

"Ah!" Rini breathed with sparkling eyes. "If someone got arrested in the city, we could find them!"

"Exactly. And we'd come and get them out, even if we had to put the *whole* city to sleep . . . which this ship is quite capable of doing."

Boro grinned at the thought.

＊

Ilika wrote names on the little pill containers as he handed them out. "Each of these has a unique number, which I'll put in your Nebador knowledge accounts. Everyone in my civilization has an account where both public and private information is stored."

"Ilika, don't you mean your *planet*?" Boro asked.

"No. My civilization includes tens of thousands of planets, and hundreds of star stations and other artificial spheres. I was born on a planet, but haven't been back since I was eight. Today there's no planet I call home, although there are some I *love* to visit whenever I can."

"What goes in these . . . knowledge accounts?" Mati asked.

"Necessary information, like your name, your job, and the number of your tracer molecule. You can add anything you want."

"Like what?" Rini asked.

"Writings, sound recordings, pictures, video, structured knowledge tables . . . anything that is information, and not substance."

Sata looked puzzled. "Sound . . . recordings?"

"You could capture speech, music, or any other sound — the croaking of frogs if you want!"

She snickered.

"What's . . . video?" Kibi asked.

"Simultaneous multi-channel visual and sound recordings. You'll see one this evening, an introduction to our civilization."

After they swallowed their pills, Ilika led them to Rini's station, made some selections, and a plan of the upper deck of the ship appeared. Six symbols could be seen gathered around the watch console.

"Those symbols are contractions of our names in the language of Nebador," Ilika explained.

Rini dashed away. "I'm gonna hide somewhere!"

The rest watched as his symbol moved around the bridge and then seemed to merge with the engineer's console.

Boro put his hands on his hips. "Rini, are you sitting on my panel?"

"No. I'm under it!"

Ilika smiled as Rini returned to the group. "Manessa's hatch can recognize the tracers, and still protect the ship from anyone else."

Kibi chuckled. "You mean . . . like priests?"

With all his students seated at the large table, Ilika went to a little cabinet on the wall in the entryway, touched the symbols in a certain order, and took something out. He returned to the table and set a dark metal bracelet, just like his, in the middle.

"Our mission bracelets can do many things, which you'll learn slowly, as you need them and we practice them.

"Four of you are going into the city almost daily for the next five days. Two bracelet functions are important right now, and both can be activated by tapping a code onto the bracelet with your other hand. The first is a bright beam of light in case you're caught by darkness."

He taught them the code, and they all practiced turning the light on and off. Rini learned the hard way not to shine it into his own eyes.

"The other function is putting people or animals to sleep. I've told you this before, but I'm going to say it again — this function can kill."

He paused to let his words sink in deeply.

"Use it *only* when absolutely necessary, but *neither* is it okay to sacrifice yourselves. You are valuable. Your work is important. If you have no choice but to defend yourselves to fulfill your mission and return, then you must do that.

"If you get captured, I *will* come get you out, and many more people could get hurt that way. And I *will* be angry if you could have prevented it. In the Transport Service, we *do not* leave our people behind if there is any way to bring them home safely."

Ilika looked around the room and made eye contact with each of his students.

"To qualify to use this bracelet function, you must show me you're willing to use it, and you must experience it. That means you have to do it to one of your friends, and let them do it to you. You will be sitting down on the grass, so there's no chance of serious injury. Who is willing to learn to use, but never misuse, this power?"

Boro's hand slowly came up, followed by Kibi's. Then Sata's hand crept upward. Ilika picked up the bracelet and headed for the hatch.

They all followed, some more quickly than others.

"May I put you to sleep, Kibi?" Ilika asked.

"Yes you may, Ilika."

She sat down, and Ilika pointed the bracelet and tapped the activation code. A high-pitched sound was heard, and Kibi melted sideways onto the grass.

Sata went to Kibi and tickled her. "She's asleep!"

Ilika took the bracelet off and snapped it onto Sata's arm.

"Good night!" Boro said, sat down, and smiled.

Ilika tapped the code onto Sata's hand with his finger.

She aimed the bracelet at her friend with a shaking hand and tapped the same code onto the bracelet.

The bracelet whined and Boro flopped backwards onto the grass.

Sata frowned. "Oh . . . I hope he's okay . . ."

"I'm ready," Rini announced. "I realized that if I can't do this, then people can't count on me."

"That's right. Who are you practicing with?"

Rini looked at Mati and raised his eyebrows.

"Is *all* our training going to be this gut-wrenching?" she asked with a sour expression.

Ilika smiled kindly. "Some of it will be worse. But like using the lift, the first time is the hardest."

She hobbled over to the thick grass and Ilika helped her sit down.

"Will you be here when I wake up, Rini?"

"Right beside you!"

"Okay. I'm as ready as I'll ever be."

✳

Ilika was happy to serve a tasty dinner to his five trainees, newly qualified for two mission bracelet functions. As soon as dishes were done, he rearranged the room and started the video on the large screen above Kibi's station.

"You are about to see people and places you have never imagined, customs and practices far beyond anything in this kingdom, and technologies that might as well be magic. You will see art and architecture, and hear music, thousands of years beyond what you know. Just relax, enjoy the story, and get a sense of what the Nebador Services are all about."

The lights dimmed and the video began.

Ilika sat off to the side so he could see both the screen and his students. They experienced the story as if in the same room with the characters, leaning forward when the events were interesting, and almost hiding behind their seats when things got scary. Several of them moved to the music when it had a rhythmic beat, and wiped at tears during moments of sadness and loss.

When the story ended, most of them dashed for toilet rooms. Ilika had forgotten to mention he could pause the video.

✳

"The furry bear guy . . . he's like us, isn't he?" Boro asked. "You know . . . coming from a simple place and joining your . . . civilization."

"The furry ursine is a girl. Yes, she's very much like you."

"But she's different too . . ." Rini suggested.

"She's one of those rare people who can understand things most of us can't. Actually, quite a few people can *see* into other reality levels, but most of them suppress it, or else go insane. The girl in our video can see *and* understand other levels. In your kingdom, those people are called mystics."

"Those dreams she was having . . ." Mati began, "where did they come from?"

"Those weren't ordinary dreams. She was being prepared by those in the Nebador Services who help special people like her . . ."

"To get the heck out of there!" Sata nearly yelled.

"Yes. As you saw, she was barely ready to leave when her people turned on her."

"Why do people hate anyone who's different?" Rini asked with a twisted frown.

"Fear of the unknown is huge in most people. You guys may not understand, because you're mostly free of fear. That's one of the reasons I picked you."

"The ship that picked her up . . . was that from the Transport Service?" Kibi asked.

"Yep. That's one of the things we do. And there was a twelve-year-old watch station trainee named Ilika on that ship."

Rini smiled at his teacher and captain.

"So she's real? It's not a made-up story with players?" Mati asked.

"She's real. Her name is Ss'klexna Rrr'tak-fi. You'll probably meet her someday."

Boro rolled the name around in his mouth for a moment, but didn't try saying it. "I have a hunch she's a lot smarter than us."

"She's a lot smarter than just about everyone. She can tell you how our star drive works. I certainly can't!"

"That beautiful place the ship went to . . . where was that?" Mati asked with longing in her voice.

"That's a star station, the first place we'll go when we leave your solar system, and where your knee will be fixed."

Mati smiled dreamily.

"What about the scaly guys?" Boro asked. "They were . . . rough."

"The quanasia seem rough with each other because their thick hides can take it. It's just normal affection and play to them. Those in the Nebador Services are always gentle with us softies."

Kibi smiled. "I didn't see many . . . people . . . I mean . . . like us."

"There aren't many. Very few planets have sapient monkey mammals, so there are few in the Nebador Services."

Sata frowned for a moment, but Rini chuckled.

Ilika served a cold, sweet, creamy dessert, and the questions kept coming from his new crew members. More than anything else, the variety of people they saw on the ships and star stations fascinated them, and at the same time, bothered them.

Ilika assured them that the other races, whether mammalian, bird-like, reptilian, or insectoid, would all treat them respectfully. No one, he emphasized, worked in the Nebador Services without careful selection, thorough testing, and serious training.

"So that means . . ." Rini proposed, "to be in the Transport Service, *we* have to get along with all of *them*, even if they are green stick-creatures with claws around their mouths!"

Ilika chuckled at Rini's description of one of the insectoid races. "That's right. And if you remember nothing else from this video, I'll be very happy if you remember that one thing."

✳ ✳ ✳

## Chapter 25: Steward

After a hearty breakfast of nutty grains from a far-away planet, Rini, Sata, and Boro stepped into the entryway where Ilika snapped bracelets onto their left arms. Boots were laced and cloaks tied, but only Sata carried a coin pouch. Both boys carried empty rucksacks.

"You are crew members of the Transport Service ship Manessa Kwi. You have responsibilities and powers beyond anything the people of this country can understand, including your parents, Sata. Conduct yourselves accordingly."

Kibi and Mati waved as their friends disappeared through the hatch.

*

Mati assumed she was going to be completely bored for the next four days waiting for her turn with Ilika. She soon discovered she was wrong.

Ilika seated her at the pilot's console and showed her how to access the ship's four hundred and thirty-two piloting simulations, each with eight difficulty levels. He activated the first simulation, at level one, and a simple flight control rose from the console. With shaking fingers, she took it in hand, and was soon moving a dot around on her display screen, trying to avoid the circles and squares it couldn't go through.

"This is fun!" Mati declared after getting the hang of it.

Ilika smiled. "You can't go to the next simulation until you achieve a good score at level four."

*

Ilika began Kibi's training by strolling around the landing site and discussing geological stability, wildlife, concealment, and many other factors. The selection of a landing site was usually made, he explained, in cooperation with the captain, as some missions needed extreme secrecy, while others required a certain location regardless of the risks.

Next they walked around inside the ship, and Ilika pointed out several loose objects that could break or hurt someone if the ship was in motion.

Mati's boot and moccasin were stowed, and they worked together to put away the cooking utensils in the galley.

Back at the steward's console, he started a demonstration, narrating it himself as Kibi watched. The panel, until now almost completely dark, came to life with mysterious symbols, strange words, and images of both the inside and outside of the ship.

"Environmental changes, starting with temperature and humidity ..." They could feel the air get colder, then warmer, then thick with moisture, and finally return to normal.

"Lighting controls ..." The lights went off and on, dimmed and brightened, and changed color. Mati, concentrating on her display screen, didn't notice.

"Hatch controls ... water tanks ... waste storage ... supplies to be stocked ... sample passenger lists ... security images ..." With each item, different parts of the console glowed with information, most of it still meaningless to Kibi.

The demonstration ended and the panel went dark. Ilika taught Kibi the operating modes for the main hatch. "Manessa is smart, and can make many small decisions without help, but *we* have to make the hard choices."

Luckily for Kibi, the selections on her screen were labeled with both strange words and little pictures.

"Which mode would you use in a star station dock while receiving passengers?"

"Um ... always open?"

"What if a meteor hit the station and the docking tunnel lost air pressure?"

"Oops! Conditionally open."

"Right. Use Manessa's intelligence whenever you can. And if we're going underwater?"

"Always closed!"

Ilika nodded with a grin.

✳

The team of three crew members-in-training wandered through the farming village east of the city, waving to the residents and chatting with those they met on the road. At the city gate, they mumbled something about the marketplace and tossed a coin. Luckily no one noticed how uncomfortable two of them were as they hurried past the street to the slave market.

When Sata, grinning from ear to ear, stepped into Doko's Inn for the first time in many months, all work came to a halt as her excited family surrounded her with hugs and questions.

"Mom, dad, this is my friend Boro who ... um ... works with the sails, and my friend Rini, the watch. And I'm the navigator!"

The reunion moved into the kitchen so the stove could be tended while they talked, and Sata did her best to dance around their questions. Sweet tea was poured, and porridge scraped from the breakfast pot.

"I discovered I'm really good at arithmetic, geometry, trigonometry, all that stuff, and pretty fair at logic, but what really got me the navigator job was that I could read and write well!"

Rini and Boro nodded agreement.

They stayed for another half hour, then arranged for a mid-afternoon lunch after they had been to the market to buy supplies for the ship.

Doko watched his eleven-year-old daughter head out the door with her two shipmates. She had not grown much in height since he had last seen her, but in the way she carried herself and spoke to others, she was somehow very different, very much more grown up. He wondered how that could have happened in so short a time.

*

Kibi next learned all about the galley, including the machines that could grind grains and nuts, mix batter and dough, and puree fruits and vegetables. The refrigerator fascinated her, until Ilika pointed out that if she kept it open any longer, it wouldn't be cold inside.

She broke into a dance of joy when she discovered she could cook without fire and smoke. However, with no ingredients until her shipmates returned, she made lunch for the three of them from the ship's food stocks.

At the table, Mati shared that she was doing well at level three of the first simulation, and out of curiosity had tried level eight. Her poor little dot had been smashed between two colliding squares within seconds.

"Levels seven and eight are so extreme we would usually just avoid situations like that," Ilika explained. "Even levels five and six need very experienced pilots. Most real-life situations are similar to levels one through four."

Mati's pout changed to a sigh of relief. After lunch she went back to simulation one, but selected level four.

*

Since Boro was along, the trio in the marketplace focused on heavy grains and beans. Sata and Rini took turns handling the money and standing guard.

They remembered clearly the last time they had been in this market, newly-freed slaves, still quite skittish. Now, with money in their pouches, mission bracelets on their arms, and a magical ship to return to, they felt proud and confident. They just had to suppress the temptation to use their money or power to rescue unfortunate people or animals.

Ilika had been very clear about the situations that justified the use of their new powers. They had to admit to themselves that everything happening around them, although often unjust, was all quite normal for this kingdom, and posed no threat to any of them.

Even so, about a dozen hungry children received copper pieces, and dashed off to the bakery as fast as their little legs could carry them.

*

Kibi lay on her back on the floor, head in an access hatch under a cabinet of spare parts in the utility room, gazing up at the mysterious tubes and devices above her.

"Can you see the three solvent filters? They're the ones with the same symbol in yellow, green, and blue."

"Yeah," she said. "So the darker filter, with the yellow symbol, is older?"

"Yes. Yellow means it's working. The green one is ready to take over as soon as it's needed. Blue means completely shut down. You can also monitor them at your station. Having three gives you plenty of time to schedule a replacement. The waste collection tanks are to your right."

"I see them. One is half full."

"It will probably be full by the time we get to Satamia Star Station where it can be processed. I'll teach you that procedure when we get there."

Kibi slid out of the utility hatch. "What's next?"

After wiggling through a tiny doorway in another part of the utility room, Kibi gazed up at three large, clear water tanks. Only one contained any water.

"We'll fill them in the mountains where the water is cleanest," Ilika said, "although we could purify just about anything if we had to."

When they squeezed through the next hatch and looked at the tanks and machines within, Kibi wore a puzzled look. "I can see carrying water . . . but *air*?"

"Have you ever been trapped in a small space with too many people and no fresh air?"

"Oh, yes! Four of us slaves were sleeping under a tarp one winter when it snowed. I woke up panicking — the edges were all packed down and no air was getting in. When I finally got it off, one of the others was dead."

Ilika shivered for a moment, hearing another example of the life experiences that had made Kibi so strong. "That's what a ship would be like during a space voyage if we couldn't remove the carbon dioxide and moisture from the air. The $CO_2$ separators are more important than the ship's engines, and again you have three of them. See the little control panel? Touch the yellow symbol on the left."

"It changed to blue-green."

"It's running a test. The big tanks store extra nitrogen and oxygen so we can repressurize the ship if necessary. The small tank collects waste carbon."

Finally, back in the utility room, Kibi learned how to load the laundry machine, check chemical levels, and make control selections. "I know lots of slaves who would love one of these!"

Ilika chuckled.

They returned to the steward's console on the upper deck to finish the day's training. Ilika emphasized that the other crew members might spend lots of time planning routes and fuel supplies, but the ship couldn't go anywhere until Kibi declared it was ready with all the necessities of life.

*

Boro and Sata both moaned with relief when Ilika and Kibi helped them get the heavy rucksacks off their backs. Mati quickly finished a simulation and came up to the passenger area. Rini started unloading the new supplies.

"I'm getting a long, hot bath tonight!" Boro declared. "And I'm *so* glad I don't have to go again tomorrow."

Kibi went to work making soup using the galley's fireless cooking equipment for the first time. She listened as the trio of shoppers shared their experiences.

"There are lots of priests on the roads . . . too many if you ask me," Rini reported.

"Could you tell what they're up to?" Ilika asked.

"No. They were nice . . . but we just looked like ordinary travelers."

"My parents didn't know anything about it," Sata added. "Business has been good, and my brother's friend is a hard worker. It was great to see them . . . but . . . I was glad I was just visiting."

Boro plopped into a passenger seat and leaned back. "We didn't have to use the bracelets, but it sure felt good to have them."

"You know, Ilika," Sata began, swiveling her chair, "I'd never heard of a *pad* of paper before your test. Now they're all over the city! My parents have two, some of the vendors in the market are using them, and even the guard at the gate has a small one on his belt. I think they're status symbols now. The king probably has a dozen."

Ilika laughed deeply.

---

About an hour later, Kibi served dinner made from scratch. Mati described her piloting simulations, each one a little different and more challenging. Kibi gave them an outline of the things she had learned that day, and announced there was a big pile of clean laundry on the lower deck to be sorted.

After dinner, Ilika put on a video, a collection of stories in which stewards played key roles in dealing with difficult situations. "This is mainly for Kibi, but I want you all to have a good sense of what each of your companions will be doing."

Kibi watched intently as a large insectoid steward succeeded in comforting a group of frightened birds who were being relocated from their unstable planet. She cringed when she saw a reptilian steward quickly take command during a complex docking maneuver when the elderly captain collapsed from heart failure. She watched from the edge of her seat as a furry steward, with nothing but a breathing mask, clawed his way to the emergency air controls to repressurize the ship.

Ilika promised a similar video for each of their jobs, and sent them off to get baths and enjoy the remainder of the evening.

When he was finally alone, he sat down at a console and looked over the long checklists of training and experience his new crew members would need, step by step, phase by phase, during the coming weeks and months.

## Chapter 26: Engineer

Kibi, Rini, and Sata decided to all take rucksacks. None of them, alone, could carry as much as Boro, but they still wanted to get a fair amount of food back to the ship. Ilika, Boro, and Mati waved as the three shoppers pulled up their hoods against a light rain.

✳

"We'll start with a little demo," Ilika said as his hands moved on the engineer's console. "I'll narrate, because Manessa doesn't speak your language."

The wall behind the engineer's console came to life with a complex diagram of pathways and devices through which mysterious substances appeared to flow.

"Here's the start-up process for the atmospheric thrusters." They could hear deep humming sounds, and several devices changed color on the display. "Color gives you a quick check — blue-green means warming up or doing a self-test, and green is ready but not yet doing any work."

Boro's eyes darted around the display as colors changed and things happened more quickly than he could follow.

"Several different fuel conversions are being simulated." Some of the flows on the panel changed direction. New devices lit up and others went dark.

Boro started pointing with both hands to keep track. "That stuff used to go over there, but now it's going through that thing and winding up over here!"

Ilika smiled. "You'll soon be very glad Manessa can use many different fuels. There are parts of Nebador where only one or two are available. Now the space engines are coming up, preparing for orbit and beyond."

Boro looked at his console, full of complex graphs he didn't understand and strange symbols he couldn't read.

"Finally, the star drive is warming up," Ilika continued. "No moving parts, just the ability to do what none of the other engines can — send Manessa leaping between the stars."

A single device with no visible fuel source, high up on the display, first glowed blue-green, then a steady green.

"The star drive has engaged," Ilika narrated as it changed to a golden yellow, "and now the demonstration is over, except to show us some of the supply lists the engineer uses."

"Hurray!" Mati cheered from the pilot's chair. "I just finished simulation two, and the next one has tunnels and bridges and things!"

*

Boro's eyes grew wide as he stepped through the door beside the lift on the lower deck. He could see, for the first time, part of the engineering ring that surrounded their living quarters. The narrow walkway ahead threaded among many strange machines, large and small, of shiny metal or luminous crystal. At Ilika's invitation, they strolled around the entire ring, just to get a feel for the layout. Only one small engine glowed and displayed a yellow symbol.

"This is the matter-energy converter that powers Kibi's life support systems when nothing else is running. Today I'll teach you about two engines, the ones we'll use in just a few days. This is the first."

Boro gazed up at the complex device from which three clear tubes emerged and curved in both directions around the outside of the engineering ring.

"The anti-mass drive allows the ship, and everything in it, to ignore the effects of gravity and inertia. It lets Manessa float."

"Didn't we pass two others like it?"

"Yes, there are three, one for each of the induction tubes. Any one of them can do the job in a pinch, two of them with ease, and three gives us the finest possible control. Many things on this ship come in threes."

"Can I . . . touch it?"

"Yes. Anything of danger is completely contained within the engines — fuel, radiation, moving parts, heat, or cold — even when they're running. Just avoid touching the control symbols until you understand them."

Boro spent time getting familiar with the mysterious anti-mass engine, touching its smooth metal surfaces and gently caressing what he could reach of the long, clear tubes.

Ilika touched a symbol on the machine's small control panel, and Boro stepped back as a subtle hum began and one of the induction tubes glowed a deep purple.

"Warm-up and diagnostics," Boro guessed after seeing a blue-green symbol.

Ilika nodded as his student went back to touching the metal and crystal surfaces.

"An important tool of any engineer is to know what his engines look and sound like when they're happy and running well. That allows him to spot a problem quickly, even when diagnostics aren't available."

Boro grinned, and continued exploring the contours of the huge and powerful machine.

✳

"Something feels really funny," Rini mumbled with a frown as he gnawed the meat off a bone. "Something's different."

The corner table at Doko's Inn, with no one else in the common room, allowed them to speak freely. Their bulging rucksacks leaned against the wall nearby.

"People seem all tense," Kibi added, "as if they're expecting something to happen, but I can't figure out what. Lots of whispering going on."

Sata's mother approached. "I just got in some good mutton. Can you stay for dinner?"

Sata's face twisted with mixed feelings, so Kibi spoke. "We're expected back by dark, but thank you for the invitation."

Sata found her voice. "Mom, do you know of any big events coming up?"

"No ... the harvest festival is past ... no, nothing else for a while."

"Thanks. Is there anything for dessert?"

"There sure is! I've got some apple pie with cream!"

"We have time for that!"

Kibi nodded and Rini grinned.

The matron of the inn smiled happily as she returned to her kitchen on light feet.

"I think we need to keep our eyes open wide on the trail back to the ship," Rini suggested in a quiet voice.

Kibi nodded.

✳

"Help!" Mati called in mock distress.

Ilika stepped over from Boro's station where they had been studying the controls for the anti-mass drive. "What's up, pilot?"

"I just started simulation four. It's all funny wiggly lines."

Ilika looked. "That's a topographic map of land elevations. Each line is a constant elevation, as if you were walking around a hill or mountain without going up or down. You can add color-coding by elevation with your display mode selector."

The selector had not made any difference before. She tried it now, and her map came to life with blues for water, shades of green for low elevations, orange and brown higher up, and finally white for the highest mountains.

"Okay, this makes more sense."

"To be a good pilot, you should practice in both modes."

Mati flashed Ilika a smile. "I will."

Ilika returned to Boro's side. "Are you ready to look at the atmospheric thrusters?"

"Yeah." He pointed to an area of the wall in front of him. "That must be this group here."

"Right. Six directions, and several fuel options, as you can see. We'll use solid number two since we have plenty."

"That's the purple powdery stuff, right?"

"Yes. No conversion necessary, just select the first tank and activate the flow control. Good."

"It's got five power levels. How do I know which one to use?"

"Normally the pilot will tell you. Sometimes, for training purposes, the captain will set a different level. In any emergency, if the pilot doesn't say, give her everything you've got."

"You getting all this, Mati?" Boro called to his shipmate.

"Nope. I'm trying not to run into these stupid mountains," she replied, concentrating on the display with her eyes and the flight control with her hand.

Boro and Ilika both chuckled.

*

Kibi had dinner all planned in her head by the time they arrived back at the ship.

"Want some help?" Boro asked.

"Sure. Grab knife, chop veggies."

"*Twice*, on the way back, we were asked where we were going," Rini reported. "And both times, it was a priest."

"What did you say?" Ilika inquired.

Sata smiled with admiration. "Kibi was great. She told them our hamlet was too small to have a name, but they could come over for dinner if they wanted to see where it was. She never spoke a false word!"

"They were peering at us like they'd find forked tongues or furry tails if they looked close enough," Kibi related from the galley.

Boro laughed so deeply he almost lost his balance and had to grab the end of the galley counter.

Rini went on to describe the atmosphere of tension and expectation all over the city.

"Did you talk to the baker?" Mati asked, hobbling up from the bridge. "Remember, he always knows what's going on."

"No," Sata admitted. "We didn't think of that. We'll do it tomorrow. Oh, goodie! We get Boro again!"

Boro moaned, but they could see he wore a subtle smile of happiness as he chopped celery and carrots.

✳

During dinner, Boro shared what he had learned that day, and the shoppers related more of their impressions from the city.

The video that evening first showed a reptilian engineer whose quick thinking had saved a large passenger ship in planetary orbit. An unexpected solar eruption had suddenly threatened both planet and ship. Ilika pointed out that many people, upon seeing such an awesome danger approach, would be frozen with fear and unable to do their jobs. This engineer moved her hands and brought every engine to readiness. By the time the pilot opened his mouth to call for space engines, they were ready, and not a second too soon.

The video continued with the story of a furry ursine engineer who had bravely done his job from the engineering ring, through voice contact with the captain, as he dashed about tending his over-stressed engines.

When the video ended, Boro closed his eyes for a moment to look inside himself and see if he had what it would take.

Everyone else waited in silence.

"It's funny that an ex-slave would be asked to handle so much power," he said as he slowly opened his eyes.

"No one," Ilika responded, "is in a better position to handle power than someone who's felt the effects of its abuse."

Boro took a slow, deep breath. "In that case . . . I can do this job."

✳  ✳  ✳

## Chapter 27: Watch

When Kibi awoke, she tucked the covers closely around Ilika, kissed him lightly on the cheek, and listened as he muttered something in his dream-colored sleep. Though his words were in another language, it sounded like a good dream. She grabbed a robe before tiptoeing out and stepping into the lift.

Rini sat cross-legged on the floor gazing through the open hatch at the dawning sky. He showed no reaction to her arrival.

She got two cartons of pinkfruit juice, opened both, and sat down beside him. He received one with smiling eyes.

Kibi gave her friend the gift of silence as they both sat and contemplated the beauty of the dawn colors in the sky. The edges of the broken clouds slowly changed from orange to pink.

"Today I learn to look at the world through Manessa's eyes," Rini said softly after taking a drink of his juice. "Then I put what she sees into charts and pictures for Sata and Mati. I'm excited!"

Kibi smiled. "It sounds like fun. I'd like to learn that job someday."

"I'll teach you, and you can teach me about the galley and everything!"

"Deal!"

They fell silent again, and after a few minutes Kibi rose and went to start porridge with diced apples. Rini stayed to watch the clouds gather morning light.

*

After everyone had eaten and waved good-bye to Boro, Sata, and Kibi, Rini helped Ilika clean and put away the breakfast dishes. As they worked together, the slender lad's eyes sparkled, and he had an especially happy and mystical quality about him.

Ilika paused and looked at him. "I think you'll enjoy talking to Ss'klexna Rrr'tak-fi someday, or just sitting and meditating together."

Rini smiled without quite showing his teeth.

When they got down to business at Rini's console, the demonstration showed examples of sensory data from both matter and energy, near and far. It then highlighted some of the tools used for extracting meaningful information from that data. Finally it showed a variety of images and graphs that others could read.

"First we'll take a peek at some of the sensors that allow Manessa to see and feel what's out there," Ilika explained as they headed for the lift.

For the next hour, Rini squeezed into little openings all over the ship to see the strange devices embedded in Manessa's flexible outer hull. While looking at a complex blue crystal that ended in a fluid-filled tube that snaked off toward the watch console, Rini asked the question that Ilika hoped wouldn't come up so soon.

"How can Manessa change shape on the outside without crushing us on the inside?"

Ilika was silent for a moment. "You'll have to take what I say on faith. It will make better sense as you learn more."

"Okay . . ."

"The interior of the ship is made from two different levels of reality woven together — normal matter you know, and something closer to pure abstract meaning. You with me so far?"

Rini grinned. "Just on faith."

Ilika chuckled. "But Manessa's hull is different still, a mixture of three realities that come from a far-away place. None of them are physical matter as you know it. That makes for an extremely flexible ship. I know this won't make much sense, but it's accurate to say that the interior of the ship — the seats, walls, consoles, everything — isn't really *inside* the hull. It's somewhere else."

Rini looked quite puzzled, and didn't ask any more questions.

✳

The baker pulled a half dozen loaves out of the oven with his large wooden board, slid them onto the cooling table, and turned to see who was at the counter.

"Sata! Your mother told me you got that job you wanted. Did I hear right that you're gonna be a navigator?"

She nodded with pride. "This is Boro, my dear friend and shipmate, and this is Kibi, the steward who looks after the passengers."

"Happy to see you folks again! Were you some of those Captain Loki bought from the block?"

"Yes," Kibi replied, trying not to laugh.

Boro just smiled and nodded.

"Tori, we want to buy some bread and tarts a little later," Sata began, "but we came to you because you always know the talk of the town. We can feel something strange is going on. Something is bothering people, but we can't figure out what."

"Oh, it's just the demon monster by the little lake in the hills to the east."

All three crew members were stunned into absolute silence. Luckily the baker kept talking.

"That high priest, the same one that has it out for Captain Loki, went to the king yesterday, asked him to send soldiers. Word out of the court is that the king asked if the beast had hurt anyone or anything, at which the high priest started making up vague bullshit. The king said 'no' until he gets word that it's harming someone or burning crops. But, they say, he gave the religious orders leave to do whatever *they* wanted with the beast . . . if they could."

"Do you . . . hear what they might do?" Kibi asked.

"They're just going around stirring people up, taking up a special collection, that sort of nonsense. It's probably a sick wolf or something that ran out of the forest after the fire last summer."

When the baker had shared all the gossip he knew on the subject, and other people were gathering for the fresh loaves, the trio thanked him and wandered toward the market.

"Do you think we should hurry back and tell Ilika?" Boro asked.

Kibi thought for a moment. "I think he knows. I think he wants us to get used to doing our jobs in places where people don't understand us. Right now our job is to stock up the galley for several months of training. Let's go do our job."

✳

Rini got comfortable at his console.

"Your most important task when the ship is on or near the surface of a planet is to provide the rest of the crew with topographic information, the shapes and elevations of the land, water, or ice. Unfortunately, this is one of the hardest sensory jobs for Manessa to do, because from any one place, especially when sitting on the ground like we are now, she can't see very much of the land. Therefore, Manessa's memory is very important. Any topography the ship has ever seen was recorded, including most of your kingdom and the desert to the east, because Manessa could see all that when I descended half a year ago."

"Did you say . . . topographic?" Mati said from right behind them after hobbling over with her crutch.

Ilika looked at her. "Yes, Mati. Rini is learning topographic scanning."

A smile crept onto her face. "Just like the simulations I'm doing?"

"Yes. Except that when we fly the ship, three days from now, Rini will be giving you *real* topographics, so you can safely fly even if there's thick fog, or at night, and nothing can be seen."

Rini's and Mati's eyes met, watch and pilot, the source of essential information about their environment, and the one who would make use of that information to safely steer the ship. Mati grinned and then silently went back to her station.

Ilika showed Rini how to scan the topography, access data stored in memory, and combine the two.

"But how could they be dif . . ." Rini began, but quickly stopped himself.

"Can you answer your own question?"

He smiled sheepishly. "Tectonic plate movement, erosion, volcanic activity, glacial movement and melting, sea level changes . . ."

Ilika smiled. "And others that don't happen on this planet."

When Rini finally felt comfortable with the topographic controls, lunchtime was past and they were all quite hungry. Ilika stepped into the galley, and quickly discovered that Kibi had rearranged everything, and he couldn't find anything he wanted.

Mati and Rini chuckled from the table in the passenger area.

✳

"It's a good thing you're going west!" Doko said with wide eyes to his daughter and her shipmates as they finished their mid-afternoon meal. "Some kind of nasty business to the east."

"Please tell us about it, father," Sata coaxed with a straight face.

"I don't know much. Some kind of beast hunt, or maybe a witch hunt, I couldn't quite tell. The religious orders are working together on it, trying to get the whole city stirred up."

Boro flashed Sata a clueless look. "Doesn't sound like anything we should get mixed up in."

"Your friend is smart, Sata," her father said, nodding. "Your mother wishes to know if she can *please* make you and your friends a nice dinner on your last day here."

Sata looked at Kibi.

"That's day after tomorrow, and Rini will be here too." Kibi could see the pleading look on Sata's face. "Sure, as long as we make it kind of early, maybe just before the dinner hour."

Doko smiled. "Great! I'll tell Mosa. But she also made me promise to tell you that you *can't pay for it!*"

The three friends smiled and went back to cleaning their plates.

✳

Rini and Ilika were just about to move on to another topic when they heard a gasp from Mati, and by the time they looked, she was bouncing up and down in her chair with excitement. They went over to see.

For a minute she had trouble putting her amazement into words. "It's . . . oh my god . . . wow! . . . I never dreamed . . ."

Luckily they could see for themselves. Mati's display was no longer a flat screen, but had become a three-dimensional projection of the imaginary terrain through which she could fly.

Ilika smiled and guided Rini back to his own console.

"Will the real topographics I give her be displayed like that?" Rini asked.

"Usually, unless she selects a different mode. But most pilots work in three dimensions whenever they can."

Rini took a deep breath, and spent a moment touching his console lovingly.

"Now we turn to collecting and interpreting weather data.  The ship's memory is useless because weather changes so quickly.  Do you remember the primary factors that create weather?"

"Um . . . air pressure . . . wind . . . temperature . . . and moisture."

"Pretty good.  Don't forget topography and planetary rotation."  He activated a new section of Rini's console, and they worked through several different methods of gathering weather data.

Next came a large group of tools for taking that data and predicting future trends.

Finally, Ilika showed his student how to create the three weather charts that pilots all over Nebador could read.

Once Rini knew the most important charts, Ilika left him to experiment with his sensors on the actual weather outside the ship at that moment — heavy rain with lightning on the northern horizon.

*

Ilika helped Boro and Kibi out of their rucksacks and sopping-wet cloaks, and Rini did the same with Sata.  Mati sat on the top step and received bags and crocks as they were handed up.

"We have serious news," Boro announced as he stood in the entry shower to warm up.

"Did the baker know anything?" Mati asked.

Sata poked at Boro so she could get under the shower.  "Oh, yes.  Even my parents, who usually stay out of politics, are starting to hear things."

Kibi hung up her cloak to drip.  "It's us.  But I'm sure you knew that, right Ilika?"

"Yes, I knew, or at least strongly suspected, ever since that priest paid us a visit."

Boro pulled out a towel and began to dry himself.  "Will we *always* put the ship in places that'll get us into trouble?"

"No.  Very rarely.  But we're getting some essential training done this way.  You all need to understand that you're not here for the same reasons as most people."

Several faces wore slightly puzzled looks.

"Most people cannot see beyond the need to survive and get ahead, at the expense of anyone and anything around them.   On planets like this, everything is done by power politics, the dog-eat-dog method.   Even religion."

Kibi finished drying, pulled on a clean robe, and headed up to deal with the food and make dinner.  To her delight, she found grains in the slow-cooker, just about ready.  "Ilika, you're so sweet!"

Rini presented himself at the galley entrance to help, and Kibi handed him a cutting board and knife.

The conversation paused as everyone helped get dinner on the table.  When they were finally seated with steaming piles of grain and cooked vegetables on their trays, the topic resumed.

"We were slaves, remember, Ilika?" Boro pointed out. "We were the dogs who were eaten."

Ilika blinked several times. "Yes, but it's more than that. Very few of your fellow slaves could follow where you are going. Toli, with all his brains, could not."

"Kodi couldn't tell right from wrong," Sata remembered.

Rini looked sad. "Neti was so filled with feelings, she couldn't finish the lessons."

Ilika nodded. "Much of the difference boils down to *fear*. I have watched all five of you deal with situations that would have scared most people white . . ."

"And *did* in Toli!" Mati growled, showing her teeth and making claws with her hands.

"Yes, Mati. And in that moment you learned something very important about Rini, didn't you?"

Mati looked at the gentle, slender boy across the table. "Yeah. I learned he'll be at my side . . . in death if necessary."

Rini blushed.

"So the current situation," Ilika continued, "is teaching you how people in this kingdom think, and giving you practice at slipping through the shadows to complete your missions, and not get caught up or bothered by *anything* that's going on, even when it's directed at you."

"Like the thieves at Port Town," Kibi remembered. "You just put them to sleep and we moved on. You didn't try to punish them, or rid the town of them, or anything else that wasn't our business."

"That's right. And even though we won't usually put the ship where people can see it, they'll often try to mess with us, one way or another."

"We won't play," Rini asserted. "We're the crew of the Manessa Kwi!"

✳ ✳ ✳

## Chapter 28: Navigator

With morning sunshine streaming in over the swamp, Kibi, Boro, and Rini headed toward the city, figuring they knew a little more about what they were up against. There was going to be trouble — they just didn't know exactly what or when. Their mission was to buy groceries for the ship. They had no doubt that someday their missions would be much more important — and much more difficult.

After entering the city, the trio made a bee-line for a certain unmarked door on one of the muddy streets deep in Rumble Town.

"I had a hunch I'd be seeing you folks, considering what the religious orders are up to," Doti the healer whispered as she gestured for them to enter as quickly as possible.

✳

Sata stood beside the navigator's station. "It's nice to get a break from walking into the city, but I'm looking forward to the farewell dinner with my parents tomorrow."

"They're good people," Ilika said. "We'll keep in touch with them, and our other friends in the city, as often as possible."

Sata got comfortable in her station seat. The demonstration showed several navigation problems — on the surface of a planet, in orbit, in interplanetary space, and finally in the vast emptiness of interstellar space. In each case, the steps were shown, and the resulting flight plan displayed.

"What's orbit?" Sata asked when the demonstration ended.

"The only stable place in relation to a nearby planet or star. You'll learn all about it when we finish our planet-side training."

"Okay."

"We'll start with surface flight planning in two dimensions. Here's your list of charts, organized by solar system and planet. Here's your kingdom." A topographic map appeared on the large display screen in front of Sata.

Ilika noticed the pilot craning her neck. "Mati, you can always see a copy of the navigator's display on channel five."

She tried it. "Thanks!"

Ilika turned his attention back to Sata. "See your line-drawing tools? Straight, ellipse, parabola, and freehand. After selecting a tool, you draw by moving your finger on the small display on your console. Try following the path we took on our journey with the freehand tool."

Sata was not one to giggle very often, but neither she nor Mati could keep straight faces as the navigator struggled to get used to her drawing tools. Ilika smiled, and only spoke when Sata was ready for another tool.

About mid-morning, Ilika gave Sata the first of five navigation problems. Each required her to plot a course to several destinations in a certain order, taking into account land elevations, cities, bodies of water, and roads. Sometimes he asked her to seek out certain map features, at other times avoid them. Sata quickly discovered that solutions to Ilika's problems were not easy to find.

Mati went back and forth, working on her own simulations when Sata was silently concentrating on her assignments, switching to the navigator's display when her friend announced a possible solution.

Ilika and Sata were discussing her solution to the last problem when they heard a sound of amazement from Mati. They both turned to see.

Mati, in three dimensions, rode the back of a dragonfly, darting among the leaves and flowers of a lush garden. "In such a beautiful place, I wonder what level eight is like . . ."

Ilika kept his mouth shut.

Mati switched to the highest difficulty level. She only saw the frog hiding among the leaves for a fraction of a second before its long tongue shot out toward her. The screen went black except for the purple symbol she had seen many times before.

*

The healer led her three young friends into the clean and tidy streets of Cobble Town, along an alley, up a stone stairway, under an arch, and along a dim passageway to the door at the end, upon which she knocked.

The old woman who opened the door seemed to converse with Doti by sheer eye contact, and no spoken words were exchanged that could be heard. The woman turned and led them into a room, up another stairway, and out onto a small flat roof.

The two women bent low as they crept to the wall surrounding the little roof, and kept their faces hidden among the vases and pots that lined the edge. All three crew members did likewise.

From here they could look down into the grounds of one of the religious orders, currently filled with several hundred people, many carrying torches even in broad daylight.

A high priest, dressed in his most impressive robes, stood on a raised platform speaking to those assembled. The listeners on the rooftop could not hear every word, but some were emphasized, and these came floating up from below.

"... UNDERWORLD ... DEMON ... CRIMINALS ... WITCHES ...

SORCERERS . . . MONSTER . . . BURN THEM!"

The hidden listeners got the general idea. Although they heard things that identified Ilika, and perhaps Mati if still on donkey-back, they heard nothing that made them think two lads and a lass with rucksacks were in any danger.

After a while, the old woman crept back down the stairs and the rest followed. She made tea, and they sat at her round table discussing what they had seen.

"What do you think they'll do?" Boro asked.

"They'll try to make it a public event," Doti explained, "get the whole city marching out there with bundles of wood and torches."

"You'll probably be questioned if you go that way," the old woman warned. "Have your stories ready."

Kibi nodded. "We got some questions two days ago, but yesterday the weather was so bad, we were the only ones on the road."

"This is what happens when people, usually men, get the notion that *they* are in charge of the realm of the gods," the woman said in disgust. "Nothing could be further from the truth!"

"We were at the aurora ritual last summer at the monastery in the mountains," Rini mentioned. "All the priestesses were humble and kind."

The old woman and the healer both looked at Rini with amazement. "You are a rare and lucky young man to have witnessed that ritual," Doti said.

"We had to meditate with them for days before they trusted us," Boro explained.

"You have seen the best, and now you are seeing the worst," the old woman said, gesturing toward the nearby gathering. "Be careful on the roads until they do . . . whatever evil they are planning."

✳

Mati was having great fun with the many simulations that put her in the place of some creature, from tiny insect to majestic bird, always in a rich three-dimensional environment. She knew from experience that level eight was always deadly, and level seven not much better. She could see herself possibly surviving levels five or six someday in the future, when she was an experienced pilot. Right now, levels one and two were easy, three and four were hard.

Ilika assured her she was doing just fine, and that most piloting accidents happened in situations like level one when the pilot became careless.

"More than anything else, I want you to be completely honest about your own limitations. If I hear you say 'This is too hard for me,' I will smile and bake you sweet biscuits, and of course help you improve you skills when we have time.

"Also, the pilot should never be at the flight controls while sleepy, hungry, sick, emotional, or anything else distracting. I can pilot, or the mission can wait.

"But if you *ever* fail to be honest about your skills or your health in a real piloting situation, you will find yourself off the bridge, and possibly looking for Buna to learn how to be a shepherdess."

Mati looked into Ilika's eyes and saw the gentleness she had always seen before, and the firmness of a captain who was not going to let *anyone* harm his ship, his crew, or his passengers.

Ilika smiled, touched her on the shoulder, and went back to working with Sata.

*

For the next couple of hours, Sata learned all about adding the third dimension to her surface flight plans. The ship displayed a cross-section of the proposed path, and they discussed the obvious goal of avoiding the ground, and also the need to stay above or below certain types of weather. They considered the issue of letting people see the ship. Finally, they discussed the native creatures of the air, who always had the right-of-way, and what altitudes they used.

When Ilika declared they had finished for the day, Sata had one more question.

"That stuff you said to Mati about reporting her skills and health . . . that applies to all of us, right?"

"In general, yes, although it's much more critical for the pilot. One reason Mati is our pilot is that she is very even-tempered and doesn't get flustered."

Mati smiled with pride and went on guiding her golden eagle through a narrow mountain pass, catching an updraft on the south side where the simulated afternoon air was rising.

*

When Kibi, Boro, and Rini came staggering through the hatch more than an hour after dark, Ilika could tell by their wide eyes and troubled breathing that they had been tested. He knew this might happen, and he and Sata had dinner all prepared. Little was said as packs were unloaded. Everyone gathered at the table as Sata passed out trays.

"We had to *fight* our way back," was all Boro said before inhaling his dinner.

After getting some nutrition into himself, Rini elaborated. "The road is being guarded by priests and farmers with pitchforks. Four times we tried to talk our way through, but they weren't budging, and we had to put them to sleep. Luckily we got past the last ones, at the top of the hill, before it was too dark and we had to use a light."

They ate in silence awhile.

"Did you consider going around the hills on the grassland trails?" Ilika asked.

Kibi, who had not yet spoken a word, suddenly stopped eating and looked daggers at Ilika, but somehow she found the strength to remain silent.

Rini knew it had not been easy for Kibi to use her bracelet at the first roadblock. It had bothered her deeply, but she had made the decision and was now living with it. Rini could see that Ilika's question had struck a nerve. "Ilika isn't saying we should have gone the other way. He's just asking if we thought about it."

"That's right," Ilika said. "I am happy with the decisions you made. But as your captain and teacher, I have to help you see anywhere your decisions could have been even better, and point out any options you didn't consider. I will have to do this every time you make a big decision, and you will have to do it any time you are in command."

Kibi started to relax. Mati reached across and touched her friend on the hand, and could feel Kibi trembling slightly.

"I . . . had to make the decision . . . very quickly . . ." Kibi began, "and didn't have time to . . . think about the grassland trails . . . but as I think about it now . . . I know that way would have been two or three times as long . . . and it was almost dark and we were very tired . . . and we don't know those trails and could have gotten lost . . . and so I think I took all that into account . . . in the back of my mind . . . when I made the decision I had to make . . ."

Ilika waited a moment and then said, "Thank you. I figured you would have. You're a strong intuitive, and so am I. Others who are less intuitive will appreciate hearing how we make decisions. One thing we have to learn to do, as a crew, is spread around our knowledge and our abilities as much as possible, every day, every decision."

A slight smile appeared on Kibi's face.

"Did you consider the possibility of spending the night at the inn and returning tomorrow morning?" Ilika asked.

Kibi brightened. "Yes, I did think of that! But I realized we had an advantage in the late evening. With our hoods up, they couldn't see our faces. If they did, it would be harder to get back to the city tomorrow."

"Good thinking, and again, I agree."

Kibi took a deep breath and went back to eating her dinner.

Ilika looked around the table with pride. "Tomorrow is your last day of shopping, and I hear you're having a special dinner."

Kibi nodded. "And we're visiting Pica in the morning, before we go shopping."

"Tell her I wish I could join you," Ilika said.

"Me too," Mati added. But her smile showed she would not give up her first training day for anything.

✳

Ilika was very sweet that evening when he and Kibi retired to their cabin, gently combing her hair and massaging her tight shoulders with scented oil. Soon they both started yawning, and curled up together in tender silence.

Kibi lay awake for a long time, going over in her mind the decisions she made that day, and the feelings she experienced when she thought she was being criticized.

Eventually she smiled, and fell asleep in Ilika's arms.

✳  ✳  ✳

## Chapter 29: Pilot

Even though the porridge contained plenty of raisins and honey, the four who were going into the city poked at their bowls and wore glum expressions.

Ilika looked around the table. "This is the last trip. Our food stocks are looking very good. Relax, enjoy the day, visit, eat tarts, pick up a few things that look good, and come back safely. You all made good decisions yesterday, and I have no doubt you will again today. Tomorrow we fly the Manessa Kwi."

Smiles crept onto their faces.

Kibi took a deep breath. "I have an announcement. We're going *into* the city by the grassland trails so we'll be familiar with them. I don't yet know which way we're coming back. But I promise, we will get back."

✳

"This demo," Ilika began, "shows what the pilot would see if she was guiding the ship from the surface to a station in orbit."

Mati heard conversation among the simulated crew members, but couldn't understand a word. She watched the screen, and soon felt the hum of powerful engines. After floating upward, the ship began to move forward, faster and faster. Beautiful red-rock canyon walls streaked by on both sides, then the surface of an ocean, dotted with forested islands, zoomed by beneath the ship. Finally they angled up and the sky slowly darkened to star-studded velvet. Mati grinned with delight as the simulated ship slowed and approached the glistening orbital station, like a cluster of jewels floating in space.

"Ready to go to work?" Ilika asked when the demonstration ended.

Mati nodded excitedly.

"First, close your eyes and picture all the things you need to make Manessa fly."

Mati, seated in her pilot's chair, soon frowned with guilt. "Except for Kibi, it seems like everyone's working for me!"

"That's right. And even Kibi would have little purpose if it wasn't for you. The others will be primarily *listening* for instructions, and only occasionally making requests themselves. You are different. As soon as you have the flight objective from the commander, you will be calling on others for information or actions. That's called *flight command.* The pilot always has flight command, regardless of who is in command of the ship."

"Let me see . . . from Boro I need engines . . ."

"And Boro needs a little time to get those engines fueled and warmed-up."

"From Rini I need topographics and weather . . ."

"And he needs time to scan the terrain, update the ship's memory, and select the best format for the information."

"From Sata I need charts and a flight plan . . ."

"She needs lots of time to do that, but will usually have it ready beforehand. In an emergency, you can fly without a plan, of course."

Mati was thoughtful for a moment. "I have to ask for all that, every time?"

"No. At first, I'll prompt everyone. As they gain experience, they'll do most of it automatically. But it remains your responsibility to *make sure* you have what you need.

"Mostly you'll use flight command for unexpected things. If you suddenly realize you need a different engine to avoid crashing into a mountain, you don't have *time* to ask the commander. You just yell 'I need . . . whatever,' and the engineer gets it for you as fast as possible. If you ever give a bad flight command, I'll butt in and fix it."

"I think I understand."

"You're going to learn two engines today, the same two Boro has studied. The first is the anti-mass drive. It lets you go up, hover at a constant altitude, or come down slowly and gently. Here are your controls and indicators," he said, pointing to an area of her console. "Seven power levels, but we'll just use level one in simulations today and in flight tomorrow."

"Boro! Anti-mass drive, level one!" Mati commanded, grinning.

Ilika went to the engineer's station, made some selections, and mimicked Boro's deep voice. "Anti-mass drive, level one, warming up."

Mati giggled, and could see the proper control group on her console light up blue-green. "When that's green, my engine's ready, right?"

"Exactly. Wait if you can, use it sooner if you need."

"There. It's green."

Ilika returned to Mati's side and made another selection at her console. "Here's a simple landscape." A three-D projection appeared in front of Mati's main display screen, and her flight control extended itself. "Only that one engine is being simulated. See what it will do."

"This is like some I've already done."

"But now the exact response and feel of the anti-mass drive is being simulated, not just movement."

Mati found she could control the engine's power in fine steps from barely-perceptible floating, to a moderately rapid climb. Soon she discovered it took more power to hover at lower altitudes, and the memory of a lesson came to her. "Um, um . . . inverse square law?"

"Yes. Gravity is a form of radiation."

Mati smiled as she took another step toward being a real pilot. But, she soon discovered, she was powerless to make her simulated ship move over the land in any direction.

＊

Pica sat wide-eyed as the four shipmates filled her in on the doings of the religious orders. They only left out the fact that they were the cause of it all.

They broke bread and ate cheese together, and reminisced about that fateful day when Ilika, with Pica's help, had tested them from morning until evening.

"I could have predicted you four would wind up on Ilika's crew. I must admit I don't understand how poor crippled Mati could pilot a ship."

"Shall we tell her?" Rini asked.

Boro and Sata nodded. Kibi thought a little longer, then nodded also.

"In Ilika's . . . country . . . there are healers who can fix her knee so she'll be able to do everything!"

"Okay, *now* I understand!" Pica said with a smile.

"She's doing her first training session today," Rini added.

"Wow. It's still a little hard to imagine Mati up there on the deck, in the wind and sun and spray, wrestling with the ship's wheel."

The four crew members grinned, but said no more on the subject.

＊

"This simulation has more . . . what do you call it when you can't get going, or you can't stop?" Mati asked.

"Inertia," Ilika replied.

"Yeah. Much more inertia than my other simulations." Mati frowned slightly as she pushed the flight control forward, then waited several seconds for the simulated ship to pick up speed.

"That time lag makes it easy to over-control," Ilika explained.

"Yeah. But only when I'm not under-controlling!"

Ilika laughed.

Mati worked with the atmospheric thrusters at their lowest power setting. Ilika watched for a minute. "Find a hill you can go all the way around, and pick an unusual tree."

"Okay. Here's one."

"Your task is to fly around the hill, and then come to a full stop right over the tree without undershooting or overshooting."

Mati tried it, and laughed when she coasted right past the tree even with full reverse thrusters.

"Once you can nail that three times in a row, you will have passed your first thruster lesson."

She smiled up at her captain, and then pushed the flight control forward for another try.

Ilika went over to the watch station and requested a local scan. The number of people near the little lake was up to six, and none of them were his crew members.

✳

Sata and her friends stepped into Doko's Inn about an hour before most people would arrive for dinner. They found a large table in the common room already set with seven places. After helping each other to unshoulder their bulging rucksacks and set them by the wall, they got comfortable, leaving spaces around Sata so her family members could sit with her.

Soon father, mother, and brother came bustling out of the kitchen carrying trays with greens, bread and cheese, and ale. They arranged the trays on the table and greeted their daughter with hugs and handclasps.

"No, no, no!" Doko boomed with a smile. "This is all wrong! Sata is at the head of the table today, not me!"

Sata grinned and blushed as she moved over.

"Your pack looks so heavy!" her mother said with concern.

"Not really. Mostly dried fruit and spices and things. And remember, I've been carrying a pack all summer. I can carry almost as much as Boro!"

Doko laughed.

Mosa had noticed how friendly Boro was with her daughter. "Sweetie, you get your own bunk on the ship, don't you?"

"Of course. I get half a nice, roomy cabin."

"You . . . um . . . share a cabin with . . ."

"With Mati. Remember the girl with the crutch? She's our pilot now!"

Mosa was visibly relieved.

The lad who now worked at the inn served the rest of the meal. First he brought spiced meat and pot herbs, followed by cooked greens with soft cheese.

Sata, Boro, and Rini did a good job of answering all the questions put to them, without revealing the qualities of the Manessa Kwi they couldn't talk about, and that wouldn't make sense anyway.

Kibi, however, was very quiet. She enjoyed the tasty meal, but was pondering how they would get home. They had already heard from several sources that the religious orders were planning some "holy" action in the hills to the east of the city. Their sources, whether Pica, Tori, the friendly guard in the marketplace, or Sata's parents, always brushed it off, assuming they would be going west to return to their ship. But everyone thought it would take place very soon, probably that night.

Finally, a large pudding covered with berry sauce was brought to the table. As Sata savored spoonfuls of the delicious dessert, she exchanged glances with her mother, her father, even her brother, and tried to keep tears from forming in her eyes.

Then she looked at Boro, Rini, and Kibi, none of whom had parents to visit, and her sad face quickly changed to a smile.

Her mother sensed the mixed emotions her daughter was feeling. "We are so proud of you! We want you to journey far and see the whole world . . . and . . . maybe someday you'll settle down with some nice, sweet man." She glanced at Boro again.

It wasn't long before hungry customers began to fill the common room. The fifteen-year-old lad, currently working alone, stood at the kitchen door with a tinge of fear in his eyes as people started demanding food and drink.

Sata shared a last embrace with each of her family members as they rose to return to work, and was then left to finish her meal with her fellow crew members.

✳   ✳   ✳

## Chapter 30: Holy Cause

The high priest waited until just the right amount of tension had built among the assembled priests and monks, then strutted into the room with an air of urgent but dignified purpose.

"Silence!" he commanded, then waited until he had their full attention. "This is the Day of Reckoning to which we have all been called, the Final Battle when Evil has come to our very doorstep. Every trial, from the day you took your vows, has been in preparation for this day, the Ultimate Pruning of the Tree of Life. Your actions today, your ability to inspire and lead the Faithful in this Holy Cause, will go far in establishing your worth when you knock at the Gates of Paradise."

He scrutinized their faces during a long moment of silence, finally focusing on one. "Brother Bako, are the bundles of sticks ready?"

"Yes, Holy Father, nearly a hundred, and more coming in all the time."

"And the oil, Brother Muni?"

"Five barrels, as you requested, Holy Father."

An elderly hand went into the air.

"Brother Kado?"

"We anticipate far more Faithful willing to carry the wood and oil than we have supplies."

The high priest considered the situation, and the answer came to him quickly. "Good Brother Kado, these sticks and oil are commissioned by the Church for a Holy Purpose. They are Sacred Weapons in the holiest of Holy Wars. It is only right that the Church be supported for its leadership in dispatching the Great Evil that lurks so near. The honor of carrying the first bundles and oil cans to the Beast's Lair should go to the Faithful who will support the Church with . . . a great silver piece."

A rumble of amazement rippled through the room.

"The second positions of honor go to those who will give a small silver piece. And finally, whatever's left over will go for a copper piece.

"Understand!" he boomed, silencing the murmur, "that when I say Church, I mean all three Brotherhoods of the One True God, who are working together in this Supernal Task!"

Now he stood stoically with eyes raised, but let the priests and brothers talk. He knew that no better situation could be contrived by man or God to reunite the three orders . . . under his leadership.

＊

As the sun approached the horizon on that gloomy autumn day, Kibi, Sata, Rini, and Boro had no difficulty leaving the city.

However, the road into the eastern hills looked like an armed encampment. Fires burned and tents were set up for the priests. Firewood was brought in from many directions, broken, bundled, and stacked. On the back of a wagon, small cans and buckets were filled with smelly oil from big wooden barrels.

The four crew members of the Manessa Kwi observed the scene for a few minutes, as did many other people.

"Well . . . at least we know the grassland trails now," Boro said softly at Kibi's side.

Soon a crier started moving among the people.

"Let's listen before we go," Kibi said.

They found a place to sit near the city wall and focused on the crier's voice. The purpose of the firewood and oil was soon clear.

Rini chuckled. "That's our ticket for the short way home! The bundles are small, not much extra weight."

Kibi saw his point, but wore a frown.

"We'd learn more about what they're up to," Sata pointed out, "and could tell Ilika."

Kibi swallowed several times. "It just makes me sick to give them money."

Rini nodded agreement. "Ilika felt the same when he had to buy us out of slavery."

Boro could see Kibi weighing the options. "We have the money . . ."

"Okay," Kibi said with a sigh, "but I think we shouldn't be in the first group who pay a great silver. Too conspicuous. Nor the last group, 'cause they might run out."

The others nodded.

"And the stuff we carry does NOT go under the Manessa Kwi. We leave the trail above the lake, dump the stuff, and circle around from the north. It'll be completely dark by then."

Boro nodded. "Good idea."

＊

The sun set just as the Holy Weapons went on sale.

The four shipmates worked their way closer, but waited until everyone who could pay a great silver had done so. There was plenty left for those of lesser means.

The four friends got in line.  The boys received bundles of wood, the girls were handed cans of oil.

They soon found that the hardest part was not carrying a little extra weight.  It was listening to the priests goading on the people with promises of divine favor if they completed their missions faithfully, warnings of eternal damnation if they failed.

It was, Sata realized, all about *fear*.  Fear the monster.  Fear what it might do.  Fear it because it was not like them.  Fear the priests and the religious orders.  Fear God.  Fear each other because there might be unfaithful among you.

Rini wondered why this felt so different from the beautiful ritual he had witnessed at the monastery in the mountains.  If he ever had to choose, he knew which one he would prefer.

Boro was watching everyone and everything like a hawk.  He knew that Kibi was uncomfortable with this option, and that her feelings were, the vast majority of the time, very accurate indicators of what was to come.

As they passed the little farming vale on the road to the hills, Kibi noticed that the people who lived there were hiding in their cottages, and that many of their fruit trees and fences had been raided for the wood collecting effort.  For a moment, she was sorely tempted to use her bracelet to bring an end to the whole operation, force the priests to give the money they had collected to those they had harmed, and send all of them cowering behind the walls of their orders.

But after a few deep breaths, she remembered that it was not her job, as a crew member of the Manessa Kwi, to undo human follies.  It was her job, right now, to get the four of them safely back to the ship.

She took a good look around her at each of her friends, and at the other people nearby, as they began the steep climb over the hills, in the evening twilight, with their silly burdens of wood and oil.

✳

Slowly, bit by bit, Kibi began to slow her pace.  With a torch-bearing priest and other people ahead of them, and more people behind, they could not openly discuss their plans.

Kibi noticed a large gap in the line of people below the three men directly behind them.  As soon as she heard grumbling from those men about the speed of their march, she stepped off the trail and pretended to be exhausted.  Her friends joined her.

She guessed the priest would quickly investigate if he thought he had slackers, so as soon as the three men passed, she retook the trail.

The priest looked, but seemed satisfied.  When he reached the summit, he paused to let all those gather who were counting on his torch light.  As they began moving once more, Kibi made sure she and her friends remained at the back of the group.

The long, steep stretch of trail just beyond the summit, on the opposite side of the hill from the fading sunset light, was now utterly dark.  Three or four torches spread out along the trail, and a dozen more lit up the area around the little lake.

Nothing but intuition told Kibi it was time to leave the path. She stepped off so quickly and quietly that Rini almost passed her in the darkness, then followed her barely-seen form onto the grassy hillside.

Kibi set down her oil can behind a small bush and held out her hand to Rini. He tossed his bundle of sticks and added himself to the chain. Sata came next and cringed when her can rolled a few feet, but no one seemed to hear over the scraping of boots on the steep trail. Boro tossed his sticks and completed the line.

They moved slowly and carefully through the darkness, hand in hand. About a quarter hour later, their feet found the crest of the next ridge. No word floated up to them that their absence had been noted.

"I think we can talk a little now," Boro whispered.

"Yes," Kibi said in a low voice. "Thank you all for following my lead. I'm sorry I couldn't explain it better before we started."

"We understand," Sata assured. "You were great."

"Nice of them to burn torches around the lake so we can see our destination," Rini's voice whispered from the darkness.

Kibi asked sure-footed Sata to lead them down the ridge. Sata felt the way with her boots, more blinded than aided by the torches ahead. Although the slow journey down the dark hillside seemed to take forever, no one complained.

\*

Most of an hour later, the four shadows carefully left the ridge and angled down a slope toward the lake. Its surface reflected the torches of those strutting around. Stern voices in the still night air ordered the stacking of wood in one area, the collection of oil buckets in another.

Finally, with only a stretch of torch-lit grass between them and the ship, Sata looked at Kibi, and she gestured toward a shallow ditch behind some low bushes. They crouched down to watch and listen.

The priests were the only ones approaching the monster with the bundles of wood, and they were obviously afraid for their lives, tossing the sticks from several yards away and running back to the safety of their huddled groups.

The main hatch of the Manessa Kwi was closed and invisible, and the ramp nowhere to be seen.

As the wood under the Dreaded Beast became thick and the supply dwindled, the priests started tossing the cans and buckets of oil into the mix. Some of the simple monks asked why the Beast made no attempt to move or fight back, but were told to be silent, that it was not their place to question the Church's strategy.

Finally the high priest came forward, surrounded by a semi-circle of priests holding torches. He stopped about twenty feet from the Demon and raised his arms.

"In the name of the One, True, Holy Church, I, as Avatar of God Himself, command you to remove your Filthy Presence from our Sovereign Realm forthwith, or you shall be BURNED and sent back to the Underworld from whence you came!"

Neither Manessa Kwi Habishu Glinta, deep-space response ship of the Nebador Transport Service, nor Ilika Imni Zalara Sim, the captain, were impressed. Neither made any response.

"SO BE IT!" the high priest boomed, grabbed a torch from one of the priests, strode forward, and thrust it into the wood and oil.

✳

As the flames leapt and crackled under their beloved ship, Rini could feel Kibi trembling. "Remember, Kibi, Ilika could fly Manessa away any time he wanted."

"I know, but I can't stop worrying. This isn't right." Kibi's whispered voice became broken. "Ilika's done nothing but be nice to people ever since he came here."

"No, this isn't right," Rini agreed. "I don't think the people doing it know or care about right and wrong. This is all some kind of show, but I don't understand it either."

Kibi's face revealed an intense struggle. A moment later she whispered, "All I can think about is storming out there with my bracelet and putting them all to sleep. Boro, you're in command."

He nodded and smiled. "Ilika knows we're here. We wait. Keep your packs on."

✳

In other circumstances, Ilika might have just sat tight and let the fire burn itself out and the people get bored and go home.

But he had four crew members hiding in the darkness less than a hundred feet away, and he worried that if the priests and the people became too bored, they might take out their frustrations on anyone they could find.

He decided a bit of a display was in order, and hopefully the rest of his crew would take the opportunity to slip in.

✳

The fire still burned strong and the high priest chanted threats from a safe distance when a new sound was heard by all, a low rushing that reminded them of a powerful wind blowing through a mountain pass.

"Everybody duck down!" Boro whisper-shouted.

A few seconds later a tremendous blast of air shot out in all directions from the bottom of the ship, sending wood, fire, ashes, oil cans, torches, and priests flying backward away from the little lake.

The blast of air ended as quickly as it started, the main hatch opened, and the ramp appeared.

"Run!" Boro barked even before all the burning debris had landed. He helped get Rini on his feet and pointed toward the ship, then Sata. Kibi seemed to be in a daze, so he grabbed her hand and pulled her up. "I want you in that ship in five seconds, Kibi!"

Kibi knew from Boro's voice that he was going to *throw* her into the ship if she didn't run, so she quickly found her feet.

Boro was the last one through the hatch, and the moment his rucksack cleared the hull, Mati hit the emergency-close symbol.

✳ ✳ ✳

## Chapter 31: Flight Preparations

Kibi spent the next quarter hour in Ilika's arms, crying softly and kissing him at the same time, but saying little.

Rini was completely embarrassed when Mati wrapped her arms around him. She didn't let go for a long time.

Boro and Sata, who had been together the entire day, smiled at each other and started unpacking the rucksacks.

Once everyone was settled, Ilika brought an assortment of snacks and beverages to the table and listened as stories from the day were told. The leadership decisions of both Kibi and Boro, as witnessed by the others, made him smile.

"Was it *really* okay that I gave up my command?" Kibi asked with a slight frown.

"Your willingness to do that makes you a *better* commander," Ilika assured her.

"I'd do the same thing," Boro admitted, "if Sata was in danger and I couldn't think straight."

Sata blushed, and Ilika smiled.

"Manessa's hull . . ." Rini began with a puzzled look, ". . . I have a hunch that fire was like . . . nothing . . ."

"That's right, just like warming your hands at a campfire. Manessa can handle the surface of a star."

Boro whistled.

Mati and Sata looked at each other.

"After a leisurely breakfast tomorrow, I propose we fly Manessa away from here . . . unless any of you would like to stay a little longer, go to church or something . . ."

The dirty looks and snickers all around the table told Ilika they would quickly recover from their trying day. He wasn't sure the priests, however, would forgive and forget so easily.

Ilika knew of several items on his training checklists he could now check off. In addition, each of his crew members had completed their initial day of instruction. And as a bonus, the galley was brimming with food.

＊

When Ilika awoke early the following morning, vaguely remembering a dream about flames licking at his feet, Kibi wasn't in the cabin. He presumed she was taking a bath, and since he felt rested, he hopped out of bed to look over the training recommendations for a new crew's first flight.

When he arrived on the upper deck, he found all five of his crew members at their stations.

"Well, well. Do you guys know it's barely sunrise?"

"Yeah, we know," Sata began. "We're just excited, and want to get going!"

"We looked outside," Kibi reported. "It rained last night and all the fires are out. No priests anywhere. But the lake's a mess with charred wood all over the place."

"Ready to go, huh? Have you all had baths?"

The girls raised their hands, but the boys wore guilty looks.

"Have you had breakfast?"

The girls joined the boys wearing sheepish grins.

"Okay, let's get organized. We have a long day ahead of us, and we'll be visiting some friends. Boro, Rini, get baths while I look over my training manual, then I'll get one. Kibi and Sata, a hearty breakfast, and begin teaching Sata the galley, Kibi, now that you know all about it."

"Who are we visiting?" Rini asked.

"Whoever we find at your favorite place in the kingdom."

"The monastery!" Rini breathed, his eyes sparkling.

Ilika nodded. "Go, go, go! If we all work at it, we can be in the air in a couple of hours."

＊

After doing his reading, Ilika grabbed a bracelet and strolled around the landing site. As Kibi had described, it was a mess, but nothing that wouldn't vanish by next summer's growing season. The little oil buckets were just low-grade iron and would quickly rust and rejoin the soil. Manessa's hull showed no signs of the fire that had burned underneath.

Soon Rini emerged from his bath in a robe, and Ilika went in. He could smell porridge grains cooking when he returned to the passenger area, and Kibi and Sata had their heads in a cabinet, discussing the contents. Boro appeared in the lift.

"That felt good!" Boro said. "Thanks for making us slow down and do it right."

"Don't worry, Boro, there will be plenty of times we'll have to go to work without bathing or eating."

＊

As breakfast was being served, Ilika went to the navigator's station and made a hardcopy of the chart that included this kingdom. He laid it in the middle of the table as he sat down. Only Sata and Mati had seen it before.

"I want to visit the monastery again," he began, "although I won't be surprised if most of the sisters have left for the winter. I want each of you to pick a place you'd like to visit today — somewhere we've been, or a new place."

They all searched the map with their eyes while finishing breakfast. With pointers from Sata and Mati, everyone was soon able to relate the colored, shaded topographic map to their memories of the countryside.

Ilika took notes as they made their selections. Some choices made him raise his eyebrows.

As Boro helped Kibi do the dishes, Ilika worked with Sata at her station to develop the flight plan. First they marked all the locations, then planned a route without too much back-tracking. Others watched as Sata used her drawing tools to connect the dots on her display.

Next, with the ship's help, Sata examined each leg of the plan for the highest land elevation it crossed, and anything else of concern. Ilika had to interpret what Manessa reported, and guide the selection of altitudes. Soon their first real flight plan was ready.

They all looked at Ilika, and he softly spoke one word. "Stations."

Never, except in the most dire of emergencies, had a deep-space response ship experienced its crew jumping into their seats so quickly.

☀

They all hoped their captain's first command would be 'Fly!'

"Kibi, landing site status?"

"Um . . . about like it was before . . . I think . . ."

"I need to know how it really is, right now, for sure."

"Um . . . should I go look again?"

"No, your personal inspection earlier just needs to be updated with some current information from your console."

A smile appeared on Kibi's face, but it faded as she looked down. "I . . . don't remember how."

Ilika went to her side and pointed to different controls. "Visual appearance?"

"Looks the same. No one around."

"Nearest large animal?"

"Um . . . way over on the edge of the screen, by the swamp, something four-legged."

Ilika knew he had to cut them lots of slack at this point because they couldn't yet read the words and numbers on their consoles. He walked Kibi through the same process for the main hatch, the internal air system, the water and waste systems, and the food stocks in the galley. Finally, she looked at him with expectant eyes.

"Cabins secured for flight?"

"Um . . . I think so."

"You have to know."

"I'll go look . . ."

"Not necessary. The owners of all the cabins are right here. Just ask them."

"Okay . . . anybody have anything heavy or breakable in their cabins?"

They all shook their heads.

"There's still one person who hasn't answered," Kibi said, looking at Ilika with a slight snarl.

Ilika smiled back at her. "I have a few breakables, but they are all well-secured."

"All cabins secured for flight!" Kibi announced.

"Galley secured for flight?"

"Um . . . I'll have to check that one . . ."

Ilika came along, barely holding in a smirk.

Kibi chuckled with embarrassment when she found a knife on the counter. "What would have happened?"

"Today, at thruster level one, nothing. On another day . . ." Ilika paused and flashed her a devious grin. "You're the closest one to the galley!"

Kibi grinned back and returned to her station.

"I know that was tedious," he began. "The next time we fly, how much of that will you be able to do without me asking?"

"All of it! I think . . ."

Everyone on the bridge started clapping, and Kibi turned bright red.

✳

Boro went through a similar process checking the status of fuel tanks, flow controls, and the engines themselves. Finally, to his relief, Ilika said the magic words.

"Anti-mass drive, power level one, warm-up and diagnostics."

With some hesitation, Boro touched the symbols on his console that would select the right fuel and bring the mysterious engines to life. They could all feel subtle vibrations.

"Narrate engine status," Ilika ordered.

"Diagnostics okay, warm-up . . . done. Anti-mass drive ready for flight!"

"Atmospheric thrusters, power level one."

Boro again touched the symbols he had already studied. "Diagnostics okay, pressurizing . . . thrusters ready for flight!"

Ilika smiled, and everyone else cheered.

✳

Rini had to run tests and calibrations on several sensors before Ilika would let him get down to business.

"Begin continuous surface scanning. Automatic memory integration. Topographics to all stations on channel four."

Rini was happy. He knew how to do those things.

"Weather data, types one through eight, eleven, and fifteen."

Rini went to work. The others watched as more and more sections of the wall behind Rini's console lit up with multi-colored plots of air pressure, temperature, and other aspects of the weather.

When all of the data was gathered, Ilika gave Rini the final command. "Send weather chart to all stations."

It flashed onto their displays, and everyone clapped.

＊

"Sata, you've already done most of your work, but not quite all."

The navigator was ready, fingers poised.

"Overlay flight plan and weather, report any conflicts."

After a moment of embarrassment, she grumbled with frustration. "I . . . don't remember how . . ."

Ilika pointed to controls to jog her memory. Soon, both images appeared on the same screen and they studied the result.

Rini watched intently as the information from his station was used for the first time.

Sata pointed at her display. "Um . . . we might get a little rain on this leg of the flight plan."

Ilika nodded. "Nothing to worry about."

"The monastery looks like it's in clouds . . ."

"Truth is," Ilika began, "there's little weather on this planet that can affect us in any way. But we have to practice, because that's not true everywhere. Activate universe flight transponder."

"What's that?" Boro asked.

"It tells other ships and stations of the Transport Service who and where we are."

"Transponder active," Sata announced.

"Send the flight plan out on channel five."

They could all see it flash onto Mati's large display and merge with the chart already there.

Ilika started clapping and everyone joined him.

＊

"This is a good time to pause and think," Ilika explained, standing behind Mati. "You now have tons of information — ship status, engine status, charts, weather, flight plan . . . and yet you're missing the most important thing."

"I am?" Mati whimpered.

"You don't yet have a flight objective from the commander. You're assuming that because Sata handed you a flight plan, you're supposed to follow it. That assumption could be wrong. Same with the engines Boro warmed-up, and all the information Rini gave you. Never make assumptions like that when piloting. The commander could give you instructions that would make part or all of that stuff useless, and you'd have to call for other engines, or different information."

"I see what you mean."

"But having given you that warning . . . the flight objective really is to follow the first leg of the flight plan."

"Whew!" Mati breathed.

＊　＊　＊

## Chapter 32: First Flight

Mati swallowed and looked at the plan.

The first leg of the flight plan, at her request, was to hover over the capital city so she could see it one last time. She touched the symbol on her console that raised the flight control.

"Ilika, my hands are shaking."

"I see that, Mati. Maybe ... if they feel the controls, they'll remember their skill."

Mati carefully put her left hand on the flight control, and her right hand on the console near her engine controls. After a moment, they relaxed and a slight smile replaced the frown on the brand-new pilot's face.

"Take us up to about the height of the hills and hold position," Ilika commanded.

The other four gripped their seats as they felt the ship become light, then leave the ground entirely. Mati would have liked to grip her seat, but didn't dare let go of the controls.

"Good work, Mati," Ilika assured, still standing right behind her. "Nice, smooth ascent ... we're almost there ... good. Lock the position. Now you can release the flight control and Manessa will keep us in one place."

Mati wore an excited but worried look. "Did I do it? Did I really do it? Are we flying?"

"Kibi, remember how to open just the upper half of the main hatch?"
She nodded.

"Let's go look, pilot."

Mati extracted herself from the pilot's chair, grabbed her crutch, and accepted Ilika's help getting up the steps to the passenger area, then down to the main hatch. She grabbed the lower edge of the opening and looked out.

Her head immediately started swimming and her stomach threatened to revolt as she looked north over the swamp and grasslands far below.

Ilika held onto her as she alternated between looking at the floor beneath her feet, and peeking out the hatch. After a couple of minutes she announced she was okay, and took one more long look through the open hatch.

Ilika helped Mati back to the passenger area, then invited each of the others to come and look, one at a time.

Kibi felt a little queasy, but quickly got over it.

Boro immediately turned white and went crawling up the steps after viewing the dizzying scene for only a few seconds. Kibi got him a bowl from the galley.

Neither Rini nor Sata experienced any problem.

Ilika spent more time with Mati at the open hatchway, and then Boro.

"You guys are great!" Ilika announced. "I threw up the first time I looked out an open hatch at altitude."

Boro suddenly felt much better.

※

After gaining a little more altitude to clear the hills, Mati made quick work of the flight to the capital city, bringing the ship to a smooth stop high over the Traveler's Gate.

"Can they see us?" Rini asked.

"Most people rarely look up at the sky, and we arrived silently. Also, Manessa has changed color, and is now light blue."

Boro's eyes became large. "Smart ship!"

Ilika nodded, then worked with Rini to get the proper angle with the ship's visual sensors.

When the scene appeared on their screens, everyone gasped at the unexpected events below. One of the religious orders was in flames. Another crawled with people smashing and looting everything they could get their hands on. The one near the city gate had not yet been breached, but had a mob of people pounding at the gate, and more arriving with axes and logs.

Ilika was as shocked as the others as he stared at the mayhem below.

Boro swallowed. "I'm ... um ... sure glad we don't need any more supplies."

"Me too!" Kibi agreed. "Is this ... because of us?"

Ilika was silent for a long, thoughtful minute. "In a sense," he finally said. "You know how the priests were stirring people up. I think ... they stirred them up ... a little too much."

"I wonder why there aren't any guards trying to stop it," Rini pondered aloud. "They're at the gate and all the usual places, and are just ignoring it."

Sata scrunched her face. "I think I know. Tori told us the high priest was trying to get the king to help with the monster ... I mean us. So now he's letting them eat their mistake."

Ilika nodded at Sata. "From what I understand, there's been a power struggle between the king and the orders for many years."

"Did we ... do anything wrong, Ilika?" Mati asked with concern.

"No, Mati. I was asked by the head of the Transport Service to let our ship be seen. She, and her associates, can see deeply into these things. I think the events we set in motion were anticipated, and there is a purpose to them."

*

Their next destination, at Kibi's request, was the middle of the kingdom, at an altitude that would allow them to see everything. It took the ship several minutes to make the ascent, and Mati wore an intense expression as she held the flight control in the maximum-climb position.

"Let Manessa do the work," Ilika coaxed. "Lock your controls, stand up and stretch. Some maneuvers just take time."

Mati did as he asked, but kept an eagle-eye on her display as they climbed. About a minute later, she sat back down so they wouldn't overshoot the flight plan.

Boro wanted to look out the hatch again. Ilika glanced at Rini's console and reported the outside air pressure and temperature, both far below anything they had ever experienced. Boro grinned and shook his head.

Rini needed no further help aiming his visual sensors.

Northward they could see the mountains, now much whiter than they remembered, and wreathed in clouds about half-way up their sides.

Eastward spread the grasslands and the prairies, and beyond that, the mysterious desert. On the farthest horizon marched rugged, barren mountains.

Southward, between scattered clouds, they glimpsed the tiny capital city and the surrounding hills.  Beyond lay more green hills and forests, another realm whose name they did not know.

Finally they looked west.  Past brown hills and green valleys lay the vast ocean.  Sata's heart beat faster, knowing it was, at her request, their next destination.

✳

Mati tried to relax during the long descent, but had to keep her hands on the control to avoid wandering above or below the flight plan.

"Since you're already half-way down," Ilika informed her, "you need to reduce your speed.  The density difference between air and water, at this speed, would be like hitting a brick wall.  Manessa can handle that much inertia, but we can't."

Mati eased her flight control to full reverse, but soon looked troubled. "Ilika, I can barely make us slow down at all!"

"I see that.  You're fighting gravity.  What are you going to do about it, pilot?"

"Um . . . nothing's working!"

"You need help, but not from me.  You have flight command.  Use it."

Mati took a deep breath.  Her hands were shaking even while gripping the flight control.  She could see the ocean getting closer and closer.  "Boro, thruster power level two.  No, make it three."

Boro looked at Ilika.

"Don't look at me, engineer.  You heard the pilot.  If her flight command was bad, I'd say something."

Boro turned to his console and tapped in the higher power level.  He could see the fuel flow increase.

Mati felt the additional power in her thrusters, and quickly used it. During one of the most intense minutes of her life, comparable to a certain minute in the forest near Lumber Town, she brought the Manessa Kwi to a dead stop high over the beach.

Scowling, Mati locked her controls and turned to Ilika, but when she saw his smile of pride, she took some deep breaths and relaxed.  "Did you . . . know that was going to happen?"

"I was pretty sure.  You and Boro just earned check marks for some very important lessons."

✳

Ilika stepped over to the watch station.  "Rini, while Mati eases us down to the water, I'll show you how to scan for submarine topography.  Sata and Mati are going to need that information in a minute."

Rini watched as Ilika demonstrated, then nodded and went to work.

"Kibi, switch to internal air and lock the main hatch," Ilika instructed, going up to her station.  When she had completed those items, he showed her how to run a hull diagnostic.  She was happy to see the yellow symbol that meant Manessa was tight as a drum.

"Mati, how's the approach going?"

"Good.  My thrusters are actually too strong and hard to control now.  Let's try level two, Boro."

"You've got it."

"Sata, as soon as you get that underwater topographic, select a landing site, somewhere level, and modify the flight plan."

A moment later Sata had the map.  "Here's a nice place."

"Approaching the water," Mati announced.

"Nudge Manessa in . . ." Ilika started to say.

The ship hit the water with a jolt, Mati jerked on the flight control, and a moment later they were back in the air.  "Sorry!"

"That's okay," Ilika assured.  "It's just one of those things you have to do by feel.  You did better than I did my first time."

Mati smiled sheepishly and lowered Manessa back to the water.

Ilika watched.  "The top layer is usually pretty choppy."  Even as he spoke, they all felt the rising and falling motion of the waves.  "Take Manessa down before we get seasick.  Since we're not much heavier than water, you'll need very little anti-mass."

The pilot nodded and pushed down on her flight control.

Sata touched some symbols.  "Here's the new flight plan to a level place."

Mati looked up at her chart and noticed a jog to the right that hadn't been there before.  She followed it as they slowly moved deeper into the water, soon leaving all wave motion behind.

"I wish we could see better . . ." Rini muttered, staring at his murky visual display.

Ilika stepped to the watch station again.  "We can.  Here are your image processors.  I think . . . this one."

Suddenly the forward view became crystal clear.  Some fish darted out of the way.

"It's so beautiful!" Rini breathed as he touched the symbol that sent it to all stations.

Boro's face lit up.  "Nice!  Now if we could just net those fish for dinner . . ."

Ilika laughed.

"I can see the bottom," Sata announced.

"Dead slow to the landing site, Mati.  There's usually mud on the bottom, and the less you stir up, the better we can see.  You won't have any responsibilities at this landing site, Kibi."

"No picnic outside the ship?" she asked with a grin.

"How about at our next stop?"

"Yeah!"

"Landing is the most dangerous maneuver any craft can do," Ilika explained, standing behind the pilot.  "Even for a sailing ship, coming to dock is always tricky.  Bring in enough anti-mass to let your descent rate approach zero, then let Manessa do the rest with her landing struts.  Your strut control is right here."

Mati concentrated, watching both the visual and the topographic. A few seconds later she touched the strut control, the symbol became blue-green, then green. They felt a very slight bump and the symbol changed to yellow.

"The Manessa Kwi has arrived at the bottom of the ocean," Ilika announced.

Everyone clapped and cheered. Mati smiled with contentment, and Sata looked like she had just conquered another demon.

✳

"We're not at the bottom, as in the deepest place, are we?" Kibi asked.

"Far from it. We're on a continental shelf, part of the land that just happens to be flooded by shallow water right now. The deep ocean basins and trenches are several miles deep."

"Can we go there?"

"Yes, after some training in the desert."

"I was noticing," Boro began, "that for a while there, Mati was the only one working, and then all of a sudden we all had things to do again."

"Life on a ship is like that. The rhythm of work can change in an instant. That's why it's absolutely essential to never leave your station without the commander's knowledge. In an emergency, there may not be time to look and see who's there. If the pilot calls for engines, your fingers had better be moving on your console, or the ship could be in trouble.

"Most of the time it's no problem to go to the toilet, get a snack, go check on equipment in the utility room or the engineering ring. Sometimes there's so little to do that some of us can go off-duty, sleep, eat, play games, whatever. But the commander has to release you, whether it's a one minute toilet break or a one month vacation, so he or she is prepared to cover your station.

"As you have seen, Mati gets most of the work during surface flight. But when we get into space, she'll be off-duty for long stretches, and Rini's job becomes more important. Sata has the biggest part of her job before a flight begins, like today. Right now, Kibi is just doing some little things that almost seem unnecessary. When we take on passengers, she'll wish she had a twin!"

Kibi grinned from her station.

"You, Boro, will tend to be busy during any transition, and also when the ship has landed for maintenance. But on a long flight leg, you'll often get time off."

✳

They all just gazed at their visual displays, watching long strands of seaweed gently wave back and forth. Fish darted about in groups, as if one creature with one mind.

Mati had more things to learn as they made the transition from water back to air, then everyone relaxed while they floated above the hills and valleys to the place Boro had requested. On the way, he spent time at the half-open hatch trying to master his stomach.

After Kibi checked the area for people or large animals, Mati made the final descent into the geothermal area slowly and carefully, setting the Manessa Kwi down about where they camped many months before. Ilika guided Boro through his engine shut-down procedures.

They discussed the first four legs of their flight while sitting in the hot water of the colorful terraces. The steam vent hissed in the background, bringing up memories of Miko.

After drying off and dressing on that cool but pleasant autumn day, four ex-slaves, an innkeeper's daughter, and a young captain just beginning his first command, all sat in a circle on the grass. Bread from the medieval capital city was broken, a crock of butter from Cattle Town passed, and refrigerated apples sliced. A gleaming ship from a far-distant place perched nearby, hatch open and ramp extended. Mineral-laden water trickled from pool to pool in the terraces above, while squirrels and chipmunks stood witness to this unusual gathering of humans.

✻   ✻   ✻

## Chapter 33: An Old Friend

The next time they prepared to fly the Manessa Kwi, right after lunch, flight preparations went much more smoothly.  The flight plan had already been made, the five students remembered most of their pre-flight procedures, and they were fresh from a relaxing hot spring soak and a hearty meal.

Ilika decided it was time for a slightly new experience.  "Rini, cancel all information channels except visual.  Sata, cancel flight plan display."

Mati turned and looked at Ilika with narrowed eyes.

"The flight objective is to fly by visual references to a suitable landing place," he went on, "to be decided by the steward, somewhere close to Port Town.  Since you don't have a chart and flight plan to follow, Mati, you will probably be tempted to stay near the ground, but you will actually be able to see more and make better decisions if you fly high."

Mati took a deep breath, activated her flight control, and began her ascent.  Everyone studied their visual displays, the only information coming from the watch station.

"Help me out, guys," Mati pleaded.  "Down river, right?"

"Yeah," Boro confirmed.  "We passed several farms."

"Then the river angled south," Sata remembered, "and the road went straight west to the north-south road."

"And the town was north of there," Kibi finished.  "We could use the beach near the cave . . . if the tide is out."

Mati followed Ilika's advice and took the ship up high so she could see well.  With help from her shipmates, she easily found the coast.

Kibi chuckled.  "Oops, high tide!  Let's look at the bushy area north of town, where the trail to the beach goes through.  Ilika, how small can you make Manessa?"

"Small enough to easily hide in those bushes," he assured, tapping at the little control pad on the arm of his chair.

Mati began her descent, then remembered the danger.  "Boro, give me level two thrusters, please."

"Warming up . . . ready."

"See that little clearing in the bushes north of the trail, near those rocks?" Kibi asked.

"Yes . . ."  Mati slowed her forward speed while descending carefully. Everyone was quiet while their pilot made the final approach.  She was a little too careful, and lost all motion twice, but eventually coaxed the ship down and extended the landing struts.

"Shut-down procedures," Ilika ordered, and they could feel the engines fall silent.  "Rini, you are in command of the team going into town."

"Um . . . we need a couple of rucksacks, and a few coppers and silvers."

＊

A quarter hour later, Rini, Kibi, Boro, and Sata were ready in boots, cloaks, packs, and bracelets.  Ilika opened the main hatch and the four filed out.

The captain enjoyed the looks of astonishment as they turned and gawked at their ship.

Finally Rini said, "Oh . . . let's go!"  They wound their way through the bushes, still shaking their heads.

"What's *their* problem?" Mati asked, leaning on the steward's console.

"I'll show you," Ilika said with a smile.

After hobbling outside with his help, she too had trouble closing her mouth.  The Manessa Kwi had shrunk to a shiny ball not much larger than the hatch itself.

Mati hurried back inside, just to be sure it was still there.  "Rini told me you said the inside was . . . somewhere else.  You were serious, weren't you?"

"Mati, I would never lie to any of you."

＊

Mati and Ilika enjoyed their time together, sitting on nearby rocks and watching seagulls wheel in the air.  They chatted about visual reference flying, and about the thieves who had once surrounded them near this very place.

Mati felt the bracelet on her arm, and realized how far she had come from the early days of their journey, struggling every day to learn to read and do arithmetic.

When they grew tired of sitting on rocks, they poked around in the bushes, looking for anything of interest.  A snake slithered away and dashed into a hole.  Some dark purple berries were past their prime, but still edible. A dog or fox had once come this way to die, and had left its bones behind.

"I probably wouldn't have lived very long if I'd stayed a slave," Mati admitted. "If I get my knee fixed, I can live a pretty normal life, can't I?"

"I think you will *like* your life in the Transport Service, but it'll be far from normal. Being a slave ... or a goatherd's wife ... is closer to normal. A deep-space response ship pilot is a very, very rare thing."

Mati smiled at her captain.

\*

Ilika and Mati could see that the expedition had been quite successful even before anyone spoke. Mati was especially curious about the wooden box Rini carried.

"Good news!" Kibi announced as she bounded up the four steps after removing her boots. "Kit found a home!"

Mati grinned. "Fantastic! No more sleeping in the graveyard?"

"Almost none," Sata replied. "He didn't understand that someone else had paid for his bread and sweet biscuits . . ."

". . . so he kept bringing the baker mussels and clams and things . . ." Kibi added.

". . . and they finally got so fond of him, they invited him to stay with them and work at the bakery . . ." Sata continued.

". . . and there he was, stoking the oven when we arrived!" Kibi concluded.

Rini glowed with happiness. "He remembered us and gave us all hugs."

"But what about the graveyard?" Mati pressed as they gathered in the passenger area.

"The baker says he still disappears about one day a week," Boro explained. "*He* has no idea where Kit goes, but *we* do."

"Any problems?" Ilika asked after all the exciting news was shared.

"One nosy guard on the way out of town should be waking up about now," Rini said with a slight cringe. "I did it this time. I thought it was going to be hard, but when someone was standing in the way of getting back to the ship . . . and you and Mati . . . all of a sudden it was pretty easy."

Mati smiled with embarrassment.

"The old healer died last summer," Boro reported with a note of sadness.

Ilika was silent for a moment. "I'm sorry. He was a good man."

Kibi nodded slowly. "No other problems. We stayed in pairs. Having those bracelets is great for self-confidence. When you act like you own the place, people naturally respect you."

Ilika nodded.

"We got a bunch of dried fish, clams, squid, seaweed, and a few spices we didn't have," Sata announced, pulling stuff out of a rucksack and stacking it on the galley counter.

"What's in the mystery box?" Ilika finally asked.

Rini hovered over it protectively. "This just came off a ship from another land, and it cost us *four* silver pieces." He carefully opened the top and lovingly pulled out something round wrapped in a piece of cloth. "We get to share one piece. The rest are for the sisters at the monastery."

Kibi got a cutting board and knife from the galley as Rini unwrapped the treasure, a piece of rough-skinned golden fruit that none of them had ever seen before.

Mati grinned. "It looks like Manessa!"

Rini carefully sliced the fruit into six wedges. The skin released a pungent aroma with each cut that made their mouths water.

"The merchant said you can eat a little of the skin," Boro explained, "but the really good part is inside."

As each of them touched tongue, then teeth, to the juicy flesh, their taste buds were overwhelmed by the delicious sweet-tart flavor of the mysterious fruit.

"Mmmmmm . . ." they all said at once, and then started laughing as the juice squirted all over the table and each other.

✳ ✳ ✳

## Chapter 34: The Last Stop

"What shape is Manessa when we fly?" Sata asked as she sent the flight plan to the pilot.

"It depends on our speed and the density of whatever we're flying through," Ilika explained. "In air, usually a thin, low-friction shape."

"Anti-mass and thrusters, level one?" Boro proposed.

"It's a long flight, and then we'll be in the mountains. I suggest level two on both engines. Your call, pilot."

Mati's eyes became wide. "I'm new, remember!"

Boro smiled. "Warming-up."

Ilika grinned.

"Is that treasure box of yours secure somewhere, Rini?" Kibi asked.

"I strapped it into a passenger seat."

"As you probably all saw," Ilika began as he took the command chair, "a heavy overcast cloud layer is developing, and it's probably worse in the mountains. When we're in it, you'll be flying by your topographic information, Mati. In bad weather, trust your instruments. Turn off your visual displays if they're confusing."

The pilot nodded.

"Weather map coming out," Rini announced. "The clouds are thickening fast."

"Landing site, hatch, and ship are secure," Kibi reported.

"Flight objective is the monastery," Ilika began, "that level field right in front of the main building, if it's clear."

Mati could feel the extra power in both her lift and thrusters, and a minute later they entered the clouds. She discovered her captain was right — the white mist was rapidly making her dizzy, and had to go.

Everyone was quiet for the next few minutes.

After studying the chart and watching the ship's position indicator, Sata announced, "The remains of Lumber Town are below us and a little to the left. I wonder if they'll rebuild . . ."

"Lots of people there were loggers and sawyers," Boro remembered.

"I bet Misa will go back someday to look for her parents," Rini mused. "Maybe after Buna finds Noni."

The quiet hum of the engines continued. Ilika wore a contented look.

"We're entering the mountains," Mati announced as she gained altitude to follow the flight plan.

A minute later, they suddenly burst through the top of the clouds into bright sunshine with a vivid blue sky overhead. Hearing sounds of delight from everyone else, Mati selected her visual displays again. She glanced back and forth from the forward view to her chart until she knew which mountain was which.

Ilika stepped to the watch station. "We're looking for a wooden building in a cloud, so we'll need high-resolution topographics."

Rini watched as Ilika demonstrated the procedure, then nodded and took over.

"We're getting close," Ilika said, keeping an eye on Sata's chart and going to the pilot's chair. "Time to slow down, Mati."

"Okay . . . and we're back in the clouds." Mati tapped her display selector until she found the high-resolution chart.

"Flight plan off, Sata," Ilika ordered. "It can't get us any closer. We'll have to find the exact spot by Rini's sensors and our memories. As soon as we go over the next ridge, Mati, swing around and approach low and slow from the north."

"This is great!" Mati declared. "I can make out individual rocks and trees!"

"Everyone, help look for buildings or trails," Ilika requested. "Kibi, scan for people and large animals."

"Bingo!" she said a moment later. "Several animals, goats I think, in a shed, almost directly below us."

"I see it," Mati confirmed. "So the monastery should be uphill?"

"Yeah," Boro remembered. "All their animal sheds were downhill from the main hall, except where they put Tera."

The fond memory of her faithful donkey colored Mati's thoughts for a moment. "I see a barn!"

"Two people in it," Kibi announced, "and about seven more on the very edge of my screen."

"Try your visual, Mati," Ilika said.

Though still very white and misty, the faint outline of a structure, about three stories high, started to appear. She compared that to her three-D projection. "Got it! The main hall is directly ahead."

Ilika studied the pilot's display from just behind her chair. "Looks like they've had some snow. The field looks clear of people and animals. Can you confirm that, Kibi?"

"Yeah. The people are all in the buildings."

"Land by instruments, Mati. Don't trust your visual when everything is just shades of white."

"Okay. I hope Manessa doesn't mind cold toes. Getting close . . . struts down. The Manessa Kwi has come to the monastery."

"Engines off."

Boro confirmed, then added, "I wonder what they'll think of us . . ."

Ilika smiled. "I think we'll have a better reception than we did near the capital city."

Everyone laughed at the painful memory of priests trying to burn their ship.

✳

During the long evenings that followed that eventful day, the nine sisters staying over the winter added a complete description of the Blessed Event to the record books of the order.

They told of how the Heavenly Chariot descended from the sky in all its shining Glory, and then gave birth to six Angels, one of whom was wounded from her battles with Evil and walked with a crutch. The novice Kali recognized the Angels first, and found the courage to go out and greet them, silently inviting them in to warm and nourish themselves. A priestess soon recognized them as some of the strangers who had visited the monastery the summer before, had willingly meditated with the sisters in the guest house, and had joined them for the Aurora Festival, the first visitors to be so honored in living memory.

The record was clear that the Angels respected the order's rule of silence, but that good feelings and affection were freely shared with the novice they knew, and anyone else who found the courage to approach. They partook of tea and stew, and left a box of fruit from Heaven itself, fruit that had never been seen in the world before. That fruit, used sparingly, lasted the entire winter and brought unusually good health to all the sisters.

Finally the Angels, with gestures and embraces, indicated that they had to return to the Chariot and depart. The novice walked with them as far as they would allow, and the other sisters watched from the edge of the ritual field. The Heavenly Chariot ascended back into the clouds in Power and Glory.

During the year that followed, the novice Kali was quickly taught all the lessons, and advanced to the status of full priestess long before other novices her age.

✳

Ilika slowly and carefully guided their departure from the monastery ritual field, knowing his crew members were experiencing deep feelings after visiting Kali and the sisters again.

He went from station to station. Kibi had tears on her face, but was smiling, and hadn't missed any of her tasks as steward. Ilika remembered that the plan to refer Kali to the monastery had been her idea.

"Ilika, if we get to go around doing wonderful things like helping Kali, then I *never* want to leave the Transport Service."

He spoke so they could all hear him. "We will often get to do wonderful things. We will also have to do many routine things that aren't so rewarding. But remember, even when we offer to help people, they will not always accept our help. Sometimes they will choose a different path, and we will have to respect that choice." He looked at Kibi to see her reaction.

She nodded with understanding.

"We're breaking through the clouds and are back on the flight plan," Mati announced. "Objective?"

"We need a nice, clear alpine lake, preferably on our course."

Sata peered at the chart on her display. "No problem. Not far from here."

"I see it on my three-D," Mati confirmed.

"Slow and careful instrument flying, Mati. Come to a hover just above the middle of the lake."

As Mati maneuvered the ship to the lake, Ilika showed Kibi how to fill the water tanks. "Here are your siphon and pump controls, and this is basic filtration, which should be all it needs."

Kibi nodded.

Just then, the ship slipped below a cloud ceiling not far above the lake. Mists crept about, and snow covered the rocks and grass right down to the water's edge.

Rini gazed at his visual display with round eyes. "Pretty!"

Mati moved the ship into position above the surface. "How's that?" the pilot asked.

"Lock flight controls. Siphon down, Kibi. All three tanks."

Soon their water tanks were filled with some of the purest water on the planet, and they were back in the sunshine above the clouds.

Ilika sat down in the command chair. "The next and last leg of our flight plan takes us out of this kingdom . . . out of your kingdom . . . with no reason to return in the near future. We will all leave people and memories behind. Those who are friends, like Sata's family and Kali, we will try to see again someday, but I cannot promise exactly when. It could be a year or two before we can return. Nor can I promise we will find them, or that they'll even be alive. As you know, life holds many dangers for everyone.

"You have now had a small sampling of what it is like to be the crew of a deep-space response ship. Tomorrow, if you choose to remain, we will begin thorough training in all aspects of your jobs on the Manessa Kwi, and in the many things you need to know to become citizens of Nebador.

"You are not slaves. You can only do this of your own free will."

A long silence followed.

"Count *me* in!" Mati said with a grin.

"Me too!" Rini echoed.

"You couldn't pry me away," Boro asserted firmly.

"I go where you go!" Kibi said with a romantic tinge to her voice.

Sata took a deep breath. A part of her longed for her mother's hugs and the satisfaction of working with her father at the inn.  Another part of her knew she had to find her own path.  For a moment the two sides were evenly balanced, and she sat frozen with indecision.

Then she looked around and saw her dear friend Mati, Ilika her teacher and captain, mysterious Rini, Kibi looking down on them from the steward's station like a mother hen, and finally Boro — sweet Boro, the boy she liked, the boy who had already turned down another offer so he could stay with Ilika — and with her.  He wore an expectant half-smile.

"I think . . . this is where I'm supposed to be!" Sata announced with a little fear and lots of faith.

Everyone clapped.

"All stations, check flight readiness," the captain ordered.

They all quickly went over their basic diagnostics and status checks.

"Flight objective," he continued, "last leg of the flight plan, passing over the eastern boundary of this kingdom, and landing among the sand dunes in the deep desert."

Mati pushed her flight control forward, and silently promised that since Sata had given up family to be on their crew, she would always be a faithful sister to her younger friend.

*

The desert, with a clear sky overhead, was receiving its last few minutes of daylight before the sun sank into the clouds on the western horizon.  The shiny sphere circled the huge expanse of sand dunes, looking for just the right place to land.  It kept some distance from the trail that skirted one side of the dunes, even though not a soul was to be seen.

Eventually it chose a secluded little niche where some hearty cactus plants grew among the tallest dunes, far from anywhere that a person or animal would choose to be, except perhaps a snake or lizard.

It settled onto the ground, careful to not crush the plants.

Four people came running out, climbed the nearest dune, and danced for joy in the warm light of the setting sun. Two others came more slowly, one with a stick.

They would never forget the land that had given them birth, but neither did they have any intention of letting those memories keep them from the adventures that lay ahead.

                        ✳   ✳   ✳   ✳   ✳

## About the Author

Born in the Mojave Desert, J. Z. Colby now lives and writes deep in a forest of the Pacific Northwest.

He has studied many subjects, formally and informally, including psychology, philosophy, education, and performing arts, but remains a generalist. His primary profession as a mental health counselor, specializing with families and young adults, gives him many stories of personal growth, and the motivation to develop his team of young critiquers and readers.

All his life, he has been drawn toward a broad understanding of human nature, especially those physical, emotional, mental, and spiritual situations in which our capacity to function seems to reach its limits. He finds fascinating those few individuals who can transcend the limits of our common human nature and the dictates of our cultures.

In his spare time, he flies helicopters and airplanes.

He may be contacted at the email address listed on the internet site www.nebador.com.

www.ingramcontent.com/pod-product-compliance
Lightning Source LLC
Chambersburg PA
CBHW031347170626
46807CB00002B/862